Laura,

Thank you &
Confidence in me and for purchasing
this book. Thank you also for taking
such good care of my kid.

T. Z—
2/3/00

MW00830853

SHADOW SOLDIER

SHADOW SOLDIER

by

T.L. Davis

F

&

Pres S

F&S Press
P.O. Box 608
Brush, CO 80723-0608

Library of Congress Catalog Number: 97-90015

ISBN 0-9656536-4-1

First Edition

10 9 8 7 6 5 4 3 2 1

For Jennifer, Seth and Samantha and the rest of my family, who endured my relentless persistence.

For the cowboys I've known and ridden with.

And for my readers, who will ultimately determine my fate.

The War Years

1

A rhythmic drumming of cannon fire echoed from the river. Muzzle blasts could be heard near and far, respective of the side that fired: ours, or theirs. Sporadic explosions would land near the cave myself and a few others occupied, causing tiny streams of dust to issue from the ceiling.

The cave was of a better class than most of the others dug into the hillside above Vicksburg, Mississippi. The interior was lined and reinforced by planks of wood. Some canned goods were piled neatly into a corner.

The adults were somewhat solemn, or bored, or angry depending on the accuracy of the Union gunners. I shared the cave with a father, a mother and four wide-eyed children. An older couple, the grandparents, sat to one side of the cave. I was grateful to be extended the courtesy of their accommodations.

"You're Horatio Wilkes' boy, ain't ya?" asked the father.

I nodded.

"What's your name?"

"Jeff," I replied.

"Named after Jeff Davis, as I recall."

"Yes sir."

"He and your father were quite a pair, even twenty years ago. What's your father say about all of this cannon fire? Is he gonna stop it?"

I shrugged. Everyone asked if my father couldn't do something about the Union gunboats. If there was something that could be done, I imagine he would've done it. Truth was, I hadn't asked him. It seemed like a foolish question that he shouldn't be bothered with. I suppose the townspeople felt the same way and asked me instead.

The father looked from me to the opening in the cave.

"I expect we'll get along fine, anyhow. Vicksburg will never be taken. Ain't that right?"

I shrugged again.

"What's your full name?"

"Jefferson Doddridge Wilkes," I replied.

"Doddridge," he said, thoughtfully. "Your mother's folks, wasn't it?"

"Yes sir."

"Fine people. Scholarly people," he said.

"I believe so."

The father nodded and looked about at his family. It seemed that he was speaking in a casual fashion to keep from showing fear, or to ease the minds of the children.

Finally, the firing lessened and the explosions were few and far between.

"Ought to be safe enough now," the father said and rose from his place in the cave and led the way. I helped bring out the younguns, the women and the elderly.

Looking back into the empty hole, it seemed much too small to house the nine of us. We were all smudged with dirt about the face and backsides.

I picked up the squirrel gun I'd left outside and thanked the family for their hospitality. They offered my father their best. I nodded and headed down the slope of the hill to the edge of the high bluffs overlooking the river.

When I got to the blind my friends were already loading their muskets with powder, ball and patch. I don't know if we'd ever hit anything in the preceding months, but we always fired musket balls at the Union sailors when the bombardment stopped. To show our defiance.

The blind was nothing but a few logs stacked atop one another. Branches, weeds and grasses were piled in front of it so that it was hidden from the river. In our spare time we'd hacked notches in the logs through which to fire. The notches were small and didn't leave much room to aim as they were barely big enough to get a muzzle through. It was futile, I imagine, but for mere boys too young to join the army as anything other than litter bearers, stable boys or cook's helpers, it was the best we could do to strike back at the Yanks.

We fired several rounds into the river, drawing spouts of water out of the muddy flow. Once, William Flout rattled the metal of one of the ironclads with an errant ball. It was great, high fun, but had the effect of discharging muskets at a flock of geese.

That night, as we fired through the holes in the timber and poured and tamped the powder, we chuckled and nudged each other, impressed with our own audacity. Then, just as midnight approached, as our powder grew scarce and regret for lost lead began to sober our fun, a heavy musket ball plowed into the timbers with a thud. Unaware that we'd ever draw fire from the other side, we glanced at each other with wide eyes and scampered out of the blind and up toward town as fast as our legs would carry us.

We split up as we came to the city streets. It was late and most of the people had crawled out of their caves and gone back home. Groups of soldiers were starting to wander about, some of which were helping to put out small fires started by the hurtling metal balls. My fellow citizens were all fairly adept at living under the constant threat of invasion by then. Many had gone when the gunboats first arrived, but others stayed to keep Vicksburg alive.

I wandered through the town carrying my musket. It was a short walk home and I enjoyed the late summer air. The willows were heavy with Spanish Moss. I cut through the forest and made my way along the same path I'd often taken to school. I had my musket charged and awaited the approach of phantom troops through the trees, but none came. I wondered what would happen if I stumbled upon a group of Union soldiers. I emboldened myself with visions of daring. I contemplated my bravery until recalling the incident at the blind and how we'd all run. I smirked at myself and knew I'd probably hightail it home.

It was an impulse allowed to children, but I was growing older and I'd have to overcome the impulse to run if the war continued a few more years. In little over a month I'd be 15, and I'd have to start preparing myself for the inevitable command that would come, should the South need me. The idea of commanding men seemed distant as I walked through the woods. Of course, I had the training. My father saw to that.

When I was younger he put me in the cotton fields alongside his negras to pick cotton. My fingers bled and the negras taught me how to pick. I was sore and bloodied at the end of each day for a while. When I'd become proficient at picking cotton, my father put me in charge of overseeing the pickers. He just left me to my duties and berated me when production was lacking until I learned to get the field hands to produce.

The negras tried every trick in the book. They explained to me why they couldn't pick that day, or had to go slower than before. I listened and felt compassion for them, especially having been in their position. I gave them longer breaks and understood their troubles and ailments. Before long, we'd fallen several tons behind and our relaxed work habits led to the endangerment of a good portion of the crop.

Lord, my father put the fear of God into me over that. I recalled, as I walked, how he'd brought me into his study and showed me the figures of dates in the past and tons of cotton available for shipment by those previous dates.

"You're costing me a lot of money, son. I may have to sell the negra cook to make up the expense."

I stood before him, gazing at the figures and hoping to change them with my sorrowful stare. I didn't see how we'd fallen so far behind and I kept trying to reason it out, but there was only one reason for it: I'd been too easy on the field hands. I'd been too easy on myself. I wanted to be a friend they could count on. I didn't want to have to force them along. But, it wasn't working.

"You know who'll have to do all the cooking then, don't you?" He asked, staring at me with small brown eyes. His lips quivered in anger from deep inside the heavy beard and mustache. "You, that's who."

I lowered my head.

"Perhaps, I'd be a better cook than an overseer," I mumbled.

He leaned on the big, oaken desk and brought his hairy face closer to mine.

"Perhaps, you would, but I don't need a cook. I need an overseer who's able to run this farm, to run my other varied business interests. I need a son, not a cook."

I nodded, but didn't know how I'd ever become the man he wanted me to be. I enjoyed the company of the negras in the fields and didn't relish the idea of having to go out there the next day and be the type of overseer my father was. I wanted to remind him that I was just a boy, then 13, and not yet up to the task.

He sat down in his chair and studied me. I continued to stare at the desk and the figures laid out before me.

"Son, this war," he said, "this war of independence from the North, it isn't about to end soon, as I predicted. I know you had plans to further your education, but there are more pressing matters. Soon, I may have to take several trips to Richmond to consult with my old friend and new President. I have to feel confident in your abilities to run this farm. Old Ezra, he's a good negra, but he isn't kin. He can run the farm without your help, excepting the odd purchase in town and the signing of papers and deeds, but he isn't ever going to own this land. You are. I know you feel like a boy, a child, but you cannot remain so. I need a man and a man you must become. It's as simple as that."

He pushed back in his chair and waited for a response. I didn't know what to say. I wanted to reassure him, but felt that I wasn't up to the job. I didn't want to disappoint him and I didn't want to make promises that I couldn't keep.

"Maybe we could let Old Ezra run the place for a while."

"And what's to keep him from taking off for the North and taking the whole group with him?"

I grinned. "Old Ezra isn't going anywhere, father."

His massive hand slammed down hard on the desk as he rose well above my height. "Don't mistake fear for loyalty, son. Don't you ever think that any of these negras are here, because they want to be. Don't you ever think that anyone is anywhere, because they want to be. Folks are where they are, because they don't know of anywhere else to go. Now, Lincoln's offered them someplace else and they can't help but think of it every moment of their wakening."

My father began to pace about behind the desk. "It isn't any different for you, son. Tell me you haven't been thinking about going to the University, or off to war since this whole conflict began. Tell me you haven't."

"I can't tell you that."

"Of course you can't. You think of it all the time because you've been told that there's someplace else. But, you didn't think of it when you were a child."

I shook my head, slowly understanding his point.

"And we can't just turn the negras loose. I don't have enough sons to pick all the cotton. It seems now, that I don't have enough sons to oversee the picking of cotton." His energy began to slacken and he sat back down in the chair. "Son, this cotton, and all of my affairs, make money and that money goes to help pay the salaries of the soldiers. I buy goods, rifles, food and clothing for the soldiers. When you fail as an overseer, you're helping the Union boys win the war. Children think of things as if they are solitary in their effects. Men, and especially leaders of men, think of things as they're connected, one to the other. What I demand of you, at your tender age, is to become a leader of men and to think of things as they're connected."

I nodded, but this time I understood what he wanted.

"Now, you go to bed and think tonight of what you must do, how you must act to help the Confederate cause. In war, we must all do things that we dislike to ensure a future for us all. If you feel a weight on your shoulders, an obligation to the soldiers in the field taking fire from the enemy, then you're ready to become a man, a leader."

I turned away from his desk and went up the steps to my bedroom. There was more for me to do than to be a child. I had a greater responsibility than I'd ever imagined and I looked upon all of my childish thoughts with disdain.

By the summer of 1862, I'd learned how to run the farm and how to handle the negras. I was still a compassionate overseer, but I demanded certain things from the field hands and would tolerate no amount of loafing. The way I saw it, we all had jobs to do. If everyone did their jobs, so much the better for all of us. What few troubles I had at first were discussed with Old Ezra and matters were settled.

Unfortunately, the gunboats showed themselves on the river about the time I'd really learned how to do my job. The fact of it threw everything into chaos. I found myself working during the days and meeting my friends at night under the periodic bombardment of the Union troops. My father started getting regular visits from General Pemberton and from time to time General Forrest.

At first, there was a great suspicion of General Pemberton. Several of the townsfolk thought he'd trade out the Confederate cause if it got too rough. What else could they expect from a Yankee? The general's loyalty was never in question to my father. He praised the general at every opportunity to encourage the townsfolk to support him. Finally, he won the people over.

I came out of the thickness of the surrounding forest and up towards the porch. I saw my father pacing back and forth while reading a letter. Inside the still distant window, he appeared a miniature of himself searching for the way out of a tiny box. His big cigar produced a smoky atmosphere of its own and leant a dreamlike quality to the scene. I stopped where I was and watched him. I knew that I'd always remember him thus and I lingered outside.

I rested against the musket and looked into the window from afar. I was overcome by my love for the man. He was a great man and had given everything he owned for the success of the Confederacy. Already our assets were being drained and cotton was becoming nearly impossible to get past the Union lines. The blockade of the Mississippi was inhibiting all sorts of commerce.

I approached the house and entered. The smoke was a welcomed scent and the interior of our home was inviting like never before. Perhaps, the musket ball smashing into our blind gave me an unreal sense of appreciation for all that I saw and smelled of, but it was a pristine moment that I came to treasure.

I passed the door to my father's study and glanced in. He was engrossed in the sheet of paper that he held before him and failed to notice me.

I proceeded on to my room toward the back of the house where my windows were left open the whole summer. I awoke nearly every morning to the bright sounds of birds chirping in the forest. I doubt there was a better living anywhere than in Vicksburg, even with the gunboats on the river. I readied myself for bed and lay atop the mattress in long underwear. I glanced over at the musket standing sentinel in the corner, charged and ready for action should the Union soldiers make a daring attempt to capture the town.

2

Life went on in Vicksburg for a year under conditions of siege. The Union troops succeeded in making life as impossible as they could, but we held out and continued on as before. As the months passed, we came to believe that Vicksburg would survive the ordeal. Yet, the war was not going as well in other areas. I could tell that much from my father's worried expressions.

It was just before my 16th birthday and I thought more of joining the Confederate troops. It seemed to me that I'd be more valuable fighting the war than running to our blind at the conclusion of shelling and taking random shots at passing boats. I expressed my feelings to my father only to receive a quick negative reply.

"You can do more for your country by staying here and tending the farm. All my attention must be given to greater matters," he said, dismissing me with a wave of his hand.

I stumbled out of his study, and looked about the farm. There wasn't much of it left. The cotton was growing in the fields, but nothing was to ensure that it would be harvested, much less sold. The previous crop had been handed over to the Army for the making of uniforms. In trade for the cotton, we were given a bank note to provide us with the necessary funds to run our home and grow more cotton, but there was nothing left of the great profits reaped before the war.

I finished up what chores there were to be done, checked on the negras to make sure they were accommodated properly and set out, with musket in hand, to the blind. The sun was setting in the west. Rays of sunlight shone through tiny holes in the canopy of leaves above. I walked along the path and emerged on the edge of town. It was quickly growing dark by the time I met up with William Flout and Gregory Jackson.

The blind had been greatly improved over the intervening year; another row of logs had been added to the front and better notches had been carved to allow aim. We had some canned goods hidden there and had built up the sides. On quiet days we'd look at the front row of logs and count up the marks left by Union minie balls. We liked to think we were a favorite target of the Union troops, but there were so many real soldiers for them to fire at.

We fancied ourselves as sharpshooters, though we rarely hit anything. Gregory was the only one of us who could claim to have hit an enemy sailor. The truth of the matter was that Gregory fired in unison with a Confederate volley and the enemy was most likely hit by someone else.

It was a summer night in 1863. The evening was quiet except for a few cannon shots fired back and forth. There was no light from the moon and we sat in the darkness and whispered back and forth until the whispers grew louder and talking became general.

"Shhhhh!" Gregory said, peering over the top of the low blind. "There's a fire on the other side of the river."

William and I scrambled to our feet and joined Gregory. A huge fire roared on the opposite side and the faint sound of an engine could be heard pulsing with steam. I watched as the dark shape of a tug pulling three barges drifted in front of the fire. The sky burst into a show of light, fire, smoke and explosions. Great spouts of water were thrown up as a few Confederate shells missed their marks. The battle was somewhat one-sided as the Union boats only fired occasionally at the well entrenched batteries of Vicksburg.

"They'll pulverize the barges," William said. "Let's get down to the edge of the river and see what we can find."

With our muskets loaded, we charged downstream to a path that led down the bluffs. It was narrow and the footing was scarce. Thinking back on it, we probably should have unloaded our muskets before heading down the treacherous trail. But, we were in a hurry to catch whatever Union bounty might be found floating on the water.

As we rushed to the side of the river, there was a great explosion and the tug boat erupted into flame. Shattered pieces flew as close to us as 100 yards. We first saw bits of wood float by, then a Union jacket that Gregory fished out of the river with a long stick. While we were busy hauling in our trophy, a body floated into a small peninsula and cartwheeled around. I caught sight of two legs in my peripheral vision and turned to see a grisly sight.

The Union sailor was missing half his body. His left half was intact, but his right half was a confused mass of battered meat and shattered ribs. I tried not to look at it as I eased deep into the river and caught a fistful of cloth in my hand. His weight pulled me off balance in the mud and I went headfirst into the muddy waters. I regained my footing and slogged to shore pulling the man behind me. It took a minute or so to find a good enough place to land the body so that we could find something of a memorable nature.

Soaked to the skin, I checked the uniform over. Still in its holster was a Colt 1861 Navy Revolver. Behind me, I heard the splashing of my friends trying to get to my position to lay claim to a watch, or Union money, or a good pocket-knife. I lost interest in everything, except the revolver. I left the body to the devil and wandered off. I shouldn't have so treasured the Colt. The Christian side of my nature urged me to hand it over to either of my two companions, who could sell it to help provide for themselves. Instead, I admired the feel of it in my hand and the smooth toolwork which had been etched in the side.

Moments passed in a frenzy of looting and I felt pangs of guilt. I thought of how fortunate I'd been all my life and how costly the war had been for the other two. Gregory's father was killed in some of the earliest fighting and he was left to fend for his mother and four siblings. William's entire family had been killed in their home by a Union shell while he sat with us in the blind six months before.

I wanted to give the revolver to one of them, but to which one? Gregory needed the money it would bring for his family. William needed the money for his own survival. Then, I heard a whoop behind me.

"Look!" said William. "Here's his pay!" as he held up a roll of Union script.

"Probably won it gamblin'," replied Gregory, then he spit. "Let's divide it."

William dropped to his knees in the swampy marsh and began to count out three piles of notes. I looked at the growing piles of script and the few gold pieces stacked to one side.

"Divide up my share between the two of you."

Gregory and William looked up at me.

"I mean it," I said. "All I want is this revolver."

They proceeded to recount the money into two piles. When the plunder had been divided, we trekked back up the path to the woods. I thrust the Colt into my waistband and we all swaggered, jostling each other. Our spirits were well refreshed by our good fortune. I told the others of a trader who dealt in both sorts of script, though they should approach him cautiously and to have a musket handy.

The trader was a Yankee who moved down to Mississippi several years before the war to open a small store near Milldale. It was somewhat of a trading post that dealt in all sorts of items.

"Come with us," William urged.

"I have a farm to run."

"Come along, the blind won't miss us."

I thought about it. It'd be better if someone went along who knew what to expect from the trader and his band. But, my father would hang me if he knew I was going anywhere near Milldale, especially at night.

Some of the enlisted men told me of the trader while they lounged about outside as the officers entered and spoke with my father. They spoke liberally of the whiskey he brewed and the prostitutes he provided to soldiers.

"Hope he don't never sell them whores to the Yanks," one of the soldiers remarked, winking at me.

Eventually, we came to the edge of town where we usually split company.

"Let's have it, Jeff. You in, or out?" asked William.

"I'm in," I said, relenting against my better judgment.

"Tomorrow night," said William. "We'll meet here at the usual time. Someone needs to bring me a horse. I had to sell all of ours to the army."

"I'll bring a spare," offered Gregory, who worked part-time at the livery.

I nodded to each and turned to the path that led home. I carried the musket and had the revolver thrust into my waistband. I pushed my hat a little sideways on my head and felt for all the world like a regular soldier bloodied in battle.

That night, I had horrible dreams of the body coming to life as I towed it to shore. The dead man wriggled out of my grasp and tried to drown me in the water of the Mississippi. I woke up screaming so hard that my father rushed to my side dressed only in his nightshirt.

"I had a horrible dream of a dead Union soldier trying to drown me in the river."

My father glanced at the revolver on the table next to the bed.

"The previous owner of the Colt, I imagine."

"Yes sir," I said, feeling guilty and ashamed.

"Well, war isn't a pleasant thing. Pray that it won't last long. You've already seen more than you should have."

"Yes sir."

"Get some sleep, now," he said, and left.

I lay back in the bed, covered with sweat, and thought of war. I thought of death in general and hoped that the Bible was right and that all dead soldiers would find their way into heaven. I hoped that my dear mother were also in heaven where all the pain of life is washed away by the kindness of the Lord.

My mother died when I was young and my father never remarried. There was a lot of death in the world and I felt that heaven must be getting awfully crowded. It was a heavy thought and I diverted my mind to other things. I thought of all the good things the Union money would bring to the others and of the fine pistol on the table. But, before my thoughts came full circle to thinking of death again, I forced myself to sleep.

The next day, I met up with Gregory and William at the designated place. It was a fair ride to Milldale, so we started out. We followed the Yazoo river for a good piece, until it flowed into an eastern bend, then we turned our horses to the northeast. We didn't take the usual road. There'd been fighting in Jackson and the roads weren't safe.

"We need a plan," I explained to my companions. "We can't just go into the place like three dumb kids. We leave ourselves open to harassment from within and robbery without."

"What do you propose?" asked William.

"One of us has to go in and talk over the deal with the trader, a man named Orestus Langley. Another should listen at the door for any sort of ruckus and another should be posted some ways away with a musket to cover the fellows who may have to make a break."

"Wouldn't it be better to go in as a group, to show our number and thereby humble whoever might consider treachery?" asked Gregory.

"I've thought of that. The way I have it figured, if they intend to rob one youngster, what would stop them from robbing three?"

They shrugged.

"See," I continued, "if they attempt any sort of trick to the one of us, they'll reveal their number. They'll forget their backs as they rush to assault our friend on the inside. With one of us posted outside, it provides a surprise to them and a few shots, properly aimed, might repulse the attack all together. But, if that doesn't work, it might provide a break in the action during which the two might run from there. If another is stationed across the road, any pursuit might be repelled from a steady aim on those following."

They nodded in agreement.

"Who's going to wait outside the door?" Gregory asked.

"I suppose I should. I have the revolver and the ability to fire successive shots."

"Who's going to go inside?"

"The largest, oldest looking of the three."

"That's me!" shouted Gregory, who was a few inches taller and already 16 years old. "But, what would I say?"

"Inquire as to the whereabouts of Mr. Langley, pull him off into a quiet corner and ask about exchanging Union script for Confederate."

Gregory rolled his eyes. "I mean, if things go awry."

"Shout out 'ambush' and I'll come in firing."

After lengthy review of the plan in all its detail, we rode in silent contemplation of the task. It was an intimidating venture. None of us knew what to expect. I conjured up images of a rickety place with all sorts of sin occurring in and about the store. It seemed to me as if we were riding into the depths of hell itself with little more than a day's preparation. I hoped all would go smoothly. Yet, another side wished that it would go wrong and I'd be called upon to show daring bravery to save my friend. Moreover, I wanted to see if the plan would work when put to the test. I envisioned it as my first test of command.

We came upon the place slowly. We saw it first as flashes of whitewash and tethered horses appearing and disappearing among the trunks of ancient, moss covered trees. Then, a clearing opened up as we neared the road. We waited on the edge of the clearing and took a final assessment of our nerve and placed William across from the doorway.

"If something goes wrong," I told William, "we'll run directly at this position until we're clear of the horses, then we'll break in opposite directions. This is important. You're to shoot the first person who comes clear to your sights. Aim for his mid-section to ensure that you hit something. If it goes that poorly, you'll hear gunshots from inside the building, so your conscience should be clear to take whatever action you must to defend our lives. Remember, these men are sure to be armed. The longer you hesitate, the greater danger you'll put us in."

"You don't have to talk to me as if I were a coward, Jeff. I know what to do."

"It's not cowardice that I worry about, it's your proper conscience. You're a good fella, William, and these things may seem wrong to your natural sense of justice. Taking a man's life is a difficult thing," I said, as if I knew something about it.

He nodded and I left my musket with him so that he could fire two shots before reloading. I checked my revolver to ensure that it was properly charged in all cylinders. Gregory kept his rifle so as to appear a capable man instead of a child moping into the place unable to defend himself.

We all shook each other's hand, stared into one another's eyes and started off on our path toward the unknown. We left the horses in the clearing where William was to fire the rounds, scabbard the muskets and ready the horses for a quick retreat through the woods.

Gregory walked ahead so no one would see us approach the building together. As soon as he reached the walk in front of the establishment, I followed. I watched every door, every horse as I walked. I felt somewhat nauseous. My eyes were stretched wide and as much as I narrowed them, I felt that the fear showed on my face. It seemed to me that I looked suspicious to the few patrons that passed as I mounted the wooden porch and leaned against the window frame so as to hear the goings-on inside.

I waited and listened. My nerves were on edge. I heard a great roar from within and I started for the door, but it flew open just then and a man and woman appeared with smiles and low discourse. I lifted my hand from the butt of the revolver and tipped my hat. Another roar of laughter erupted from the gathering inside. I wanted desperately to enter and discover the nature of things firsthand.

What if they'd leapt upon him at the outset, before I could reach the window and I hadn't heard his pleadings for help? Perhaps they were at that moment relieving him of all his possessions.

I cupped the window to see what was taking place, but could see nothing more than merchandise piled in front of the dusty panes. Another burst of laughter came from the depths of that murky atmosphere and I literally jumped in the air with frustration and anxiety. Keeping my distance from the door was the hardest thing I'd ever had to do.

I couldn't imagine what he might be doing in there. I didn't understand the raucous nature of the situation. What's worse, I suddenly realized that I hadn't taken any precautions as what to do when he emerged peacefully from the establishment. I felt chagrined at the prospect that someone might follow us and attack us in the woods, perhaps killing us all and taking the money. Furthermore, now that I thought I should linger and ensure our rear was safe, I had no way of telling Gregory.

An eternity seemed to pass as darkness settled and lamps were lit inside. Periodic bursts of laughter would issue forth and my anger only grew at the impertinence of Gregory, who left us outside and ignorant. My thoughts alternated from thinking that I should enter and find out the status of my friend, to walking back to where William waited to tell him that I'd cover them as they left.

Not only were these things occupying my time, but I was beginning to attract some attention as I waited outside of the building. Every once in a while, one of the soldiers asked my business on his way in. I simply mentioned that my pa was inside.

After waiting for close to an hour, I walked back to the horses.

"What's going on in there?" William asked.

"I can't tell. There's a lot of laughing and carousing. I don't think Gregory's in any kind of trouble. I'm going to take my horse and move off further north into the woods to watch for someone following him out."

"What am I supposed to do?"

"Just wait here for him and then head back home. I'll watch for a while and catch up about the time you fellows hit the eastern bend of the Yazoo River."

William nodded and relaxed his grip on the musket.

I hitched myself up into the saddle and took the horse further up the road. I made sure that I stayed out of sight until the others left. I tethered the horse to a small tree and ventured closer to the road to have a look.

Gregory came through the door with a couple of well-wishers at his heels. He appeared to be intoxicated to some degree, and stumbled toward William after those behind him had mounted up and rode on.

I laid down in the tall grass and watched the store. I promised myself to wait at least 15 minutes. The time went by slowly. Mosquitoes, fireflies and gnats visited me regularly where I lay. None of them were a nuisance, excepting the gnats that entered my ears. Several groups of men, both civilian and soldier, came through the doors, but none seemed to have a plan in mind. I waited another few minutes and mounted up to start out after my friends.

The woods had an entirely different look to them in the dead of night. I felt a rush of anxiety and urged the horse on a quicker tempo. There was something eerie and close among the tall, dense trees.

I kept my eyes wide open and scoured the darkness on both sides. I had a great sense of foreboding. It wasn't until that very moment that I'd even considered the possibility of getting lost. By letting the others go first, I'd doubled the possibility that someone would lose the way. My first command was rife with failures and misjudgments.

Every few minutes I'd stop the horse and listen for the sounds of them up ahead. I didn't hear anything of interest, but the buzzing and chirping of the insects. Occasionally, I'd hear the hoot of an owl that would raise the hair on my neck. The owl sounded human, as if a human were emulating the sound of an owl. I kicked the horse and picked up the pace a little before stopping to listen again.

It seemed as if I should have come upon my friends. Perhaps, I'd passed them as each of us took different paths. I wondered if they'd been ambushed without my hearing the scuffle and lie dead a few feet away. Were those really owls that I heard? Were the ambushers surrounding me as I traveled? What if the fighting in Jackson had been finished and Union troops were now filling the woods around Vicksburg? What if we came upon them?

As I considered all of the possibilities, my breath grew short and labored. I had all I could do to keep from darting for the road and riding as hard as I could to Vicksburg and the safety of home. The only thing that kept me from it was the thought of worse dangers on the road in the middle of the night.

I stopped the horse to listen. In the distance, I heard the lapping of water.

It was all wrong. I shouldn't have been to the Yazoo for a little while yet. Maybe, I'd ridden my horse faster than I supposed. Gregory and William were probably waiting up ahead for me at the bend. I spurred my horse and rode quickly through the woods toward the sound of the water.

When I reached the river, I realized that it was just starting to bend southeast. I'd veered off too far west in my confusion. I followed the river bank hoping I'd meet up with the others in a short time.

Up ahead, I saw that the river began to take a slow curve. If all had gone well, my friends would be waiting for me at the tip of the curve. I rode along feeling much better. I urged my horse into the woods so as to come upon them as if according to plan.

I first saw the dim outlines of horses. It appeared as if there were two, each facing the other. I let out a deep breath. Then, another one appeared from behind them. I stopped my horse and eased out of the saddle. I stood quietly in the shadows and listened for whatever might be taking place up ahead. I tied the reins off to a branch and began to circle the other horses.

I had no room in my mind for guesses, or assumptions. I concentrated wholly on listening. I could hear voices to the left of the horses. The words were low, mumbling sounds, whispers in the distance. I jerked the pistol from my waistband and approached step by step.

The voices grew more audible, but no more distinguishable. Intervals of silence and mumbling were broken by grunts, and sharp ending utterances. Finally, I could see the outline of a horse and rider. As I neared, I thought about shooting him. It was obvious, by then, that there'd been some sort of ambush, or chance robbery. I could only assume that my friends were lying on the ground. I drew a steady bead on the rider's head and walked forward with caution. Another of the robbers might be stationed in the woods.

As I stepped closer, I heard the voice again. It was Gregory's voice.

"I think we ought to hang these here fellers, what's your mind, William?" Gregory asked, then kicked one of the men on the ground.

"Couple of rascals, that's for sure," William replied.

"Vermin, at the least."

I relaxed my hand on the revolver and stepped heavily onto the underbrush. William's musket, that I hadn't noticed laying across his saddle was brought eye-level to me.

"Where've you been?" William asked.

"Following behind."

"Where's your horse?"

I motioned over my shoulder.

"Better get it and let's be out of here."

I hurried back to where I'd tied the horse. I pulled myself into the saddle and started back toward them.

We rode along in the darkness. Gregory had taken the lead. He'd discovered something in the store in Milldale: he discovered he was a man. The other patrons had taken him in and gathered around to hear his fictitious story of winning the Union money in a card game on a riverboat. They'd gathered around him and asked him the details of the game, the players and the stakes. Gregory had improvised well enough to secure their trust. He was coaxed to buy drinks and received drinks in return. Whores sat on his youthful knee and kissed his cheek with every lie he told. It was the awakening of a man and by the time the ruffians ambushed them by the river, he was full of himself and took the two robbers down alone.

Gregory was six feet tall, even then, and weighed nearly two hundred pounds. For sixteen years old, Gregory was capable of a lot. It helped that the robbers were nearly drunk out of their minds and Gregory was intoxicated only to the point of bravery.

The event had solidified the friendship between Gregory and William. I soon felt the loneliness of exclusion. At first, it was a mere way of speaking to me as if I'd missed out. Later, it became an insinuation of cowardice.

"Where were you?"

"I was trying to catch up."

"Seems, you should have caught our trail by then," Gregory pointed out. "How long did you wait by the store?"

"Fifteen minutes."

Gregory shook his head. "It don't add up that way. We waited better than that at the river. We repulsed an assault by the time you arrived."

"Okay, I got a bit off the trail and wound up by the river, then followed it down."

William let his horse drift into Gregory's, who rode in the middle and a little ahead.

"Hear that, Gregory? The Colonel got lost on the way back."

"I didn't get lost, I drifted off the trail."

"Sure you weren't hiding in the woods watching the ambush from safety?"

William smiled at Gregory. "That's the way of the officer ain't it? Let the men do the fightin' and come along later to claim victory?"

"That's the officer way, all right."

I shook my head. There wasn't much to say. They were just ribbing me about my absence. They attacked my education and my father's place in society. They made references to the command I'd have someday. Everyone knew I'd start the war as a Lieutenant. It was well planned out in advance. But, unlike before, there was an edge to their words. It wasn't good natured. Perhaps, I felt a twinge of guilt for not being there, or maybe, I knew that they wouldn't listen to reason. They considered me a bit of a coward at that point and I knew there'd be no way on earth to change their minds. So, I kept my mouth shut and the conversation died of its own accord.

3

When we arrived in Vicksburg, we were met with every light burning and a great deal of confusion in the town. Some people said that Jackson had fallen and that the Union soldiers were no more than a mile away. Soldiers rushed forward to form skirmish lines. We split up. Gregory went to care for his family and William sought out a place to be near the fighting. My place was by my father.

I rode quickly to the house. Outside, a number of soldiers and officers waited patiently in the yard. Old Ezra was tending their horses and I tied mine outside the barn. I started to enter the house, but was refused entry by a short, thin sergeant. His name was Jameson.

"This is my home, let me pass," I said, determined to enter.

"Not tonight it ain't," the sergeant replied. "Tonight, this is a military installation. If'n you want to know what goes on within, you'll have to wait by the window and learn all ye can from there."

I looked to my left where a small group of soldiers stood casually by the window. I rushed over and got close to the opening. I heard my father's voice rise in anger.

"I'll not, by God, abandon my childhood home to the Union Army."

General Pemberton was inside with my father and a few of his aides were also present.

"Sir, it's not the intention of this general to allow the President's own advisor, and close friend, to fall into the hands of Union troops to satisfy your selfish, disagreeable nature. The President has given me a direct order, and a personal plea to yourself, via this cable," Pemberton said, pausing to pull a piece of paper from his woolen military jacket, "to evacuate to a safer place inland from the river."

I heard the rustling of paper as my father grabbed the cable and read as General Pemberton continued.

"I am not altogether assured of being able to hold this position, Sir. I regret that I am shamefully placed in the position of having to evacuate yourself and your family, under protection of my best troops, to a place of your choosing."

"There's only me and the boy," he said, in a somewhat more solemn voice. I heard the creaking of his chair as he slumped heavily into it. Then, he spoke in a quiet tone, almost inaudible at the window.

"Jeff Davis spoke here, in Vicksburg, as a personal honor to me. He could well have spoken in Woodville, his childhood home, but he gave me the honor of hosting his first Presidential Address in February of Eighteen hundred and fifty-nine."

"I've heard often of that day," Pemberton said, in a wistful tone. "It surely must have been a solemn, glorious moment for the South." Then his voice became stronger and wavered only a bit with emotion. "I may well have to abandon this position, Mr. Wilkes, but I will never abandon the cause."

My father's chair creaked again as he rose and hollered, "boy!"

I rushed through the front door held open by Sergeant Jameson. I entered my father's study to find General Pemberton and several high ranking members of the Confederate Army.

"Gentlemen, this is my son, Jefferson Doddridge Wilkes, a Confederate to the core, who's already relieved a Union soldier of his Colt revolver."

Hands of congratulations were thrust forward and I felt the heavy hands of others slap my back.

That night, we packed a few things for housekeeping and comfort. In the load were numerous books of my father's and other supplies from his study. We took only a few of the negras that were most loyal. The others were to stay behind and help General Pemberton in whatever way they could. Old Ezra came with us, along with a cook and a maid. Vicksburg fell that week. From then on, we moved about Mississippi and into Alabama a time, or two, to stay clear of the Union Army. My father continued his correspondence with Richmond through letters and dispatches.

My life became one of isolation. I was separated from William and Gregory while they considered me a coward. I didn't know how I'd ever reconcile myself to them. I hoped the war would bring us together. I often thought of how I'd gain a command and do everything possible to find them and bring them into my camp.

As the summer wore to its end, and fall began, I stayed by my father's side. Where a battle would encroach upon our immediate surroundings, we'd pick up and move a little further on. I found myself surrounded by soldiers and became friends with most of the men assigned to my father as guards. Sergeant Jameson was the most notable among them, but all were selected for duty from those who'd already distinguished themselves in battle.

I fancied my conversations with such men as the substitute for attendance at a military academy. I listened to the ways they had overcome bad odds, or poor positions. I asked questions whenever I thought that a particular point might help me to make the right decisions in the field. They all knew of my desire to understand the art of warfare and were generous with their time to discuss it. After months of investigation into the nature of war, I felt I was ready to receive a command and approached my father with the prospect.

"Sir," I said, assuming my most official voice. "I have studied war with the troops here, who are of the best calibre of fighting men in America, to my knowledge. I have a good understanding of tactics, formations and commands. In the absence of a good military academy, I believe I've done the best I can to prepare myself for military service as an officer. I'd like to ask your assistance in securing my first orders to join the Confederate forces."

My father looked me up and down. He pushed back in his chair and studied me. There was a different sort of look in his eyes, as if he were going to give the proposal great consideration.

"No," he said, and returned to his business.

The brevity of his answer stunned me. I stood before him as my plans and careful study became meaningless. Then, I wondered what right he had to deny the request.

"I'd like to enter the service with your blessings and your encouragement. I'd like to obtain a command," I said, pausing to gather courage. "However, I'd just as soon join the Confederate Army in the dark of night." I swallowed hard, "under an assumed name if that's the only way you'll allow me to serve."

"No!" he roared, without looking up.

"Then, I'm not asking your permission, but informing you of my intent," I said, and stormed out of the room.

I wandered down to the stables where the smell of dust and hay took me back to my childhood. I loved our fine horses in Vicksburg. I'd raced a few of them at the local track. The speed and pounding hooves stirred my blood. I realized I was homesick, but in a different way. I wanted the comfortable life I'd led as a child. I wanted not to think of being a coward and of the war that consumed my father's attention.

At the same time, however, I wanted the new freedom of adulthood. I wanted to join the Army and prove my worth. In the time since my trip to Milldale, I'd come to believe that fright skewed my judgment that evening. Worse, I hadn't been afforded a chance to prove the others wrong. The only way I saw out of it, was to go to war. If my father wouldn't endorse my choice and help me to gain a command, I'd join as an enlisted man.

I lounged in the alleyway of the stable and looked over the fine horses of the men who were stationed about the house. The horses were beautiful and spirited. They were covered with blankets monogrammed with the insignia of the Confederate States of America. My heart filled with pride. The new nation was one of my people's, not the Northerners, who ran roughshod over the old Union and treated Southerners as if they were less than human.

From the dark shade of the alleyway, the openings at either end were bright with sunlight. The dust hung illuminated in the air as if embedded with silver. When my father stepped into one of the openings, his figure was framed in the doorway as a shadow, a huge representation of the actual man who stood well over six feet to begin with.

My stomach turned over. I knew what he was about to say and there'd be hell to pay before the day was done. I'd never stood up to him before. He was not a man to be trifled with and I knew I'd stepped over the line. I was ready for whatever punishment he aimed to give.

He approached through the hanging dust, becoming slowly more visible.

"Boy!" he called out, and I felt my innards jump.

"Yes sir?"

"We have some matters to tend to."

"Yes sir."

"While I don't approve of your impertinent speech, I understand the cause of it. You're a young man and your blood runs hot these days with thoughts of war and glory. Perhaps, you feel guilty that so many others are dying while you're doing nothing. It's all perfectly understandable."

I nodded while he spoke, but wondered how he knew so much of what I felt. I thought of my emotions as being singular in nature. Most of the others I'd talked to were not anxious to join the fighting.

"I know how you feel, I want that understood," he said, and watched me for any sign of denial before he continued. "What you don't understand, is there's more to this war than fighting. Peace is as much a part of war as guns and ammunition and when it comes, there must be enough men left to lead a new nation. I can tell that you've been led to believe that your destiny is to assume a command, but I tell you it's not."

As he finished, I shook my head and began to speak, but he held his hand up to stop me.

"Hear me out. You're too young to join the war as an officer and you'll not serve your nation well to die in some meaningless battle as an enlisted man. In the years to come, you'll be surrounded by those who've led men into battle and have become the heroes of Southern society for their bravery. As an enlisted man you'll gain no such notoriety and at your age you'll not gain the confidence of a general so that you might be placed in command. Should the war last until your eighteenth birthday, a command will be sought. But, you must think beyond your youth and the moment. The new nation will need young men of vision to keep the political goals of this war alive in the minds of the citizens. That's why I've refused to watch you seek out folly through misplaced ambition."

He took a deep breath and nodded to me for a response.

"Father, I'm a coward to some of my friends. I don't want to discuss how that's come about, but it has and unless I'm able to throw off the yoke of cowardice, how am I ever to lead men in politics? Who'd vote for a coward?"

"There are other ways of serving your nation than in battle. I am not a general, and yet, no one questions my bravery."

"That's different. You were a soldier and I've not yet been one. Now it's my turn and if I miss it I'd carry the stain of cowardice for the rest of my life," I said, pleading for understanding.

My father nodded his head, as if considering my words.

"I'm impressed with the thought that's gone into your decision. However, let me suggest another route to securing your honorable reputation. As you know, it's vital that I remain in contact with President Davis. It's becoming increasingly difficult to get letters through along the regular routes. Dispatches must often go through enemy lines, or questionable territory. Therefore, I propose you become a Presidential courier. It can be dangerous work and you must protect the documents entrusted to you at all costs. You may be called upon to give your life, if need be, to guarantee that no official message falls into the hands of the enemy. You could be responsible for the deaths of thousands of men should these letters find their way into the hands of Union troops."

I was stunned by the proposal. It seemed all too important for a youngster to be entrusted with such vital papers. I swallowed hard. The responsibility terrified me.

"You'll be forced to ride at night through woods you're not familiar with, woods that may be filled with Union troops on all sides," he said.

I didn't know if he were trying to frighten me out of the job, or talk me into it. I could only think of the ride back from Milldale and how easily I'd gotten off the path. I thought of the strange noises and the fear that gripped me that night.

"It isn't a job for a child," he said, prodding me closer to a decision.

It seemed that he was somewhat ambivalent to the answer I'd give. I wondered how he wanted me to answer. Maybe, it didn't matter to him. If I declined the offer, he'd always be able to say that I wasn't ready for battle if I were too frightened to take the messenger's post. If I took it, he'd be able to keep track of me as the war progressed.

"Well," he said, turning to leave, "you think about it for a spell. I have duties to tend to in the house."

When he'd gone, I pulled myself onto the top board of a stall and sat there thinking. If I took the job, when would I leave? What preparation would I have to undergo? Would I always have to ride at night? I knew I couldn't ask him any of these questions as they'd sound mitigating in nature, as if I were afraid of certain aspectsof the position. It was all, or nothing. I decided to talk it over with Sergeant Jameson.

I walked out of the stables and up to the porch where Jameson stood his post. He was a rather short man, not quite as tall as myself and I only 16 years of age at the time.

He was fairly thin, but for the paunch that protruded beyond his belt. A red sash encircled his waist and a sword hung from it as a deadly decoration.

Jameson, though short, was a ferocious fighter. Originally, he rode with General Forrest until receiving several wounds. Evidence of the wounds were noticeable in his halting, dragging gait. But, no man could match his movements when a serious threat presented itself. Since his assignment to my father, we'd become friends and I trusted his judgment.

He stood on the porch, scanning the area about the house with small, blue, intense eyes that shifted and darted while he spoke.

"Sergeant Jameson, may I have a word with you?"

"Go right on ahead," he said, wasting no more than a glance on me before returning his gaze to the bushes and weeds that surrounded the perimeter of the house.

"I believe that it's time for me to join the war effort. I'm only 16, but I know of others who've served at that age."

Jameson spit tobacco juice saved up in his cheek. He glanced at me again and narrowed his eyes.

"Becomin' a man, are ye?"

"I feel it's my duty."

"Fancy yourself a hero? Ye havin' dreams of gallant warfare?"

I shrugged.

"Let me tell you something about yonder war, son. It's a filthy business having to cut a man's throat who wants to live as much as yourself. It's hard to watch the life go out of his eyes while keepin' the life in yourn."

I kicked at the dirt under my feet. I understood his position in the matter, but he had my intentions all wrong. I didn't seek glory. I sought solace and peace of mind. I knew that death might find me in the war, but hiding was eating my guts out like a cancer.

"I'm not looking for this war to be a pleasure. Yet, as long as I remain safely behind the lines, I feel like a coward."

Jameson roared with laughter. "Don't worry none about them lines, son. Afore this one's over, the lines will get in behind ye, whether you move, or don't."

"My father has offered to make me a Presidential courier to run the first leg of his correspondence with the President."

"That's worse yet."

"I don't imagine it's much more dangerous than carrying the mail."

Jameson was shocked. "No sir, I don't believe a word of it. Ye might as well make out your will as we stand. Why, a courier is treated with utmost distaste by soldiers as they're liable to be spies as well and most are tortured before being hung. No sir, that ain't no calling for you to be courtin'," he said, with a glimmer of a smile in his eyes. "I'd rather stand unarmed before a direct charge of cavalry than become a Presidential courier."

"You're having quite a time at my expense, Sgt. Jameson."

"No sir, ask any one of the men here. I'll not speak to them a second and you can gain whatever intelligence you might, free of all coercion. They'll all say the same thing. Why, just go up to any of them and inform them that they're to become a courier and see if their tempers don't flare."

"I doubt my father would place me in such jeopardy," I countered, trying to break him of teasing me.

Jameson shook his head as he kept a faithful watch on the surroundings. He spit a long, arcing stream of tobacco juice.

"It just ain't right," he said, sneaking a look at the position of the sun. "Unless, of course, he has some mighty plan for you after the war. That is, should it end while you breathe the good Lord's air. No sir, I think he was teasing you a bit. If'n it were me, I'd offer ye the most dangerous assignment the army had to offer to make you sit still at home, as rightfully you should."

Jameson had me confused. I didn't know whether to believe him, or not. I thought it might be a plan conjured up by the two of them. But, some of what he said made a great deal of sense.

"Yonder's Corporal Donnigan, ask him what he thinks of taking a job as a courier."

I searched the woods beyond the house for a sign of the Corporal, but couldn't locate him.

"I don't see him."

Jameson grabbed my neck and pointed my head in the direction I'd been looking, then tilted my head up until I saw, between the branches and leaves of a tree, Donnigan sitting idly upon a limb.

"But, don't look up into the tree when you speak to him. Look out onto the road." He gave me a little push on the back. "Go on, now."

"I don't have to do that. I believe what you say."

"Fine, then go into the house and tell your father that you'll have none of it. Remind him that you're his only son and that you'll not stick your neck out to be severed. Tell him that your life is much more valuable than for it to be wasted on such foolishness. Tell him, from me, that I'm ashamed to serve a father that would suggest such a thing to his own flesh and blood."

I stumbled across the door frame unsatisfied that Sgt. Jameson was being completely honest. My mind swam in confusion trying to sort out the pieces and decide whether I were being manipulated, or not. Either way, I knew I'd take the assignment. If it were truly dangerous, I'd establish my bravery. If it weren't dangerous, I'd have the satisfaction that I'd served my nation in the best way I could.

I strode stiffly into my father's study and announced that I'd become a courier for the Confederate States of America. A flash of amusement sped across his face and I knew I'd been had.

4

Corporal Donnigan taught me the finer points of being a courier. He was a tall, lanky man with red hair and a heavy beard. He seemed old to me, but I was surprised to hear he was only 22.

Donnigan began the training by showing me how to lie, should I meet up with Union troops. He said that I should stick as close to the truth as possible, altering only slightly the real intentions. I'd be on business for my father taking a message to one of his partners. I learned the names of businessmen in towns that corresponded with the general directions that I'd travel. A week was spent on developing logical and factually supported stories.

Then, we got into the part I wanted to know most about: physical defense. Donnigan was a master at it. He was a true pugilist. He was also a sneak.

"Nay, see, you be thinkin' all wrong," he admonished once, when I'd suggested keeping my Colt revolver in the saddlebag where decoy contracts were stored. "Thinkin' like that'll be the end of you, sure. Keep the papers here and, when asked, you can show them. When you stick your hand inside they might get suspicious and reach in theyselves. Least ways, they'll go for their guns when you reach in. Keep the pistol in the other bag and look through the papers on this side, not finding the proper papers, you make to look in the other bag and you have them cold, lad," he said, his eyes brightening with mischief.

"Never," he said, waving a finger, "show your best hand first."

Donnigan knew his business. He taught me how to rate a command by their organization, their attitudes and dress. Which of the troops would be undisciplined and would fall for simple diversions. Most important, he told me how to tell a well prepared command that might have others in the woods.

"Now, should you ever be surrounded with no hope of escape, or if the shootin' starts, you must be prepared to destroy the most important part of the message. Hand over all of the decoy information first, then calmly and casually eat the vital portion of the message as if you were takin' a chaw of tobacco. Stare 'em right in the eyes when you do it, lad."

"Then what?"

"Then what?" he asked, laughing, "then they'll kill you."

I swallowed hard as fear revealed itself in my eyes.

"You ain't on a picnic, lad. Many better and finer men have died for a lot worse reasons. Be proud and defiant to the end. Then, you'll know that you died with a purpose and for the cause of others."

I nodded. It was hard to remember that others were depending on me for their lives. It was hard to forget myself. My selfishness got in the way of reason. The fear showed too often, at first, and betrayed my thoughts to Donnigan. Then, after a few weeks, Donnigan pulled me off behind a tree.

"It's about time for you to take some messages," he said, watching my reaction. "Aye, soon they'll be coming to you with a dispatch to carry. Are you ready, lad?"

"I think so," I replied.

"Thinkin's nothing to do with it now. You just do as I've said to do," he stared at me for a moment and pulled a bottle from inside his coat. "Have a drink of this fine whiskey."

"No, thank you, Corporal."

"Did it sound like a request? Have a drink, I say."

I looked up toward the house to see if my father might happen to take notice.

"Never mind your father. He's placed you in the position of needin' the drink, he shan't have a say any further."

I took the bottle and removed the cork. I sipped at it and handed it back. Donnigan refused to take the bottle.

"I said a drink, lad, not a drop or two."

I shrugged my shoulders and took a deep pull, then coughed and wiped my mouth. Donnigan took the bottle, drank from it and corked it. I was suddenly hit blind-side by his fist. I felt myself reel from the impact of the blow. I fell against a tree and steadied myself.

"There's only this last lesson, so mind it well," he said, replacing the bottle inside his coat. "You're dead. From this point on, you're dead and there ain't a damned thing to do about it. There's no way, twixt heaven and earth, that you'll ever live to see the end of the war. The only solace you might take from it, is that you'll die an honorable and heroic death. Get that straight in your head and act accordingly. Everything I've taught you in the past few weeks has been to keep the dispatch alive, not you, lad. Remember, you're there to keep the dispatch alive and that's the end of it."

I didn't know what he meant, exactly. I certainly didn't know why he had to hit me before he said it.

"May I have another drink, Corporal?"

"Aye, that you may," he said, his mischievous eyes watching my every move as he handed me the bottle.

I tried to pull the cork out of the bottle. I pulled on it and tugged. I angled myself against the cork in a variety of ways.

"It's stuck," I said handing back the bottle.

Donnigan's brow knotted and he gave a firm grip to the cork and it came out so easily that his arms were thrown wide apart and I hit him square in the teeth. He stumbled backward into a tree, corked the bottle and dropped it. I could see in his eyes that he was about to take after me and I sprinted away. He chased me about the front of the house until Sgt. Jameson put a stop to the tomfoolery.

When Donnigan regained control of his temper, he slapped me on the back and smiled with pride.

"You'll do fine," he said and went back into the woods to find the bottle.

Jameson stood beside me. He spit tobacco into the dirt and pulled me inside. My father sat in the study. There were several letters on the desk, along with a number of bogus contracts.

"This time," Jameson said, "you're to meet up with General Forrest's courier, who'll convey the letters from there."

I nodded. My cover story was gone over a number of times. I was asked to recite things to be said to whomever might stop me. My stomach knotted up with anxiety. I put the contracts and letters into my saddlebags along with the Colt revolver as I'd been instructed. I threw the bags over my shoulder and started out.

"Wait," my father said.

I stopped and turned around to face him. He stood up from his desk and walked to a closet. He opened one of the doors and produced a Spencer seven-shot carbine.

"You'll need more than a musket to do this duty. I'd never forgive myself if you were killed for lack of ability to load a musket. Lord knows, there's plenty of other ways to die in this day and age."

He held the rifle out. I took it gingerly and my eyes followed the length of the gleaming barrel. The rifle seemed an unwarranted extravagance.

"Father...I don't quite know what to say. It's beautiful."

I was proud in that moment, as proud as I'd ever been. I was proud of my father for the valuable service he gave to the Confederacy. I was proud that he'd willingly sacrificed all of his belongings to do the right thing. I was proud of myself, too, and that I'd become someone my father could count on.

"Just, please, be careful and avoid any confrontation if you can. Your pride must not be greater than your duty."

I nodded and turned toward the door. As I walked, it seemed that I left something of myself behind. Perhaps, it was the child that dwelt within. I felt a sense of maturity. It was a grave and terrific moment.

Outside, the others waited for me and gave their simple nod, or slight wave as I ventured down to the stables. I carried my bags and the rifle that seemed all the more beautiful for the sun shining on it. The stables were filled with the smell of grass, dust and manure that seemed always to brighten my spirits.

I saddled the horse, a gelding roan, and removed the old musket from the scabbard. I slid the Spencer in its place. The rifle was much shorter and lighter than the musket. I took my knife and cut the scabbard down to fit the carbine.

After the alterations, I mounted the horse and carried the musket to the porch. I tossed it to Jameson.

"Would you put that away for me?"

Jameson nodded and set the musket by the door. He never took his eyes off the tree line for very long, and he did the task without turning away from the perimeter. He was a gem and I felt indebted to President Davis for sending him to protect my father.

I rode off on my first assignment with the sun past its apex and heading deliberately toward the horizon. There were a few more hours of daylight, that I planned to use as efficiently as I could. The horrors of riding blind had not left me in the months since returning from Milldale. The child was gone, but not the fear of things lurking in the darkness.

I rode northeast toward the Tennessee line. It was a fairly short ride to the rendezvous point with Forrest's courier. I guessed they were testing my ability before giving me a difficult assignment. When I arrived at the appointed spot, an old Indian village long since abandoned, I sat the horse and waited for the courier.

There was a cool breeze in the November evening and the leaves upon the trees rustled with a constant surging, pulsing commotion. I heard strange noises, or imagined that they were strange. My eyes were wide to the darkness and I turned constantly around in the saddle to discover who might come upon me unexpected. I listened closely for sounds of the other courier. I thought he'd ride right up to me. He didn't.

When I'd waited a half hour, I turned my horse around to head back. I wasn't sure if I should do so, or not. I started back a few steps, then stopped and decided that I'd wait a bit longer. I strained my eyes to see beyond the foliage. Finally, I decided to return home.

As I started back along the way I'd come, I heard a voice. I don't know what was said. The words were in the form of a grunt, of sorts. I whirled around instinctively.

"Ye won't be needin' that shootin' iron," a man said from the darkness. Then he rode out into the open, where I could see him. He was a man dressed much the same as I was. I'd expected him to be in uniform.

"Depends on who you are," I replied, my mind still reeling from the fact that I'd jerked the rifle from its scabbard. I didn't recall reaching for it. It was a reflex that was untrained and unpracticed.

"Then again," he said, "it might just depend on who ye be." He narrowed his eyes and squinted as he looked me up and down. "Do you live nearby?"

"Might," I replied, thinking that it was the courier, but then, I wasn't dead sure about it and they'd often instructed me to be dead sure about everything. It dawned on me that neither of us had enough information about the other to be confident in who we'd found in the depths of the woods. Or, was it a test?

"What are ye up to in these woods, so long after dark?" he asked.

"Same thing as you, maybe. What business have you here?"

He grinned a gold-tooth grin and relaxed in the saddle. I kept my rifle pointed in his direction. His horse began to walk toward me with unguided, unprompted steps. I cocked the rifle.

"Hold on, now. You keep that rifle safe, hear?"

"Isn't much danger to me," I replied.

I couldn't tell if he were having fun at my expense, or testing me, or someone unknown to the Cause. He might be working for the Union at that. There were too many possibilities for me to trust him an inch.

"Ye best think on that some more. If'n you kill me accidental, they'd be liable to string you up just the same."

"Not in this county," I lied, playing the cards I'd been told to play. "These hereabouts are all my kinfolk, and I don't know you at all. I'd simply tell them you were trying to rob me in the dark and I had to kill you."

"Family from here, eh?"

I nodded.

"Well, I'll be," he said, letting his horse draw closer.

"Next time that horse moves a hoof, you'll be lyin' face down beside it."

He pulled up short on the reins and a serious look came over his face.

"You don't want to kill me, son."

"Yes sir, I do. Fact is, I can't think of anything I'd enjoy more than an upright killing of a robber in the woods. It'd make me a hero with my kin."

The rider seemed to lose a taste for the game at that point. I don't know if he believed me, but he suddenly changed his tone to one of serious business. Perhaps, he thought he'd come upon someone besides the courier he was supposed to meet. Unsure of his position, he began to pursue a different line of questioning.

"Let's just take a step back here," he said, spitting into the dirt. "I'm to meet someone here." He watched for my response, but I gave him none. If it were the courier, the shoe was on the other foot and it was my turn to play.

"I was just out here riding. I like this old place. Used to be Indians here, prior to the government moving them off somewhere."

His eyes narrowed. "Truly, are ye from hereabouts?"

"Yes, sir."

"Seen another rider, tonight?"

"There was a fellow who seemed lost a few miles back, but I didn't stop to ask his business."

"Damn," he said and spit. "Can ye show me there?"

"I'm headed yonder," I replied, pointing behind him with the rifle.

"Young feller?"

"Yes, sir. He seemed right spoiled. Folks must have a dollar, or two. Riding a nice horse with a fine saddle."

"Damn," he said. "How far back?"

"Mile, maybe more."

"I'll pay ye a dollar to show me."

"Confederate, or Union?"

The words stopped him dead in his motion for the dollar. He was being asked something of consequence and he knew it. His thoughts about my allegiance to the Confederacy might be source for speculation, but he knew he shouldn't show his. Even as his hand hung in the air, he was conscious of it and knew he should move it soon.

"Pays to have both," he said, with a sly grin, "which would ye ask?"

The time to put facts on the table had come. The dodging and ducking had been fun. I'd proved my ability to handle a situation, but the hour was growing late. I didn't want to be the one to give in totally, so I decided to extend an offering that he'd find amicable.

"Neither spend too well in a forest," I said, alluding to General Forrest.

"Nor in Mississippi these days," he replied.

I grinned and each of us let out a long breath. It was good to have withstood the pressure and to know the feel of solid ground for communication. Without another word, he offered up his saddlebags. I reached back and pulled the Colt from mine and tossed them to him.

"See ya next trip," he said and pulled the horse around in a tight circle.

The ride back to the house was much lighter without the damning papers carried in the saddlebags. It seemed strange that all of the dangers the darkness presented on the trip out, vanished with the exchange. So, I enjoyed the ride and took particular attention of the woods and the animal life that scurried about in the darkness.

When I returned, I was met by Donnigan and Jameson who asked me to describe the courier from Forrest. I gave as complete a description as I could. I handed them the saddlebags and put the horse in the stall as I answered question after question about my route, the things I saw and the conversation between myself and the other courier.

In describing the way I turned the table on the other fellow, Donnigan's mouth twisted into a crooked smile. He wanted to hear every word just as it was uttered by myself and by Forrest's man. Both men were delighted when I told them of asking what sort of dollar he offered.

I made a few mistakes in the discourse and they fine tuned my way of getting at the matter, but applauded my handling of the situation. I grinned like a schoolboy at every compliment they handed me.

The three of us walked back to the house, they'd been relieved of duty for the night and asked me into their quarters, but I declined. I was exhausted by the ride and the anxiety that came with the responsibility. They understood and gave my shoulders a squeeze as they made to leave. Then, Donnigan stopped and turned to me.

"You'd have shot the man, lad? Had the horse continued to near?"

"Yes, sir," I said, only then realizing it was the truth. "I certainly would've." I looked up at the night sky showered with stars. "But, I didn't want to. I lied about that part of it."

"Decency hangs in the balance of wanting to kill and not wanting to."

5

I rode as a courier from then on without much trouble. For all of the anxiety I'd suffered at first, I found little danger on the trails. The war moved away from Mississippi, leaving a minimum of troops behind to maintain order in some of the larger towns. Toward the end of the war, the dispatches became more frequent and more urgent. Often I'd have to ride for days. The rains came and I rode through it all. Sometimes, during that winter, I felt as if I were frozen to the saddle and felt more danger from temperatures than from anything else.

In April of 1865, I found myself the lone hold out of believers in the Confederacy. Even Sgt. Jameson had conceded defeat and began to think more often of how and when he'd surrender. Of course, he'd not do so until word from the President, or my father, had come that he should. He expected it to come any time.

"Yes sir, I've sure enough dug a hole here for me to rot in," Jameson said.

I looked at him from the corner of my eye. I didn't want to respond to the statement, because I knew his frame of mind. I didn't want to hear anything critical of the Confederacy.

"I'm a fightin' man, son," he said, and spit a stream of stringy, brown tobacco juice. "I don't know no other way to be and yet, none would have me now, 'cept maybe the Mexicans."

"It isn't over, yet," I replied, leaning against another support on yet another porch of another place that we'd found to inhabit. The houses were becoming of worse quality as we moved. The place we found ourselves in at the time was nothing more than a barn with windows and a poor, weather-beaten porch.

"It's over."

"It isn't over until we surrender and I have no intention of surrendering."

"Word will come any day now."

"Not today."

Jameson glanced in the direction of the North. "They got us whipped. Ain't nothin' to do now, but figure a way to stay alive afterwards. Which is what I aim to do."

His words stole my rigid determination, though I knew that I could never bring myself to surrender. I felt as if recognition of the fact would leave me broken. I was only 17, and felt my life slipping from my grasp. Without the Confederacy, life would be more than I could bear.

The notion of it was making me reckless. I saw, in the rides through the darkness, a way to end my life before I had to suffer the humiliation and horror of utter defeat. Perhaps, I felt it stronger than Jameson. For him, it was a matter of survival. For me, it took all hopes for the future with it. I was trained to be a statesman, but as the son of a traitor I'd never see office.

I took more chances as the war ground to a close. I rode the regular roads more often and stopped at public houses on my way to and from the encounter. Some might say that I was endangering the war effort, but, as far as I could see,

there was no war effort. The fighting became a mere
pretense to hold out for more favorable treatment, nothing
more.

I'm not sure if I were slowly maturing, or if the reality
of defeat were finding its way into my brain, but my
manner took on an edge. I felt betrayed and sought out
whoever might take the brunt of my temper.

"Well, I'm not giving up that easy," I said, pushing past
Jameson. I went to the stables to prepare my horse and
bags for the ride. I heard Jameson suck in a breath as I'd
nudged him. I knew he wanted to hit me for it. I also knew
he wouldn't out of respect for my father and his duty.
That's why I had the nerve to nudge him. But, I wanted
him to feel ashamed of his words. I wanted everyone to be
ashamed of losing the war. In my juvenile mind, I thought
it would make it easier to accept if those responsible were
duly ashamed of it.

I walked my horse to the front of the house. Jameson
stood his post and didn't look at me when I went in to see if
there were any final letters to take along. My father sat
behind a makeshift desk in a tiny room lit by the waning
sunlight. He had yet to light the candles and lamps. Fuel
was hard to come by and he saved everything for
emergencies.

His hand was on his forehead and he leaned heavily on
the desk. He looked much older and quieter than I'd ever
seen. Long since gone was the brusque mannered, lively
man that populated my youth. That day and for the rest
that followed, I'd know him only as an old man. His mind
was as sharp as ever, but his physical presence seemed to
grow smaller, as if he were imploding upon himself in small
degrees.

I didn't see any letters at the head of the desk and took
that for the answer I sought. I turned slowly, quietly, so as
not to be heard.

Out in front, Jameson was running his hands over the gelding and whispering to it. I untied the reins and swung aboard. My earlier words had the opposite effect of what I'd intended. Instead of making Jameson feel ashamed, I felt ashamed. I looked down on him from the saddle.

"I apologize, Sgt. Jameson. It seems I've no manners left."

"Apology accepted, Jeff," he said, without looking up.

I pulled the horse around and started off before any more was said.

I remember that night by the cool wind that smelled of rain. I looked up a number of times to see the stars, but they were hidden by low-hanging clouds. I checked the ties that held my slicker to the back of the saddle. An hour went by before I saw the moon appear on the eastern horizon. It revealed itself only as a bright spot in the clouds and rose quickly up into the sky.

As I rode, the wind began to gust and finally the rain started in. When I stopped to put the slicker on, I took the Colt out of the saddle bag and thrust it into my waistband. The slicker was a large, circular cloth, formerly a tent, sealed with oil. A hole was cut in the center for my head to fit through and it was large enough to cover myself and most of the horse.

The rain came first as drops, then as a downpour. I searched for a light in one of the houses along the path where I might stop until it lessened. I rode through the rain and wind for a long period before I came upon a small shack with a lantern in the window. I drew the horse up to it and dismounted. I gathered up the saddlebags and knocked on the door. No one came at first, and I beat harder, nearly breaking it with a thunderous pounding of my fists.

The door was jerked open and I came face to face with a stout man in his thirties. He was missing a leg and his left arm hung uselessly at his side.

"What is it?" he asked, his face twisted in an expression of anger and annoyance.

"I was hoping to get in out of the rain, to let it blow over a bit before moving on. Do you have room?"

"Late to be out riding, ain't it?"

"Yes sir, but I'm on business for my father and he wouldn't like it if I failed to meet his obligations."

The man glanced over his shoulder at the humble interior. "Well, come on in, leave that slicker for your horse."

I removed the slicker and spread it over the horse's back. I felt a bit awkward, carrying the Colt in my belt, but decided that it would be better to have it. The man watched me tend to the gelding and noticed the revolver immediately. He studied me a bit closer and stepped away from the opening of the door as I entered.

"Have a seat," he said, pointing to an empty chair. The table set in the center of the room and a small bunk set along the wall. The interior of the shack was clean and well cared for. It had the mark of a woman about it. There's a distinct difference between a home cared for by a man and that cared for by a woman. Even the house negras could do only so much for my father's taste and every time I visited friends, their homes seemed so much softer for the touch of a woman.

I adjusted the pistol and sat in the chair opposite of his. A fire was burning in the fireplace, keeping the humble quarters warm.

"Set yer hat by the fire. Let it dry some."

I did as the man asked and was grateful for the opportunity. Removing my hat gave him a better look at my features.

"You're just a young feller," he said.

"Old enough, I reckon."

He nodded. "That may be," he said. "Not in the war?"

"No sir, I'm only 17, and tending to my father's business occupies most of my time."

"I seen plenty of younguns die in that war." He narrowed his eyes, "you someone important enough to miss all the fun?"

"No sir, my father does business with the Army, but he's too old to tend to all of his doings and I help him."

"What sort of business?"

"Horses mostly, some beef and wheat. He's a broker of sorts. He puts together small buyers and offers the whole package to the Army."

"Which army?"

"Confederate."

A wry grin appeared at his lips. "That business is almost done and the whole South along with it. I reckon you'll be poor soon enough," he said.

I shrugged. "None of my concern. Rich, or poor, I have to live my life through."

He nodded at the reasonable answer. "Unfortunate, ain't it?"

"Yes sir."

"Lost my leg in the battle for Vicksburg. Arm don't work neither."

"You're a brave man."

"Ain't nothin' brave about it. They fired a cannon and when the smoke cleared, I was missin' a piece." He chuckled to a private joke.

"Sad thing."

"Yep, it tis."

His eyes seemed to gloss over and he drifted into some world of reverie. I didn't care to disturb him. I looked about the room, wondering where the woman fit into it. I wondered if he had children. It seemed as if there were missing pieces everywhere.

"Care for some coffee?"

"I'd appreciate that," I replied. I watched as he struggled to get out of the chair. "I can get it, if you'd like."

I received a cold stare in return for my polite generosity. He didn't say a word. It seemed to be a stare often used to discourage sympathy. He hobbled over to the pot brewing over the fire and took down a cup from the mantle. His movements, while clumsy, were swift. The shack was small enough that all areas were quickly accessible without a crutch.

We drank from the metal cups in silence. His eyes roamed periodically about the room, then seemed to lose focus. The man lived as much within himself as he did without.

I listened to the sounds of the storm. The winds would die down and the rain would lessen only to be suddenly enlivened. As I monitored the weather, I slipped into my own world of reverie. What dreams I'd had for my life had slipped away in the storm of war as time slipped away within the shack.

"What's the pistol for?"

I pulled my mind back to the present. "I travel a lot at night and there's robbers sometimes and Union soldiers who might take exception to my part in supplying the South."

"Now there's somethin'! A well-educated boy with a gun and on the look out for robbers and Yanks!" The grin he wore faded into a stern look. "Don't trifle with me, boy. I ain't got it all figured yet, but you're up to more than you're sayin'."

"Well sir, you could be right about that, but I only asked for a dry place to put up. If you'd rather I leave, then I'll be going." I set the coffee cup down and reached for my hat.

"Naw, don't worry yourself."

We sat again for a long time without talking. Even in the silence, there was a roaring of the mind that continued to race behind his stoic expression. On occasion, he'd wince from some pain, either physical, or emotional.

Time was eternal in the shack and when I pulled my watch out, I noticed that I'd only been inside for an hour. It seemed closer to days.

"The revolver's loaded is it?"

I nodded.

"More coffee?"

"Yes sir, if there's plenty."

"There's plenty."

He struggled up from his seat and made his way to the pot. I held out my empty cup. He took it and filled it. As he handed it back, I felt that something was wrong. It was a momentary thought that shot across my brain, a panic of understanding that I didn't have time to act on. The hot coffee spilled down my shirt, scalding my chest. As I stood up, I felt the Colt rise out of my waistband as I stumbled backward over the chair. I fell against the wall and the chair clattered. I looked up at the man, worried for my life.

He stared down at me over the barrel of the Colt. I could only think of the irony of being killed with my own weapon. A tear ran down the rugged, sun-tanned cheek of the one-legged man. Then, he raised the gun to his own temple and pulled the trigger. Pieces of his head flew against the wooden walls. I was sickened by it. My mind reeled, searching for a reason, or cause for the tragedy of his life and death, but could find none. All that could be known remained with him, hidden behind the still lips and sightless eyes.

I got up from the floor and bent to retrieve the pistol. My fingers trembled as I reached for it lying so close to his dead fingers. I brought all of my powers to bear and snatched it up from the floor. I grabbed my hat and charged out of the door. The storm continued to rage, but I was glad to be free of the shack.

I wrapped myself in the slicker and kicked the horse into a gallop. My hat was pulled low over my eyes and I struggled to see out from under the brim without getting pelted by stinging droplets of rain.

I rode without thinking. I couldn't think. The suicide haunted me. I felt guilty for my part in it. Had I not stopped, he might well have gotten through the night and found something to live for. I told myself that I should've seen it coming. I gave myself far greater powers of premonition than I possessed and cursed myself for not acting on them.

All night, I replayed the incident over and over until I came to grips with the fact that there was nothing I could have done. It was an awful pill to swallow, but the facts held that I was not God and could not pretend to have power over anyone's life, but my own. I came to think, even, that God had placed he and I together for the specific purpose of bringing his suffering to an end. I put my faith in God's will and rode on.

The morning found me near the Tennessee line. The
storm had ended before first light, but heavy clouds hung
close to the ground and threatened to begin a drizzle. An
old church, recently shattered and burnt by some military
operation, stood in a field outside of a small town. I rode
behind the church through the high grass. From out of the
trees, by a creek, another led his horse toward me.

"I figured ye for dead," the man said.

"Me too," I replied.

He cocked his head, but didn't have time to pursue the
matter. We exchanged saddlebags and broke up as soon as
possible to avoid suspicion. Any one of the townsfolk could
be a Union informer.

I stopped in at the town to roll up the slicker and feed
my horse. I'd passed the livery on the way into town and
rode up to it as if I'd been there several times. I paid for
some feed in gold and received Union military script in
return. There weren't many places to cash Confederate
script and even when some of the proprietors would take it,
they wanted great amounts for the goods they offered.

After getting a quick bite to eat, I returned to the livery
and left town. I didn't care to go back the same way I'd
come. It was a bad practice, and the idea of passing by the
shack turned my stomach. A few miles out of town, I
turned west for a few miles and then south again to put me
off my recent trail.

I arrived home in the evening. I nodded at Corporal
Donnigan who stood guard on the porch, I continued on to
the barn where I unsaddled the horse and threw the
saddlebags over a rail. After putting the saddle in the tack
room, I removed the bit and turned the horse out into the
corral. I hefted a few forks full of grass hay into the bin,
stroked the horses' neck and picked up the saddlebags. I
walked back toward the house.

I was tired. I thought about sleep, but was afraid that a recollection of the blood splattered walls would greet my unguarded mind. Drifting up to the porch, I dropped heavily into one of the wooden chairs and set the saddlebags at my feet

"There, lad," Donnigan said, "you just rest your bones a might. These days a man finds rest where he may."

I nodded and closed my eyes. Behind the lids, my eyes felt as if clogged with sand. But, all was black, no visions occurred, no thoughts raced. My brain sat atop my spine as if mush upon a stick. I felt as if I were floating in a dark sea, bobbing with the waves as a buoy. The air was cool and I pulled my jacket tighter about my body.

"Go along, now," Donnigan urged. "Get some proper rest. No one knows what tomorrow brings."

"I'm enjoying the air."

I heard the scuff of his boot as he stepped off the porch and into the night, pursuing some flash, or rustle that he might have seen, or heard. I opened one eye to see which way he'd gone, but he'd already vanished. I closed my eye again to revel in that lovely, exhaustion that obliterated thought and set the soul free.

I enjoyed the lolling, numbness and sat on the porch for some time. Donnigan came back to resume his post. Perhaps, he'd only slipped away to relieve himself in the bushes. A thump sounded in the night and suddenly I was falling, then I landed hard upon the rough boards of the porch.

"There you go, off to bed, now," Donnigan said.

"You kicked the chair over," I replied, feeling abused.

"There's one I've not heard in a while."

I dusted off my clothes, resecured my Colt in its place and gathered up the bags. I entered the house and set the bags inside my father's study, if it could be called that. I had the only real bedroom. My father slept in the room off the kitchen that he called his study. It was a small dining room when people lived there. With our coming, the house had become a command post with my father taking his dinner at his desk.

I stumbled away to the bedroom. I removed my revolver from my waistband and fell over onto the bed.

In the world of dreams, I saw all that I feared to see and more. Bloody walls, the sound of the discharge reverberating in my ears and a sense of guilt haunted the netherworld of dream. I woke, more than once, with perspiration beaded on my forehead. My neck felt cold and wet, but fatigue forced me back to sleep each time.

Morning came silently as I slept. Beyond the door, I heard the rustling of commotion. It seemed different from the normal bustling of men, but I could gain no knowledge from what was said, or done. I didn't want to rise and thought of excuses to stay in bed the whole day long. In the end, I gave in to my growling stomach and rose with a stretch.

I rubbed my face and walked into the world of my father. It was then that I realized, after all previous mornings had not brought it to mind, that my father's world and mine were distinct and separate. His centered around the business at hand, while mine was carried out in the darkness along empty roads and thick forest. I was a mere by-stander to his world and he to mine.

Breakfast was long over, but the army cook had some left-overs waiting for my arrival. The meal consisted of dry bacon, eggs and grits kept warm in the oven. I sat down ready to devour all set before me, but before I could take a bite, my father called out to join him.

I rose, angry and hungry, but I entered his study with the most pleasant appearance I could produce.

"Yes sir?"

"I've received word of a murder this morning."

I was taken aback. My thoughts encircled the word that seemed alien in a time when people died by the thousands in the most gruesome manners and the term used to describe it was "war", not murder. My thoughts were occupied with the irony and I failed to reply.

"What's your response to that?"

"Murder seems a strange term these days."

"There's death and murder, son. One is not the other," he said, looking up from his desk with a steady gaze. "Did you see anything?"

"No sir."

"I ask, because it was along your route. Or, would have been had you taken the most logical path."

"I didn't see anything. How did it happen? How many were killed?"

"At last. You must be waking up!"

I chuckled. Perhaps, I was at that.

"A man was shot to death in his home about half the way to your rendezvous point."

"Oh, that!" I said, shaking my head. "That was no murder. It was a suicide. I was there, the crazy fool used my gun. I went up to the shack to wait out the worst of the rain..."

"You aren't to do that!" my father roared. It was a clear violation of procedure, which is why I hadn't told anyone of it.

"Yes sir, I know."

"Then, what happened?"

"I beat on the door and he let me in. We made some small talk, but he seemed disturbed and distant. He asked a lot of questions about what I was doing out in the rain, and what I kept a gun for. He laughed at me when I told him. Then, he asked if I wanted more coffee, spilled it on me, grabbed my gun and shot himself in the head."

"Go on."

"Well, I couldn't go to the nearest constable, so I left him there. I assumed that someone would find his body, surely others knew he was distraught and could piece it all together."

My father tapped the desk with his index finger. "Yes, I'm sure they might have been able to do that, if they'd found the gun on the premises, if they hadn't found tracks leading away from the cabin. But, the only weapon they found was the shotgun that he used for hunting. Now, they assume that it was murder and scour the county for suspects."

"I don't think they'll find the murderer, since none exist."

"Son, they'll find the murderer, because they'll have to. They can't have people afraid to go to sleep at night. They'll find themselves a murderer and hang the poor fool sure as the sun sets in the west."

"I'd better tell them the facts of the case."

"You'll do nothing of the kind. Do that, and you'll be the murderer they find."

"We can't let someone take the blame for a crime that wasn't committed."

"Why didn't you leave the revolver for them to find?"

"I didn't think about it like that. It was a suicide for which I didn't know an accounting would be necessary."

"Son, you must consider the times we live in. That's a Union county yonder. As far as I know, the army holds trials in that section. Everything is different today, you must keep that in mind when you're out in the woods. And, stay out of people's homes. You're not to stop anywhere."

I nodded. "Okay, but what are we going to do about this?"

"Nothing."

"We have to do something."

"The time for doing something was last night and the 'something' was to leave a gun for them to find. Now, there's nothing to be done that won't endanger us, or the Confederacy, in some way. Take this as a lesson and forget it. Hopefully, they'll find some undesirable they've been trying to rid themselves of and put his name on the rope."

I turned away. My head hung when I entered the kitchen. The food had lost its appeal. All through the meal, I saw, in my mind's eye, some poor wayward soul who'd take the blame for a suicide. All, because they had to hang someone.

6

I was moved by the thought of an innocent man being hung for the fictitious murder. I knew my father wanted me to stay out of it. I hoped that it wouldn't come to a choice. If forced to choose, I'd have to disobey. Perhaps, the townspeople would rid themselves of an undesirable, and maybe they'd commit an act of injustice greater than the act they sought to punish.

I grew sullen during that time. I was forced into silence around the soldiers, who were loyal only to my father and President Davis. They had no loyalty to me and that left me with no one to tell my plans to. So, I remained silent to disguise my intent.

I had visions of riding into town as the noose was being drawn around the neck of the convicted man. I saw myself pushing through the crowd, shouting his innocence.

I rode short routes then, to the south and east. It seemed that I was being kept from the area of the murder. The search lasted for a week until all hope was lost of finding the murderer.

I learned a great deal about the man in the shack. He was a Confederate soldier who fought to save Vicksburg in '62 where he lost his leg and the use of his arm. He was married then and lived with his wife in the shack where I found him. A week before the suicide they insisted on calling a murder, his wife was killed in a socially questionable situation that the newspaper refused to give detail of other than to refer to it as "the recent scandal". It was a sad history that I hoped would not be made tragic by hanging an innocent.

As time passed, I felt as if I could breathe again. It was all going to blow over without need of my dramatic appearance. There was a bit of humor in the notion, anyway.

My routes continued to take me away from the scene of the suicide, but my direction had lost meaning as time rolled on. A full month elapsed before I confided my intentions to Donnigan, who stared at me for some time in silence.

"But, lad, they hung the scoundrel."

"What?"

"Yes, two days ago. Didn't you read the paper?"

"I haven't seen the paper in weeks. I thought the investigation was stalled."

"It was, then a Union deserter was caught in the act of another murder and presented to the constable. He had articles from the man's home on his person and was promptly convicted of both murders." He eyed me suspiciously. "And, you claim that you were there when the poor veteran took his own life?"

"Yes, I thought you knew."

"Nay, I'd not known that," he said, rubbing his red beard. "So, that's why you've been quiet as a mouse these past weeks? Because you had all of this on your mind?"

"Yes," I replied, searching the ground for some way to make it turn out as it should have.

"But, lad, he was indeed a murderer. Set your mind at ease. What difference does it make if he murdered one, or two?"

He was right. Regardless of what I knew, it made no difference to the outcome. I felt relieved they'd not run a poor beggar in for the murder. My duty was satisfied by intent alone.

The war was in its final stages, then. Alliances with my father ended and the days filled with time. Others realized the end had come long before I would. I refused to let my dreams die as easily, but after Lee surrendered a sadness and realization bore down on me with such weight that I gave in and accepted the fact.

With the war clinging to the last gasp of life, a great excitement was aroused over the President's request to be smuggled across the Mississippi, where he'd continue to resist capitulation.

Most of the soldiers returned to their homes, or what was left of them. Only Donnigan and Jameson remained. My father sent me to organize a night movement across the Mississippi with friends and business partners near Vicksburg, then we all waited patiently for Jefferson Davis to arrive. He never came. He was captured early in May of 1865. Then it was over.

I rode my horse deep into the surrounding woods. I found a small pond and dismounted. I let the horse drink. As I stood watching him with the reins held lightly in my fist, I suddenly felt light-headed and nauseous. My throat grew tight and my palms moistened. It felt like I was about to faint. Instead, I dropped to my knees and cried. My sobbing was silent, but deep and it drained my soul of the resistance that kept me going through all the dark times of the Confederate cause. I wept and let go of all I'd ever wanted from life.

I don't know how long I knelt in the woods and moistened the ground with tears. Time meant nothing to me. There was nothing to look forward to, or back on. My future and my past vanished with the defeat of my nation. I was no one. I'd been orphaned in a new world of the all-powerful Union, stripped of identity and possessions in a huge world of enemies. Even the right to battle those enemies had disappeared.

I rose and pulled on the reins. The gelding followed as I walked. I'd never felt so alone and unwanted. It was a terrible, desperate and empty feeling that I'd never forget. As hard as I might try, in the years to come, I'd never be able to rid myself of the inner belief that I was an alien in my own land.

I returned to the house as the others were making preparations to leave. The owners sent word that they'd be reclaiming the place soon and that we should vacate the premises. I joined in the work of loading what little we had left into a wagon. Most of the cargo consisted of official papers and documents that marked my father's part in the war. Perhaps, the Union would disdain his effectiveness, but the people of the South would remember and someday look forward to the memoirs of my father.

When the wagon was loaded, I went into the house and sat against the wall. My father entered, but he wouldn't look at me. We were all conspirators in an illusion that had finally burst and the debris from the explosion spread shame on all of us.

"Where will we go?"

"Home," my father said, "I still hold the deed to most of the land and the house. I'm not sure how I'll make a living, but we have time to figure that out."

I nodded. He was right. My father always had a plan and a way of making things work out for himself. But, what would become of me? Who would I become in the world left to us?

I got up from the floor and walked out of the house for the last time. It was nothing compared to our home, but it felt familiar. Outside, my horse was tied to the back of the wagon.

"I'll ride the gelding," I said over my shoulder to my father, who followed. "You can ride with Jameson."

Jameson sat atop the wagon with the reins in hand. Donnigan was to the right of the wagon on horseback. I decided to ride to the rear to watch the load. It was a slow ride and felt somewhat like a funeral march.

It was raining when we came in sight of Vicksburg. It looked much the same as always in the dark. Lights shone from several windows, but the streets were empty due to the weather. We turned off the main road and toward our home. As the large structure came into view through the trees, it seemed cold and forbidding, as if holding a grudge for being left in the hands of the Union.

We camped out in the front room like vagabonds and left the unloading for morning in hopes that the rain would clear. I was restless, but tired enough to sleep and drifted off soon after lying down. But, my dreams held me captive in a mournful setting of emptiness. Visions of what had taken place over the years appeared before me in slumber and startled me from sleep. When I woke during the night, I stared up at the dark ceiling and listened to the sounds of the others snoring. Then, I'd fade from consciousness and awake again in a few hours.

Several days later, when we'd reestablished ourselves in the place and Donnigan and Jameson had gone home to wherever they lived, or would live, I confronted my father about my future. I sat in the front room of the house. I shifted the Colt and leaned the Spencer into a corner. It was hot inside and sweat rolled down my jaw. The front door stood open. I saw my father come across the lawn and duck under the bows of the willow.

He held a sadness, and if not an uncertain air, at least a more cautious one. He glanced about and strode up the steps. He walked on past me as if not seeing my ragged, skinny frame piled on top of the chair.

"Boy!" he yelled, from the other room.

I gathered my Spencer and carried it loosely in my hand with the barrel wavering floorward. I stood before him in the all but empty room with the massive desk of old being practically the only thing that remained of our lives there.

"You'll not be needing your arms, son. The war's over. It's time to put the weapons away and find employment of another kind."

"I've not learned another way," I said, hoping to hurt him for neglecting my education during the war years.

He leapt from his chair, knocking it backward, squeaking along the floor. His massive hands thundered down upon the old, familiar desk.

"I'll not have that tone, nor that attitude from you." He trembled with anger. "Whatever we fought for, we've lost. There won't be any need of carrying on with regret, or revenge. We all made our stake and spoke our will and the good Lord, for whatever indecipherable reasons, has gone against our cause. You must recognize the fact and live life by whatever manner He allows."

"Were we wrong?"

"I imagine so," he said, looking down, "for it was not His will that we should have won."

"Have you lied to me then?"

"I've not. But, neither do I know the power of the Almighty. I've not lied to you concerning the cause of our actions, nor the need to defend our beliefs and having put

all that I owned and all my thoughts to the outcome, as did
millions of others with their belongings and families and
lives, it was not to be. Perhaps, the injustice of slavery,
however humanely applied, is a greater sin than all the
good of all the people of the South. I honestly don't know,
son. But, I do know, and believe, that the Lord would not
have let us lose unless it were so."

"Or, God is unjust."

A thunderbolt crashed against the side of my head as if
the Lord, himself, had struck me down with a mighty blow
of lighting. I found myself thrust violently against the
wall, where I collapsed, and sat with folded legs in a corner.
A couple of feet away, where I'd been standing, the Spencer
stood on it's barrel a moment before falling over.

My mind swam in a liquid world. Roaring words came
to my ringing ears as muffled grunts and deep rumblings.
My eyes were uncontrollable and searched randomly about
the room until massive, powerful hands lifted my limp body
from the floor and my legs dangled. The toes of my boots
brushed lightly against the floor from time to time. I felt
the breath being squeezed from my lungs and I came to my
senses in the strong embrace of my father's arms.

"Forgive me, forgive me," he said, his words
penetrating the fog as my senses cleared. He set me down
on my legs and held me in place while my knees stiffened to
support my weight. Suddenly, there was a pounding at the
side of my head and I reached up to brush my swollen
cheek. My tongue explored the torn skin inside my mouth
and I spit out a molar.

He spoke to me, with his hands still clutching my
shoulders.

"My son," he whispered, "you're all that I have. Forgive
me and repent your brash words of atheist intent."

"I repent."

He clutched me to him then until I felt the air float from my aching mouth.

"All will be right in Heaven. Repent such thoughts and find His glory again in your heart. Your journey through life will follow a hard and difficult road. I dare not send you forward without knowing that God rides with you."

"Send me forward?"

My father let his grip ease and thrust me back to arms length, still clutching my shoulders.

"There's no future in Mississippi, or any of the South. Your only hope is to ride West, to the Frontier."

"But, what will you do? I'd better stay and look after you."

He smiled at the statement. "I'll work something out for myself, but you shall not stay."

He let go of me then, and picked up my carbine. He laid it on his desk. He strolled behind the desk and turned to face me. "War is war, son. Had we won, we'd have taken control of the Northern ports and garrisons and rebuilt the nation over in our design. The North will undoubtedly do the same to us."

He mused to himself and a smile broke across his face. "They believe that I'm a traitor. It amuses them to think of me as such, but I can handle it. You, however, must not be branded by the same iron. As an old man, I can handle their taunts, but it would stand as a mark against you no matter what occupation you found. They'd bring you down, Son, simply for the fun of it."

"I'm not afraid of them."

"No, I know you're not, but it doesn't matter."

"Where should I go?"

"Texas, most likely. Cotton will grow, should you decide to pursue that way of life. If not, there's the cattle business which is still fairly easy to involve oneself in. Not that it will amount to much, but it's an option. Mining seems fairly lucrative in the West."

I was silent as I thought of life anew.

"I'll not leave Mississippi!" I shouted, in panic.

"You must, or you'll have no life worth living. The privileges we've known have become our curse. Bear yours where it can least hinder your youth and the lives of your children. You must think of the future. It's all that's left."

"Now? You want me to go, now?"

"There's no better time. The longer you linger, the harder it'll be to leave."

I reached for the carbine and he laid his hands on it.

"I'll need a rifle...for game and self-defense," I said.

"And, you may have it, but take it without malice. We can't be blamed for losing a war God would not have us win. They can not be blamed for winning a war that God would not have them lose," he said. He placed a bible atop the carbine, "one is no good without the other."

I looked at the Bible and the carbine. "Can I stay the night?" I asked.

"Of course," he smiled, "your wagon doesn't leave until tomorrow."

"My wagon?"

"I've enlisted you to escort a family to Texas. You'll see to their safety. In trade, they'll provide food and shelter."

I pulled the Spencer from the desk and lifted the bible. I stared at the heavy book and wandered off. I felt stunned and betrayed, as if I were being kicked out of the home that I'd longed to see all those years. I went to my room and sat down in the straight backed chair. I put the carbine in the corner and opened the bible. I thought of the horrible things that might befall me in Texas, or on the way. My father would be sorry, then.

I laughed at the thought. I was pouting. I'd soon be 18 years old and my first instinct was to pout. I roared with laughter. No sir, pouting would solve none of my problems. It was time to face the world with my chin up and take whatever it had. The training I'd received as a courier would take me a long way in dealing with the world.

I read the bible and found inspiration in its pages. God would deal with me as he might, but no man could alter His plan. I'd venture out into the world knowing that God's will would be done, in Texas, or Mississippi. It didn't matter to God, and I felt that He'd provide, or deprive, as he saw fit.

Later, I checked to make sure that the carbine was loaded and the revolver was charged. I put what few valuables I wanted to keep in the saddlebags along with the bible.

My father came to my room that night and presented me with a new set of clothes.

"Travel as a gentleman, speak as a gentleman and you'll most likely be treated as a gentleman."

"Yes sir," I said, nodding. I took the clothes, a white shirt, dark jacket, tie and britches. I looked with a degree of shame at my hat. My father glanced in its direction as well.

"I'm sorry that I don't have the money for a hat," he said.

"The one I have keeps the sun out of my eyes. That's all it's supposed to do."

He looked at the floor and backed out of the room. I felt sorry for him, then. He saw his inability to afford better clothes as a sign of failure. Grown men had wept at receiving his supplies during the war. To them, he was as much a hero as he was to me. But, in that moment, he seemed less a hero and more a man. It pained me to see him that way and I prayed for the day he would regain his pride.

The night was cool and long and filled with sounds of insects and birds. I lay awake until late that night listening to the sounds of the night beyond the window. I thought of my future. I didn't know very much about Texas, and less about the Frontier. It seemed to me a wasteland of butchers, thieves and Indians. It seemed an unlikely place for a father to send a son, but I trusted my father's instincts.

My father often regaled me with tales of business dealings that were shrewd and clever. He talked romantically of the days when fortunes were built out of nothing, but hard work and negotiations. He spoke of risks and profits, of supply and demand, but always of how men had made their mark in life by securing something worthless where it was and taking it to sell to those most starved for it. To be honest, it bored the life out of me.

7

I woke early the next morning and had breakfast with my father. After all the years we lived in the same house, I found he was quite a cook. I remarked a number of times about the quality of the meal.

"All men should know how to cook," he said. "It helps one to make a more rational decision about marriage."

When he smiled, I realized that it was the first time in years I'd seen a trace of mirth in him. I only then understood the strain he'd been under during the war. He was, for a moment, the father I adored as a child. The smiled faded and the serious lines in his face resumed command of his features. As the change came over his face, I felt my adoration melt into a deep sense of respect.

We ate in silence and lingered over the last scraps. Then, with plates clean and bellies full, we looked into each other's eyes.

"You're to meet the wagon at the livery. The man's name is Sheppard, can't miss him. He's a short fellow, beard and forever on the move, though he achieves less than his ambitions."

I nodded.

"He knows the situation," my father continued. "He's glad to have your company."

"What have you told him about me?"

"Just that you are my son and an able man."

Pride welled up inside. Did my father consider me an able man? Obviously, I'd come far in his judgment.

"It seems strange that you consider me a man. I am, you know."

"I can see it plain enough. You did fine work for the Cause."

I looked down at the napkin on my lap. Shame surrounded mention of the Confederacy. It seemed as if it were becoming a dark secret. No one wanted to talk of the defeat, especially myself. I felt as if I'd lost the war for the South, because I hadn't joined the regular army, but hid out in the special service of the President.

"Well," my father said, rising and stretching, "off you go."

I rose from the seat and set the napkin on my empty plate. I took up the Spencer from the corner where it stood. I'd left my bedroll, pistol and saddlebags by the front door. As I walked over to pick them up, my father joined me and hefted the saddlebags.

The gelding stood patiently outside tied to the handrail of the porch. We loaded him down with my possessions. With nothing left to say, or do, my father embraced me.

"Keep the Bible close, son. Out there in Texas, you'll find plenty of diversions from it, but if you read it and learn from it, you'll make out. I hope to set things right while you're gone. In a few years you may be able to come back and pick up where you left off before the war. Good luck to you."

My throat was choked with emotion. I struggled to find confidence in my voice.

"Good luck to you, father," I said, safely. I backed away from his embrace and shook hands with him, hoping the doubt didn't show on my face. I took one last look around at the place and mounted up. I wanted to stay in the safety and security of my father's shadow, but I knew it was time to go.

I turned the horse and rode toward town. I was scared, but I looked forward to what I'd find further down the trail. I looked forward to seeing the world through a man's eyes. Only when I thought of the dangers that accompanied the adventure did I swallow hard. There were stories of ungraceful death and common murder in the Frontier. As I rode, my thoughts alternated from success to death. Strong emotions came with these thoughts and by the time I reached town I was drenched with sweat.

I met Mr. Sheppard at the livery. He was just as my father described him. He was busy circling the wagon, checking every article for secure placement. The wagon was new and four oxen stood ready in the front.

"Murphy makes the best wagons," Sheppard said, walking up to me. He wiped his brow with a handkerchief and thrust forward a hand.

"Mr. Sheppard, I assume?" I asked.

"That's me," he replied, shaking my hand. He pointed over his shoulder. "My wife, Ophelia and the younguns: Jack and Melissa."

I nodded in each person's direction as their names were listed.

"You must be young Wilkes," he declared. We let our hands drop to our sides.

"Yes sir, the name's Jeff."

"Jeff Wilkes, eh?" He glanced up and down my frame.

"Yes sir."

"You can fire a rifle, I take it?"

"Yes sir."

"Good, good, that's what I need, someone to lend a hand if things get rough."

A great and familiar roar of laughter came from within the stable. I looked into the darkness trying to determine the source, but could see nothing in the black, hollow depths. Gregory emerged from the doorway and into the sunlight. I smiled and took a few steps toward him, before I noticed the malice in his expression.

"You shouldn't count on the valor of a coward, Mister."

"I'm no coward," I said, baffled by the comment. "Why would you say such a thing?"

"This boy left myself and another to fight the war, while he stayed with his rich and powerful father," he said, staring at me, but speaking to Sheppard. "Another time, earlier and when he had the excuse of being a child, he left the two of us to face robbers and murderers in the woods while he hid to await the outcome."

"Are these charges true?" Sheppard asked, his face knotted in concern and anger.

"No, and I take great exception at my friend's accusations."

"You see this scar?" Gregory asked, pointing to a scar on his cheek just below the ear. It was an ugly, gouged wound dried by time into a rough patchwork of skin.

The man nodded.

"This is a bullet wound received during the battle of Atlanta. Ask the boy if he has any such scars. Go ahead, ask him."

"Do you?"

"No sir, I don't, but..."

"You see there? Where was he when the fighting was done? I'll tell you where, he was hiding behind the britches of his father. You've met the elder Wilkes?"

"Yes, I have. Pleasant fellow, who claims that his son did remarkable service as a courier for President Davis."

Gregory thought a moment. "A father's opinion is tainted by affection, isn't it? You're a father," he said, glancing at the children, who sat wide-eyed in the back of the wagon. "Aren't your opinions likewise tainted for your children? Where are his medals? What campaigns did he participate in? What wounds can he attest to? Speaking from experience, Mister, I'd not stake my safety on this one."

"How do you respond, Wilkes?"

"I'm at a loss how to respond. My service was done for my country in a less dramatic way than Gregory. I've known him to be a brave person and probably a fine soldier. His assessment of me is incorrect and I'm deeply wounded by his words, but I cannot attest to my bravery, only to my lack of cowardice."

"You see, Mister, he can't attest to his bravery, because he knows I can prove his cowardice. Tell him to go on, I'll find you another escort for your trip. Perhaps, I'll do it myself."

"I need a man to help. I have a family to consider," he said, searching the ground, "but I don't have time for another to replace this one. I must be going." He looked over at his family, "they're set and ready, everything is sold and I've spent enough daylight as it is."

"Take him, then," Gregory said, hatred permeating his words, "but blame yourself when he leads you right into the mouth of hell." Gregory retreated into the stable and disappeared into the darkness.

"Trust me, Mr. Sheppard, I'll not disappoint you."

Sheppard couldn't look me in the face. He scoured the ground with his sight and rubbed his whiskered jaw. "God help me, I want to believe you."

"You can, sir. I'm not a coward."

"Mount-up then, and follow," he said, walking toward the wagon, but beneath his breath he cussed himself for his poor luck.

I gathered my reins and mounted the gelding. I looked into the dark doorway of the livery, sensing that Gregory watched my every move with loathing and contempt. His hatred was unjust, but I was helpless to explain. His mind was set and nothing I could do, or say, would change the fact of it. I should have been angry, but my heart was overwhelmed with shame and regret.

The whole incident was made worse by the senselessness of it. If only Gregory were willing to listen. If only the details of what I'd done could be known, but I didn't even know the value of my service, or what I'd accomplished. Secrecy was the premium of the courier and it thwarted the arguments I'd have otherwise had. Sadly, the facts of my actions, as seen through the eyes of a brave soldier, such as Gregory, seemed to indicate cowardice. It pained my heart that he knew no different and could discover nothing to the contrary.

I left Vicksburg and crossed the Mississippi into Louisiana with the wagon. I found myself under the cursory and suspicious eye of Sheppard. He'd occasionally peer out from under a worried brow and quickly look away when I turned to meet his gaze. Oddly, to observe the scene from a distance, one would think it were he that had been referred to as a coward, and I, as the brave pioneer.

We traveled far into Louisiana and camped that night near the Tensas River beyond Richmond. Sheppard and I ventured near the bank of the river and fished. I tried to strike up a conversation in order to learn more about him and his family, but was met with silence. Later, Sheppard moved further upstream from my position, effectively ending any opportunity for conversation. In a few hours time, we'd caught enough fish to feed the party. Mrs. Sheppard produced some cornbread from her provisions and it accompanied fish on a plate that her husband thrust toward me with the abruptness of a man throwing food on the ground.

I took a deep breath and turned away to keep from lashing out at him. I moved further from them and sat at the edge of camp to eat. I looked out into the dark night and shook my head. How wrong they were to hate me, to suspect me. I ate quietly and washed my plate at the river before handing it back clean. I unsaddled my horse and laid out my bedroll. I took up a blanket and my rifle and walked away from the fire.

"Hey, where you headed?" Sheppard asked.

"Stand guard."

"No need," he said, "I'll tend to it myself."

"I have to earn my supper, Mr. Sheppard, or I may as well turn back directly."

Sheppard scampered after me with short strides, looking back toward the camp on occasion, as if his family and possessions were liable to disappear any moment.

"Look here, now," he said, "I've got the first watch. You just go on back and get some sleep. We're leaving early in the morning."

I studied his manner for signs of what he thought. He fidgeted and could stand my look for only short periods at a time.

"Everything Gregory said..." I started, but was cut off.

"Never mind that, it doesn't change a thing, like it, or don't like it."

"It isn't true, Mr. Sheppard."

"Yes, son, I heard you say all that before. Don't waste the night tellin' me things I've heard."

"You've heard it, but you didn't believe it."

"No, but I ain't going to believe it any sooner tonight than I did this morning. Bravery ain't everything neither. Right now, you'd be as brave as anyone if you just tried to save yourself when the time came. I'll worry about myself and my family. You just protect yourself and you'll reduce those tryin' to hurt me and mine."

I could see that talking would have little effect on Sheppard until he came to know me.

"Okay, you wake me when it's my turn."

"Surely."

I nodded and returned to the bedroll. Sheppard's family were preparing for bed near the fire. I listened to the squabbling of the children and smiled. What would it have been like to have brothers and sisters? When I was younger, I made up an imaginary brother that I'd talk to when the night storms came and bent the trees in the yard. I'd talk to him about the storm and how he shouldn't be afraid, that our dead mother sat in heaven and protected us from harm on such nights. I talked and talked to the imaginary sibling until I fell asleep. What would it have been like to have a real brother? What would have been his reply? I pulled the blanket close under my chin and closed my eyes.

Morning came and I jerked awake. I looked about, knowing that I should've been keeping guard. Where was Sheppard? I searched the ground and found the family still asleep in their blankets. I peered into the woods in the direction I'd left Sheppard. I first saw the barrel of his musket emerge from behind a tree, followed directly by himself. I got up and walked to meet him.

"Why didn't you wake me?"

Sheppard avoided my stare.

"I know you're concerned about me. I don't blame you for it, but if you don't allow me to pull my weight, you'll get so tired driving the team all day and watching all night, you'll find yourself sleeping behind a tree and ensure the danger you hope to avoid."

"This is my family, Mr. Wilkes," he said, finally allowing his shifting gaze to stop on my face. "They're all I have beyond the wagon. I want to trust you. I'm just not sure how to do that."

"That man in Vicksburg knew me as a child. I didn't hide, as he assumes, I was put off the trail in the dark of night through unfamiliar territory. Since that time, I've served the President of the Confederacy. The war changed us all, Mr. Sheppard, myself, as well as Gregory."

He threw the musket over his shoulder and ran his thumb up and back along the stock, thinking.

"I don't like it, son. I don't like it none at all, but I suppose you're right. I can't do it all and I am feedin' you."

"Yes sir, I imagine that covers it."

"Saddle up," he said, "we'll be leaving as soon as we've eaten."

We followed the railroad most the way through Louisiana, except where it was left unfinished. We picked it back up in Shreveport and followed it into Texas. My first opinion of the state was a pleasant one. It didn't seem much different from Louisiana, which wasn't much different from Mississippi.

During the two weeks it took to cross Louisiana, I spent most of the time riding behind the wagon. The Sheppards were nice folks. They didn't talk very much, except to each other. The children were fashioned after their parents and spoke very little to me and referred to me only as Mr. Wilkes. I tried to get them to call me Jeff, but they'd have none of it.

The passage to Texas was fairly mundane and offered little excitement. I stood guard at night and picked the trail ahead when we came to a river. Mr. Sheppard had grown to trust me enough to get the job done. I kept hoping for a moment when I could prove to him that I was worthy of trust, but none came.

We parted company in a town called Port Caddo along the shore of Lake Caddo. It was a fine, small town with a hotel, saloon and livery. There were other stores well stocked with dry goods and other merchandise. Farming seemed to be the main occupation.

The wagon was pulled up to the livery and instructions were left to have the oxen fed and turned loose into the corral. The Sheppards and I walked to the hotel across the street. Mr. Sheppard invited me to dine with them one last evening. I didn't have any other plans and agreed to do so.

What little money I had would have to be spent on a bath and supplies for my further wanderings about the state. I looked forward to a warm bath after having spent so much time in rivers and ponds the past few weeks. When I'd secured a bath, I settled into it and gave a groan of satisfaction as I lowered myself into the water up to my waist. I rested my head on the rim of the tub and thought of where I'd go from there.

The romance of travel had worn off completely, and I was starting to worry about what I'd do to survive. I didn't know where I'd go, or what I'd do for money beyond the few gold pieces I had. I thought I should find work, but I was afraid to until I'd found a place I wanted to be. At the time,

I'd only seen a small piece of Texas. Surely, somewhere, there was a place more suited to me.

I was troubled by the prospect of a career. It dawned on me that I didn't have a career, nor a proper education. Was I to work for someone else the rest of my life? Where were the opportunities? I tried to think the problem through, but my head felt as if it were filled with cotton. Finally, I fell asleep.

When I woke, I rose out of the tub and dried off. I beat the dust off my suit and put it on. It smelled of smoke from the many fires built over the journey. The cuffs were dirty, as was the collar, but it was all I had. Finally dressed, I ventured downstairs to find the Sheppards engaged in supper. A plate was set aside for me with beef and potatoes heaped onto it.

"We tried to wait," Sheppard said.

"That's fine, I dozed a bit in the tub."

I sat down and ate silently with the family. They seemed as strangers, though we'd spent a good deal of time together. I ate and stretched and looked about at the interior. It was a plain sort of place that served its purpose.

When the others had finished their meal, Mrs. Sheppard and the children went up to their rooms. Mr. Sheppard and I sat at the table.

"Care for a drink?"

"I might have a taste of beer," I replied.

The bartender, a gruff looking man, came over to our table. Mr. Sheppard ordered two glasses of beer. The bartender was quite polite and cordial. He seemed eager to please, though he appeared hostile. Perhaps, the naturally cocked eyebrow and perpetual frown gave the bartender a sense of anger that did not fit his personality. He brought two glasses of beer to the table, which Mr. Sheppard paid for with Union script.

"Well, here's to ya, young man," Sheppard said, raising his glass.

I raised my own and drank.

We talked a little about the journey from Mississippi and drank the rest of the beer. Sheppard left shortly after and I stayed in the saloon trying to think of what I'd do next. The bartender came over to clear the table.

"Might you know of anyone looking for help in town?"

The bartender looked me up and down.

"What can you do?"

"I've no particular trade, if that's what you mean."

"That's what I mean."

I realized that there was not much use for a courier, but it was the only skill I had.

"I've ridden the post roads," I said.

"Stagecoach brings the mail," he replied.

I nodded. "Is there someone I could ask to find if the coaches are in need of drivers?"

"How would I know? Do I look like a teamster?"

"No sir."

"Well, there ya have it," he said, turning away from me with the glasses.

I didn't want to ask him any more questions, but he was the only one I'd met from town. I walked to the bar, feeling like a kid. I stood there for some time before he looked at me.

"What now?"

"When does the coach arrive?"

The big man put his hands on his hips. His cordiality seemed to extend only to those who had money. He pointed toward the door.

"Go down the street and ask at the livery."

I nodded and turned toward the door.

Down at the livery, I asked my questions and got answers to them. While I waited to ask the stage drivers for a job, the livery owner put me to work cleaning stalls and feeding the animals for room and board. Every time the stage would come in, I'd ask about a job, but there didn't seem to be any openings. The stable owner told me to wait it out.

"Them Injuns, or the Mexicans'll get frisky in a bit and there'll be more jobs open on the stages than a man could imagine."

With that in mind, I settled down to my job as a stableboy.

8

I worked at the livery and barely made enough to feed myself and board the gelding. Mostly, I dreamed of the things I'd do in the future. I thought of the opportunities available to a teamster who could watch the flow of commerce and decide which path to take and where to settle. Then again, a teamster may not live long enough to reap the rewards.

One day, as I fed the horses and cleaned the stalls, a group of men rode into town. They charged their mounts through the street and pulled up suddenly at the livery stable. Clouds of dust rose from their clothes as they dismounted. They were in a hurry, but their business wasn't urgent. It seemed as if they'd been racing.

"Take care of the horses, boy," one of them said, tossing a set of reins to me. He was taller than average, heavyset and had a thick beard. He tossed me a five cent piece. "That coin ain't for nothing," he said, meaning that I should take extra care with their mounts. I was eager to do it.

Then, the group of them, five it seemed, jostled each other and laughed as they swaggered to the saloon. I watched as they burst through the door and seconds later the piano started. Right in broad daylight. It impressed me, if I cared to admit it. I couldn't help but wonder what sort of men they were. I might have gone over to have a look, out of curiosity, but the owner of the livery, Ben, hurried me about my duties.

"You never know when men like those are going to need those horses, son, and you don't want to leave them unbrushed and unfed."

"What sort of men are they?" I asked, revealing my ignorance.

"Lord knows, but I've seen a few like 'em."

I unsaddled, brushed and fed the horses. I laid new straw down in their stalls. When I'd finished, I found Ben sitting out front watching the saloon.

"You best go ask if they'd like to keep their mounts saddled," he said.

I looked at the saloon and back at Ben. He'd never sat so long on the porch before, not without whittling, or something to keep his hands busy. But, all he did was sit and stare at the saloon. I looked back at the saloon.

"What're you thinking about?" I asked, turning back to him.

"I'm thinking that I'm gonna be here when they want those horses and I'm gonna get my money before they get 'em back."

I looked at the saloon and started across the street. It was getting close to late afternoon. I listened to the plinking of the piano and the roars of laughter that issued from the open doorway. It felt awkward to enter the place on business, but I had my job to do.

I stepped into the darkened saloon, alive only with the piano and those gathered at the bar. Light shafts pierced the darkness at sharp angles, illuminating the dust in the air. I let my eyes adjust to the darkness and picked out the man who'd tossed me the coin. I walked up to him. His back was turned to me and I could only see his face in profile when he'd glance at one of his companions.

He seemed impenetrable. I certainly didn't want to disturb his fun, but was forced on by duty.

"Pardon me, sir. If I might have a moment of your time."

"What is it?"

"My boss wonders if you'd like to have your horses saddled, or unsaddled."

The man looked at the others.

"How on earth do you plan to brush 'em with the saddles on?" he asked, as the others chuckled. He glanced about at them and let a smile appear briefly at the corners of his mouth.

"No, sir. I've taken care of that and I'd like to know if you'd prefer that I now saddle them again, or leave them be for the evening."

The man squinted his eyes, then glanced at the others. "Listen to the way this one talks. Where'd you learn to talk that way, boy? In a stable?"

"No, sir. My father saw to it that I was given a good education."

"And, where's yur pa now?"

"In Mississippi."

"A Confederate?"

"Yes, sir."

"I don't know that I'd be too proud of that."

"Well, that may be, but I'm proud of my father, regardless."

"Regardless of what?"

"Regardless of the war."

"How old are you?"

"Seventeen," I said, and tried to get the conversation back to the subject, "but, all I really wanted to know is about the saddles."

"Never mind them saddles for now," he said, narrowing his eyes. "Were you in the war?"

"Everyone was in the war."

My response was greeted with the back of his hand across my teeth. It knocked me back a few steps.

"Don't take to smart-mouthing me, boy!" He drew himself up and wiped his mouth. He stared at me with evil little eyes.

I touched my lips and looked at my bloodstained fingertips. Then I laughed a small laugh.

"What are you gigglin' at?" he demanded.

"My father hit me that way once. He left me on the floor wondering who and what I was. Now, you clip me with the back of your hand as if to impress me, as if you could with such a mild swipe."

Rage burned in his eyes. Across the bar, his companions repressed their grins as they thought of the whipping I was about to take.

"I suppose I ought to strike you proper, then," he said.

"Perhaps, you should try."

I could tell the man was about to do as he suggested and I only hoped the things Donnigan taught me would work as well in practice as they had in theory. He took a big draw backwards with his fist and as he threw it forward, I easily ducked it and moved to his right. His face flushed with embarrassment. He drew himself upright and charged me. I pushed one of the tables in front of him and he flopped on top of it, taking it to the floor. He rolled over with his gun in his hand and got to his feet. I stood there, unarmed. I didn't need a gun to clean the stables and care for horses, so I left my weapons in the stall where I slept.

While I tried to sort the situation out, one of the others moved slowly between myself and the man with the gun.

"That's enough, Ned. This boy's unarmed. Hell, you ought to be hirin' him, not shootin' him."

Ned put his revolver away and spit.

"What would I hire him for? What can he do, besides take care of horses and talk smart?"

"The boy talks good, that's for sure. He talks like a banker, but he ain't no coward like some of the others you've been hirin'. He'll stick it out in a fight."

"'Til someone shoots him," he said, then looked at me. "You own a pistol, a rifle, anything?"

"Yes, sir, a Colt."

"Why ain't you wearing it?"

"I've never gotten into a fight with a horse, or hay, or straw..."

Ned came after me then, but I stood my ground and the man in front of me pushed him backward.

"You see there, Clyde. Smart mouth is all he's got."

Clyde looked back at me, studying my face. "That may be, but hire him all the same. He'll make a good one 'til you kill him." Clyde put his hand on my shoulder. "You can make a lot more money than shovelin' stalls and if you keep yur mouth shut, you might even live through it."

I nodded. "What should I do with the horses?"

"Saddle 'em, and yours too. You have a horse, don't ya?"

"Yes, sir."

"Good. Here's some money for the horses. Make that old man do the work. You come back here and have a drink. It'll be a long time between 'em where we're going."

I stumbled out of the saloon and into the bright sunshine. Across the street, I saw Ben sitting in his chair. I knew how he'd react to the news. He didn't trust the men. The fact is, I didn't either, but it was an opportunity to make some money.

Walking up to him, I noticed his curious expression.

"What happened to your face?" he asked.

I rubbed the swollen lip and caught a trace of blood on my finger. "One of them hit me. It was just a slap, really."

"What for?"

"He thought I was being smart with him. Maybe I was, he was asking too many questions, anyway."

Ben looked at me as if he'd never seen me before. To him, I was a young man in need of protection. Suddenly, he was forced to think twice about it.

I dug in my pocket and pulled out the money given to me. "Here's the money for care of the horses."

"Thanks, Jeff," he said, taking the money. "You didn't have to..."

"I didn't, they gave it to me of themselves...just after they hired me to ride with them."

Ben's face went pale. He looked about him quickly, as if the answers to his questions could be found lying about. "Well, they hired you?"

I nodded.

"To do what?"

"I don't know. It doesn't matter. They offered me money and somewhere to go and I don't think the stage company is ever going to hire me."

"Them fellas are wild, Jeff. They may be wanted by the law, for all you know. They might even kill you as soon as you get out of town."

"What for? My money?" I asked, unable to hold back a chuckle.

"Well," he said, but seemed unable to find anything else to say.

"Look, they asked me to tell you to saddle the horses, mine too. I'm going back over there for a drink before we leave."

Ben thrust forward a hand. "It's been a pleasure, Jeff. I sure hope you know what you're doing."

"I don't know what I'm doing," I said, shaking his hand, "but I can be that way here, or there and 'there' pays more than 'here'. It's simple," I said, moving back into the stable. I put the Spencer in the scabbard of the saddle and thrust the Colt into my waistband.

"Listen," Ben said, "if you're goin' with them men, you'd better have a saddle suited to the work and a pair of chaps. You'll be in the saddle more than out of it."

We traded saddles, and he handed me a pair of chaps that were worn and greasy, but they were better than what I had. I put them on.

I walked back across the street toward the saloon. Suddenly, I felt as if I had a direction, even if it was the wrong direction. Ben was right, I didn't know anything about their business, or what I was getting myself into. But, Port Caddo had lost its luster and I was bored. The men waiting in the saloon offered somplace else to be and I was going to go.

I paused at the doorway and let my eyes adjust. The scene was just as before, but I saw that the men were edgy, looking more over their shoulders than before. The piano still plinked out a song and the drinks were being spilled, and swallowed in equal amounts. It was a sight much the same as Gregory must have seen long ago in Milldale. But, like Gregory, I'd see it through for the money.

"Here he is!" called Clyde.

"The smart-mouthing little snake," Ned added.

"Better watch out, Ned. He's packing a hog-leg this time," one of the others said.

Ned looked over his shoulder and sized me up. "Still don't make him a man."

"God made me a man," I replied.

Ned couldn't contain his anger and whirled around, reaching for his pistol, but he hadn't even cleared leather when he stopped. I noticed that the men were staring wide-eyed at me, especially Ned. The piano stopped playing. In my hand was the heavy Colt. I wanted to put it back. In a matter of seconds my life was put in play, like a poker chip lying on a table waiting for someone to claim it.

Clyde seemed to sense my predicament. He could see something in my eyes that told him I didn't want to be in that position, so he eased over to Ned and whispered.

"The boy's fast as lightning, Ned. Let go of it. You may not like him, but if I had to put a gun on our side, his would do."

"He's a smart-mouthing snake," Ned whispered.

Clyde let his weight fall back against the bar. He was enjoying himself, reveling in the critical moment that hangs between life and death. He wanted to savor the smell of fear and the rush of blood. I'd never seen such a look in a man's eyes before.

"The way I see it," Clyde whispered, "you can pull the rest of that gun out, or you can let it back down. It don't seem to matter to the boy, seein's how he's out-pulled you, Ned."

"How do you know he won't shoot me?"

"Well, he might do that. I can't vouch for him, but I think he figures you're his boss and he don't really want to kill you and go back to the stables with his hat in his hand begging for his job back."

Ned seemed to realize that he was the boss, and I'd do what I was told.

"Put that damned Colt away," he said, in a booming voice.

"Gladly," I replied, uncocking the gun, which allowed him to let his weapon fall back into the holster. I shoved the Colt into my waistband. The others let out a sigh of relief.

Clyde bought me a beer and I drank it slowly. The others shot glances at me from time to time. Then, Ned moved closer and leaned against me. I could smell the long-dried sweat in his clothes. He smelled of horseflesh, as did the rest of them. It seemed more offensive on him.

"You're pretty fast with that iron. You practice it?"

"Nope."

"Well, you keep that thing holstered until I tell you to unholster it. Got me?"

"Yes, sir."

Ned nodded and walked over to the piano and put a coin on it. "Let's go, boys."

The others gulped their drinks and dropped coins on the bar. There was a shuffling of boots on the saloon floor, and the event was over. The horses were waiting for us when we got back to the livery stable.

"The boy paid ya?" Ned asked.

Ben nodded.

We all mounted up and rode out of town. It was slick and neat and suddenly, I was on the frontier with a job. Though, I didn't know how much I'd be paid. If they gave me any money at all, it'd be better than lying about in Port

Caddo with never a penny more than what it took to keep myself alive.

I rode close to Clyde. Not so close as to be a bother, but close enough that I could read which way the winds were blowing by watching him. None of them talked very much. Clyde and Ned seemed to be the most familiar with each other and seemed somewhat on equal footing.

We rode following the lake the rest of the day and into evening when we stopped and made camp. One of the others had purchased supplies before they started drinking and there was plenty to eat. I was informed that until I earned something, my supplies would be owed to the group and taken out of my first pay. After that, I could buy what I wanted to eat, or kill it.

After the meal, I poured myself a cup of coffee and went to sit beside Clyde.

"I'm a hard worker, and I don't complain, but I'd like to know what sort of work I've signed up for."

"Nothing to it, kid. All you have to do is help us herd some cows, drive 'em up into Indian Territory and sell 'em to the government."

"Well, I can do that, but I don't know anything about cattle. My family was in cotton."

"Quit worrying, there ain't nothin' dumber than cattle. If you get the leader headed one way, most of them will just follow along. You just have to be there in case there's stragglers, or those with their own minds. You'll get the hang of it."

I nodded. "Where are these cattle?"

"All about."

"They're Ned's?"

Clyde shot me a strange look, then nodded. "Most of 'em. The others ain't owned by nobody. A lot of people were killed in that war and many of the cattle were born when they left and more was born long after they were dead and their families had been killed by Injuns."

It made sense.

"Well, how do you know which ones are orphaned, so to speak, and which belong to others who've come back for their herd?"

"They got brands and the ones without brands don't belong to anyone."

I nodded. "Kind of like picking berries," I said.

"Yep, like pickin' berries. Ain't that right, Ned?"

"What's that?"

"Our business is like pickin' berries."

Ned wrinkled his brow in confusion and waved a hand at Clyde. Clyde laughed until he began to cough.

It didn't seem right to me, but I didn't have any idea how the world worked since the end of the war. So many had died. So many had been maimed and the laws had all changed in the former Confederate States. I figured that these boys were living in the margins of the laws and in the confusion of the times. I didn't care. Union law was no law at all, to me. I followed moral law and I couldn't find anything immoral in picking up strays and orphans along with Ned's cattle and selling them all together. The way I understood it, there were dangers in roaming the frontier looking for cattle, dangers that the owners might not be willing to brave. It was our reward for our bravery and ingenuity, the way gold can be found and the miner is rewarded for his perseverance and risk.

9

I rode with Ned Smith, Clyde and the boys for several weeks. I learned my job as we went and kept a constant eye on Ned whenever he came close to me.

As I rode, I noticed there was something curious going on that I had no business with. Every day or so, we'd change directions. We'd come upon some tracks of one kind, or another and break off in a different direction. I thought for a long time that we were avoiding Indians. Indeed, that may have been true much of the time, but there were other instances when the faces of Ned and Clyde would grow dark and their tempers would shorten. It seemed apparent to me that there was someone in particular they were trying to avoid.

All this time, we rode across North-Central Texas. We'd drifted all over and were gaining quite a herd of cattle. Most were ragged looking animals, but some of them were prime beef.

I was starting to believe that Ned didn't own a single steer. But, there was nothing to keep us from taking the ones we found. They were scattered all over the country without a soul interested in their welfare.

Yet, I had the distinct impression that we were doing something wrong. I promised myself that if we were ever accused of stealing cattle, I'd kill Ned for getting me to do his thieving. As long as no one seemed to care, I'd keep my mouth shut and take care of my responsibilities.

After a month or better, we made camp one night on the East Fork of the Trinidad River, which would have been called a creek where I was raised. Ned was in a surly mood after finding more tracks and being forced to change direction, again.

I stood by myself, as usual, with a cup of coffee and thought about my turn to stand watch. I always got the late part of the evening that stretched into morning.

"Get your eyes off'n me, boy!" Ned roared from the other side of the fire.

My eyes had lost focus, as I thought, and they happened to be pointed at Ned. I should have just looked away, but I'd done nothing wrong. There'd been other times like this. Times when Ned was angry, or worked up over something. Like always, he found a reason to start in on me. If it hadn't been staring, it would've been something else. There was no way around it. I knew no one in the party would jump in on his side, so I pushed it a little.

"I said, get your eyes off'n me!"

"I heard you the first time."

"What?" Ned asked, rising from his seat. Clyde grabbed at his arm, but he pulled free. "Look here smart-mouth, I've had about all I can take from you."

"Make your move, Ned," I said, moving the cup to my left hand.

Ned looked me over for a bit, then rubbed his whiskers and turned away. I let out a breath. Every time Ned got nervous he tried his luck.

I threw my coffee on the fire and eased back into the shadows where I liked to sleep. I laid out my bedroll and lay down on it in a way that I could watch Ned. I didn't trust him any more than he liked me. It was a bad situation to be in, but my only option was to ride off alone.

I waited until I could hear Ned snoring before I went to sleep. I woke up near midnight and moved the bedroll. I slept in it for a while, then got up and made it look as if I were still there. I sat beside a tree. Soon, I'd have to go out and keep watch on the cattle.

I dozed a bit, leaning against the bark, and when I opened my eyes Ned was standing above my bedroll with a knife in his hand. I eased the Colt out of my waistband and cocked it. Ned froze.

"Looking for me, Ned?"

"No..., I, uh..."

"Am I going to have to kill you?"

"No."

"Then, stop trying to sneak up on me."

"Okay," he said, and walked off.

I might've taken off when we came to a town, or disappeared in the night to keep from getting killed, but Ned was a simple man. He didn't have any profound abilities of mind, either for general business, or for outlawry. He was, therefore, predictable and it was only when he'd tried to take me face to face and failed that he'd take it into his mind to kill me in my sleep.

I saw through his plans. When I knew he'd come for me, I stayed awake and moved about. Aside from that, I found it a bit amusing to watch him sulk off, defeated.

Ned was fair with me most of the time, but there were times when he had to needle someone. Some people were like that. They needed to bully. The man I replaced was most likely Ned's last target. I figured he'd either gotten tired of it and left, or Ned killed him on the silent prairie in the deep of night. But, I kept my guard up and stood up to him and that frustrated him all the more. There'd come a time when he could stand it no longer and he'd even accept his own death in order to kill me.

In the morning, when the sun rose up bright and cast long, red fingers across the plain, I rode into camp and got a cup of coffee. Clyde was bent over the pot. He held the reins of his horse in his hand and the mare stomped impatiently behind him. I held out my cup. He poured it full and tossed the rest over the fire.

"Ride close to me today," he mumbled.

"I'll come up before noon."

Clyde nodded and withdrew to mount up. Ned was riding a little ways from camp. He stared hard at the two of us as he passed. Ol' Ned was working on something in his mind and I didn't like it.

The morning sun grew hot. It was August, then. I was drenched by sweat early on and rode to the back of the herd. I kept a constant lookout for Indians. We were close to the border and there were several bands of Indians who'd shoot across to steal anything they could get their hands on. They killed whomever they found and took a few steers back to feed their people.

By the time the sun had risen high into the sky, I eased up towards Clyde. Clyde slowed and I caught him.

"You're a good boy. I like the way you handle yourself, so listen hard. You need to look for other work. Ned's gone as far as he will with you. We're coming to a town called Sherman. He means to kill you there and hire another."

"What makes you think he can kill me?"

"That gun ain't fast if you never get a chance to pull it."

I nodded and slowed my mount. Clyde nudged his and we took up our usual positions.

We arrived near Sherman toward dusk. We stationed the cattle outside of town a few miles and all but myself, and one other, went into town. The two of us were left to hold the herd and keep it safe from Indians while the others were gone.

The sun slipped behind the horizon and the darkness came fast. I kept an eye open for anything unusual. I jumped at the slightest sound and nearly drove myself crazy the first few hours of the night. I envisioned and created dangers everywhere.

I let the gelding wander away from the herd. I planned on leaving, but I had to do it in a gradual manner and at the right time. If the other fellow knew I was going to leave, he might raise a ruckus at being left alone with the herd.

I began to circle the herd at a great distance and dipped into several hollows in the land. When I was a good two miles off, I saw a flickering of orange light. It was still several hundred yards away. I dismounted and walked my horse toward the camp in a roundabout fashion. As I neared, I felt a strange sensation at the back of my neck and whipped my head around to look behind me. My eyes were wide open to the black night, but there was nothing to see. I felt desperate and scared all of a sudden, as if I'd fallen into a trap. I decided I had no business there, and reached up to the saddle. The sound of a cocking pistol stopped me dead with one foot in the stirrup and both hands on the saddlehorn.

"Leaving so soon?" a voice whispered from out of the void.

I felt a great sense of helplessness. I'd never been caught at such a disadvantage. My throat was dry, and when I began to speak, my voice broke.

"I saw the fire and thought I'd stop in for coffee," I said over my shoulder.

"Perhaps," the man said. "And, maybe you thought you'd sneak up and cut my throat."

"What for?"

"You're a cow thief."

"I am not!"

"Who's herd is that, then?"

"Ned's."

"Ned doesn't own any cattle."

I kept trying to think of a way to make a move on the man, but I was stuck with both hands clutching the saddlehorn.

"Then, who's cattle are they?"

"Several men. They're camped out on the other side of Sherman waiting for Ned to try and take 'em to Indian Territory."

"A man can't trust a soul out here! Look, Mister, I just hired on for a wage. I didn't know anything about this."

"So you say," he grinned.

"What would I gain by lying?"

"Your life, for one."

"You saying those ranchers aim to kill me for it?"

"That's what they do with cow thieves in this country."

"You've never heard of a trial?"

"Ain't no trial for cow thieving. We just toss a rope over anything sturdy and string 'em up."

My mouth hung open. I wanted to close it, but it astonished me.

"For stealing cows?"

"Where do you think you are? Boston?" he asked, a big grin spreading across his face.

I took the opportunity to raise myself back up into the saddle.

"Where you goin'?"

"I have my honor to protect," I replied.

"Get off that horse!"

"Well, how would you feel? I'm an honest man, Mister. I don't like being associated with thieves of any sort. The thought of it gets my dander up."

"Get off the horse," he repeated, without an ouce of give in his voice.

I swung down to face the man. He was my height, in his twenties, with a face made for a grin. He wore a slick looking black hat.

"Hand me that revolver."

I took the Colt and tossed it underhand to him. He caught it and put it in his waistband.

"What are you going to do? Shoot me?"

"Not yet."

"When?"

"I wouldn't be so anxious," he said, a grin pushing at his mouth.

"I should've killed him when I had the chance," I said to myself.

"Who?"

"Ned!"

"What did you want to kill him for?"

"Have you ever met him?"

"No."

"If you had, you'd know in a minute."

"Get over there by the fire."

I led the horse over to the fire. It was still somewhat of a walk. I could feel the aim of the revolver at my back the whole distance. I sat down heavily before the flame, while the man started looking through my saddlebags.

"Hey, that's none of your business, in there."

"I say what's my business," he called back. He pulled the Bible out and looked it over, then put it back. He dug out my coffee cup and walked back to the fire.

"What are you? A preacher?"

"No, sir. I read the Bible some, though."

"How old are you, son?"

"Seventeen."

"What brings you out this way?"

"I'm trying to earn a living, like every other honest soul."

"Stealin' cattle ain't honest."

"I didn't know I was."

"I can believe it, now," he said, laughing again.

"This may be funny to you, Mister, but I'm about to hang."

"Maybe, not," he said, and I saw his mind working.

"You thinking of letting me go?"

"In a manner of speaking," he replied, glancing at me. "Here, build yourself some coffee." He tossed the cup, his canteen and a bag of coffee to me.

I did as I was told and set it to boiling.

"You see, I have a hard time trusting folks out here. It's easy to trust a man in town, because you always know where to find him, but out here, a man could tell you anything and you'd never see him again."

"I told the truth," I said.

"Don't rush me, boy." He fixed himself a cup of coffee and set it to boiling. He looked up at me. "You have to do something to prove you're telling the truth."

"Anything."

"You say you'd like to kill Ned?"

"Yes, sir."

"Well, here's what I have in mind. The only way I can believe you're telling me square, that you didn't know you were stealing those cows, is if you kill Ned," he said, watching for my reaction. "See, you could save your life that way. If you go in there with this Colt blazing and kill Ned, and maybe a few others, I could believe you. Otherwise, you hang along with them tomorrow. What do you think about that?"

"Well," I said, swallowing hard. "First, it's immoral to kill. Second, I don't want to hang."

"I agree completely," he said, grinning.

"What would I have to do?"

"You go into their camp tonight and shoot 'em."

"Then, you could have me hung for murder."

"What for? That doesn't help me any. Ned and his bunch are who I'm after, not some seventeen year old kid."

"Why not just let me go, then?"

"As it stands, you're one of them. If you kill them, you're not. It's as simple as that."

"I don't like it."

"Like it, or don't," he said, pulling his cup off the fire and motioning for me to do the same. I took the cup and set it aside to cool. "It doesn't matter to me. I aim to put an end to Ned and his bunch either way."

He watched me for signs of a decision.

"I'm in a fix, aren't I?"

"Yes, sir, you surely are."

"What do you get out of it?"

"What makes you think I get anything?"

"I know I'm a kid," I said, "but, I've learned something in the time I've been out here. I've learned no one does anything in this country that it doesn't benefit them in some way. What's your angle on this?"

"The fact is, if you kill a couple of Ned's bunch, it's less to be shooting at us tomorrow when we take to hang 'em."

"What's to keep me from telling Ned all about it? What's to keep us from getting away from it all?"

"You can tell Ned, and you don't have to shoot him. But, as sure as I've got them now, I'll get them later. But you, I'll hunt you down like a dog and make your last hours the worst a man's seen since Christ."

"That settles that," I said.

"Pretty much," he grinned.

"It's not like I have a real choice, but I'll do it," I said, then thought about Clyde. "There's only one other thing."

"What's that?"

"I don't want to shoot Clyde."

"Then don't. The only one I care about is Ned. But, they aren't going to sit there and wait for you to pull the trigger. Could be, this Clyde is going to shoot you."

"He won't."

"How do you know that?"

"Because, he saved my life by telling me Ned was going to kill me tonight. That's what I was doing out here."

"Why's Ned want to kill you?"

"I make him mad."

"That'll do it," he said, nodding.

I came to know the man as Tom Garfield. He was a tracker during the war. We talked until I didn't feel like it anymore. I drank the coffee and thought. It was a hard bit of country, Texas. No law, but what men thought up on the spur of the moment. No one to stop people from doing whatever they decided was right.

I felt nauseous when I thought of how I rode with Ned the whole time thinking out my trial, if we were accused of being thieves. I thought I could just explain to the jury how I was hired on for a wage and didn't know what they were doing. I was going to explain about being young and needing the work and how surprised I was when people said we were stealing the cattle. I had to rub my neck when I thought of how close I'd come to being hung. I got the shivers just thinking about it.

10

I sat in the glow of the fire thinking about the task ahead. Before the night was out, I'd have to kill someone, or be killed. I never killed anyone before, though I thought of it often during the war. But, the war was different, there was a reason for killing then, an important reason. The political life of the Confederacy was on the line. There were political questions to be answered about the rights of states and citizens. It was acceptable to kill under those circumstances and always had been.

The sort of killing Tom suggested had none of those implications. It was killing to achieve a personal goal. It seemed selfish and impulsive and wrong.

The men I'd met on the Frontier were quite a bunch. It seemed to me that a lot of trouble could be avoided if more of them went to church. That'd give them one day of rest before they started another week of lying, stealing and killing. Lord knows, the Devil could use the rest.

Tom was leaning back on his elbows, looking up at the sky. He stayed that way for quite a while.

"What're you looking at?"

"I'm waiting to see if St. Peter's up there somewhere waiting for Ned."

"I doubt it," I said.

"It's almost time to go," he remarked, looking at me. "You going to be able to shoot a man?"

"I'll be able to shoot Ned."

"Well, there's more than Ned there."

"I'll shoot Ned first, then I'll shoot someone else."

Tom nodded. "You take Ned then, but kill him."

"I'll kill him."

"You don't sound too sure."

"I'll kill him. I already said that. I don't have to like it as well, do I?"

"I hope you never learn to like it, but you have to learn to do it. Either white men, or red, black, or brown. You can't let it make a difference."

Some time passed since our last words and he seemed in deep thought. By his expression, he didn't like what he was thinking about. He shook his head.

"You're from the Southern states?"

"Yes, sir."

"I'm from up North, at least my kin are. Ohio, but they moved to Texas long before the Rebellion. Moved here after the war with Mexico." He drank from his cup and swirled the contents. "I fought on the side of the Confederacy. How about you?"

"Too young," I said.

"Officially," he said, "but I saw younguns fight. Saw 'em die, too."

"I was a courier for the President."

He whistled. "There's some dangerous duty."

"It had it's moments," I said, angry at the presumed implications.

"No, I meant it," he replied. "All the couriers I heard of got hung, captured, or both. Some lived, I guess, but I never heard of any."

"Heard of one now," I replied.

"If you're telling the truth."

"I'm a cow thief, sir! Not a liar," I declared with as much mock dignity as I could and we both laughed.

We drank our coffee, periodically laughing at my joke as we thought of it. Then, the air seemed to die. Clarity came to my sight like I'd never known before. Everything appeared fleeting and temporary, lasting only the next few hours. Then, it'd disappear into the air as if it never happened and I'd be dead.

"Let's go," he said.

I stood and followed.

"Picket them horses. We'll have to walk in."

I did as he asked and checked my weapons.

"Don't play around," he said, under his breath. "If you shoot someone, kill them."

"Stop worrying about me."

"I'm trying to," he replied.

We met scattered cattle as we moved closer to the camp. We could see the fire every time we topped a rise in the landscape. It grew closer each time. We often laid down on the ground to keep track of the men watching the cattle.

"When we get to the camp," he whispered. "You go in alone. I'll take the riders as they come in."

"What?" I asked in panic.

"Do as I say."

"You want me to face the whole camp?"

"There won't be more than three, or four and Clyde's liable to be one of those. The thing you can't do, is talk.

Shoot the first man you see. If you start talking to them, you lose the edge. They'll go for their weapons as soon as they see you."

When we were within fifty yards of the camp, we heard hurried, excited talking. Ned was yelling at someone for losing me. I felt sorry for the other man. He'd done nothing wrong. I felt sorry for the whole camp. They were about to be killed, either tonight, or tomorrow. There was no way out of it and I could have been one of them. I had a lot to be grateful for, but there was a sense of betrayal in my heart.

"No fooling now, kid. Can you do it, or not?"

"Yes," I replied with resolution.

We neared the camp slowly.

"Okay, you go in alone from here on. I have the other men located. If they start in, I'll knock 'em down."

I thought of something all of a sudden. What if this was just a ploy to get me killed? When I heard the firing from behind, would it be directed at me? I lost my nerve and wanted to stop and go back and reassure myself. I looked over my shoulder. Tom had his rifle shouldered and shifted it to different places on the horizon.

I walked right toward their camp. I could see the men more clearly. I could tell who was who. Clyde was off to my right. Ned was in the middle with his back toward me. Butch was to the left. I pulled the revolver from my waistband. I could hardly breath. I kept walking toward the fire and got so close, I thought I could sit down and have a cup of coffee.

Then everything started to happen. I cocked my revolver when Butch saw me. He scrambled to get his weapon out of the holster. I squeezed the trigger, but the Colt remained silent. It missed fire and I thumbed the hammer back. Butch had his revolver out and Ned was turning around. I shot Butch in the shoulder and he shot me a grazing wound on my neck. I heard Tom's rifle go off behind me. I didn't even look at Clyde. I wasn't going to shoot him and I didn't have time to look at people I wasn't going to shoot.

Ned lifted his revolver and I shot him in the chest. Then, as he fell backward, I turned my attention to Butch. I heard the rifle go off behind me again. I thumbed back the hammer of the Colt just as I saw Butch do the same. We aimed at each other and I just saw the flash from my revolver in the darkness and felt my head snap straight back. I fell, without knowing if I hit Butch, or not.

I lay in the grass, staring upward at my closed lids. It was dark inside my head, a darkness that had an incomprehensible depth to it. I heard Clyde talking, but not to me. He was talking to Tom. Their conversation was taking place in a world that I barely hung onto through consciousness. As I listened to their words, I felt myself drifting away into another world and I didn't care. Whatever they were saying, it wouldn't matter to a dying man.

I felt the division and understood the world of the dead and that of the living as two separate things. Nothing existed to connect one to the other. All the worries and cares and troubles of one were the pleasures of the other. I gave myself up to the new world and embraced my own death. I was comforted in the thought that even in the last act, I was moral and tried to save my friend, Clyde, from certain death. I knew that God would know the reason I'd killed Butch and Ned, if indeed I had.

And then, darkness and void and I recalled nothing of the former life. All was black until I woke in bed. I felt first the softness of the mattress under my body and then the pressure of bandages about my neck. I couldn't open my eyes, but I sensed the room around me. It had room smells that didn't exist in the open. I could smell someone cooking and my stomach felt shrunken and empty.

All was quiet. There was no one in the room. I was alone and alive and felt a disappointment that I didn't awake in the arms of the Lord, but was left to battle my conscience for killing those men.

I was awake for a very short time. I slipped back into the void and dreamt of my father in Mississippi. I saw him as I'd seen him that night in the window. He was small and paced back and forth with the cigar. I dreamt of the trees and the horses. In the dream, there was still a Confederacy and then, the shame when the war was over. The dream turned wicked and I woke later with perspiration rolling off my forehead.

I stayed awake longer than before. It was daylight, then, and I could see only the ceiling. I couldn't move my head. I was either too weak, or the bandages were too tight about my neck. Soon, my eyes grew tired and I slept again.

Later, I heard voices in my room and tried to wake-up. I wanted to know who stood over me. I fought to open my eyes, but it was no use. I could hear the voices, but the language made no sense. The voices sounded busy, efficient, as if a doctor were examining me, but I didn't know.

Sometime later, I woke up and was able to raise my head. I pushed myself up to an angle that allowed me to see the door with little effort. I noticed a bell beside the bed and thought it was there for me to ring. But, I wouldn't ring it. There was a sense of danger, yet. I could still be hung for my part in killing Ned's bunch. Thomas could have left me in the room to die, or hang, depending on whether I ever woke up, or not. There was so much I didn't know about my current predicament.

Outside, it was evening. I noticed a lamp on the dresser across the room. Soon, someone would be in to light the lamp. Or, maybe they wouldn't. Did they even bother to light the lamp for a person who always slept? I thought that I'd like to pretend to be asleep when they came in, so I could better determine my situation before revealing my actual state, in case I had to escape.

I'm not going anywhere on this empty stomach, I thought. Even if I hang, they'll feed me first. I sat there waiting for someone to come in. I looked at the bell.

I thought I was awake the whole time, but I must have dozed off because I heard noises in the room and opened my eyes. There was a heavyset woman standing there with a tray of food. A thin, tall, old man with a badge stood by the dresser. The woman was just about to set the tray on the dresser. The lawman had his hat in his hand and talked to her. He glanced at me and saw that my eyes were open.

"He's awake," he said, jutting his chin toward me. The woman whirled around so quickly, the bowl moved on the tray and soup splashed over the side.

"Thank the Lord," she said.

I didn't know if I agreed with her, or not. It depended on what the Sheriff wanted.

The woman rushed to my side and adjusted my blankets.

"Do you think you can eat something?"

"Could eat...a horse," I said, surprised that it was so much work to speak. It wasn't painful, like from a wound, but rather like my muscles were tired. My tongue stuck to the side of my mouth now, and again.

"Don't try to talk. Simply move your head."

I nodded and she set the tray on my legs. She tucked a napkin over the bed spread and under my chin. The lawman helped to pull me up into a more practical eating posture. Then, he backed away and looked at me with a bit of curiosity. I looked back at him.

"Well, he looks as if he'll get better. I'll be going for now."

"Okay, Bill. I'll let you know when he's well enough to talk."

The lawman nodded at the woman and myself and left. I tried to nod to him, but he was gone by the time I finished. I pointed to the door.

"What?"

"Never mind him," she said, lifting a spoonful of the soup toward my lips. "You have to use your strength to eat. Look at you, you're all bones. When you're fat you can talk."

I opened my lips and felt the warm soup slide down my scorched throat and into my belly. Warmth emanated from the soup and I felt much stronger. I ate most of the soup and some of the bread, but found that I'd become quite full on it. The woman didn't argue with me when I indicated that I'd had enough.

The woman packed up the meal and fluffed my pillows. She left me with instructions concerning the bell.

I thought about all of it. It was a good sign that the lawman left me with her, once he realized I was awake. The way I had it figured, if I was wanted he'd have been more protective of her. That, or I was hurt much worse than I believed.

With that thought in mind, I tried to move all my arms and legs to make sure they worked. I wiggled my fingers, toes and felt of my stomach for bullet holes. Everything seemed fine and I fell asleep, assured that I'd re-awaken.

11

As I grew stronger, I began to get visitors. The first, and most important, was Sheriff Bill Dixon. He came in one morning shortly after my breakfast tray had been removed. It was a good breakfast and I felt robust and healthy. When the Sheriff entered, my stomach tightened.

Dixon held his hat in his hand as before. He looked at me with sad and tired eyes. He was thin and old, but there was a severity about the man that couldn't be mistaken.

My future hinged on what the man would say. I was still unaware of what'd taken place after I was shot in the head. I know I suffered a serious injury, but that was all the information that my nurse, Mrs. Beaufont, would reveal. Everything else was left to my nightmares and dreams. But, Dixon held the answers.

"What's your name?" the Sheriff asked.

"Jeff."

"I've heard that name. I meant your full name."

"Am I in some trouble?"

"Not that I know of, but I have reason to believe you might be. At the very least, I have to satisfy myself that you aren't wanted in the neighboring counties."

"Wanted? For what?"

"That's what I'd like to know."

"What makes you so sure there's a reason for such an inquiry? I know for a fact that I've done nothing in this town to warrant suspicion."

"Not in town, but in the county, maybe."

"What makes you think so? It seems that I'm the one who's wounded and lying in bed."

The Sheriff lost all patience with me.

"Not telling me your name is suspicious, but let me tell you what I do know. Thomas Garfield and his partner, Clyde, brought you into town in your current condition. Actually, you were much worse than now. But, they brought you in wounded. We found, by their direction, four bodies. The bodies of Ned Smith, Butch Reynolds and Jose Gallegos and some other no-account.

"Tom and Clyde, I know. They're trackers. They're working for the ranchers, who've lost a lot of cattle during and since the war. I've also heard tell of Ned Smith and his bunch. Some of them were in town before the trouble started, but I didn't come across them then. I wouldn't have known them to look at them anyway. But, you. I don't know you. I've never heard tell of you. I don't know where you came from, or what you were doing out on the prairie that night. I don't know what part you played in the killing of Ned and the rest."

It was the first I'd heard that Tom and Clyde were known to each other. I wondered if Tom would've said something about Clyde if I hadn't mentioned sparing him.

"What about those who found me, didn't they tell you anything?"

"Nothing," he said, becoming frustrated. "They brought you into town and left you here, then rode off

again. Simple as that. Now, something happened out
there the other night, and I want to know about it."

"Well, perhaps you should speak with Tom and Clyde. I
was unconscious when they brought me in. By the way, did
they bring my horse?"

"He's down at the livery."

"As for my name, I'd rather not give it unless forced to.
I have family that wouldn't care to be associated with me if
I'm to be charged with a crime. I'd not bring that disgrace
on them."

"I could put you in jail until you talked."

"That you could, Sheriff."

"One thing's for sure, you're not leaving town until I get
some answers."

I nodded agreement with an inclination toward escape.

The Sheriff, turned and left me to the silence of the
room. A few minutes later, Mrs. Beaufont entered with a
cross look on her face. She arranged certain things about
the room, avoiding my stare.

"It's unfortunate that you've decided to be stubborn,"
she said, in a low whisper. "I find that sort of behavior
unbecoming."

"I'm sorry to disappoint you, Ma'am. My father is a
man of consequence and I'd rather not muddy his name
without proper cause. If I've committed a crime, I'll pay for
it anonymously, even if I'm to be hung."

"Pshaw," she said, waving her hand. "They wouldn't
hang you. I doubt the Sheriff cares one iota about you,
except that he must protect his neighbors and you're only
delaying the process."

"Be that as it may, I have reasons."

"Make up a name, if you must."

"And, what if the name I make up is wanted? What then? I'd have gotten myself hung for someone else's crime."

"Oooo!" she said, stomping her foot. "You're a very frustrating young man!"

"I apologize, Ma'am. It's not my nature, but I find myself in strange circumstances."

"Well, I'll not feed a man who has no name. Think about that," she said, storming out of the room.

"My name's Jeff," I whispered to the sound of the slamming door.

As stern as Mrs. Beaufont was, or wanted to be, she brought dinner that night. Skipping lunch was all her good heart could bear, but her mood was as surly as before.

"There," she said, setting the tray down. "You'll not make a poor Christian of me with your stubbornness." She threw her nose in the air and stormed out again. The meals all came in a like manner after that, but I felt myself growing stronger all the time and looked forward to the time when I could get up and do things for myself.

The next afternoon the Sheriff brought a number of men into my room. All of them carried posters. I assumed the others were local lawmen determined to settle the question of my identity.

"There he is, boys," the Sheriff said. "Take him if you think you can get someone to swear that he did something, anything."

All of the other men looked me over and thought. They looked through their posters and back at me.

"How tall is he?"

"He ain't six feet, yet," the Sheriff responded.

"Don't suppose you could keep him locked up 'til he's full growed, could ya?"

The Sheriff fought back a smile at the thought of it, but slowly shook his head. "Well," he said, finally, "looks like I drug y'all over here for nothin'."

"I could cut a scar into his face and he'd fit this here character," one of the other lawmen said, in all seriousness and holding up a poster.

"Tempting idea, Fred," the Sheriff replied, "but, I ain't looking to get him hung for just any reason." He stared at me for a moment. "Y'all go on down to the saloon, I'll be there directly to buy a round."

The other lawmen shuffled out of the room and the Sheriff moved closer to my bed.

"It seems that you've been cleared of any charges. In this part of Texas, anyway." He shifted the hat in his hand. "Mrs. Beaufont tells me that your father is someone of consequence. Is that true?"

"Yes, sir."

"So what brings you out here? I know something of your predicament, I've discovered enough without your help. But, for the life of me, I can't figure your part in it, or what you were doing out there."

"Well, sir, I can tell you that my father suggested that Texas was a place where a man could make his mark. I've come here to make an honest living and hope to die with my good name intact."

"If that's your intent, it seems that you were in the wrong company."

"A man rarely gets an opportunity to pick his travelling companions and even when he does, that doesn't guarantee that he'll make the right choice."

The Sheriff seemed to weigh my words. "No, I suppose not," he said, moving toward the door. Then he stopped.

"Of course, you still owe a lot of money for your care and this room. I assume you'll want to work off your debt before you leave. To protect your good name and all."

I nodded and he left. Well, there it was. I knew I wouldn't get out of town as easy as I'd hoped. But, the fact was, I owed Mrs. Beaufont my life and that was worth a few weeks of work.

When I was better and felt I could work, I went to see Sheriff Dixon. His office was in the post office, that was a part of the hotel I'd been staying in. He was out at the moment, but Mrs. Beaufont directed me to a chair where I could wait. I sat for a long time reading the wanted posters. Most of them were crude drawings of Indians, negras and Mexicans. It seemed to me they were being blamed for a lot of crimes.

I watched flies buzz in and out of the room. There was a rack for rifles against the wall, but only a shotgun and a Sharps were in the rack. The desk was nothing more than several crude boards nailed together. There was no cell, only an iron bar with a set of shackles dangling from it and a chair beneath the shackles.

I sat and waited and adjusted the bandage still wrapped about my head. I couldn't wear a hat, which was just as well, because no one bothered to pick mine up. I began to curse Tom and Clyde for it, until I realized they'd been kind enough to pick me up. Then I felt guilty about my rush to curse them. They could have said something to the authorities here, though. That would've saved a lot of trouble.

"Up and about, are ya?" Dixon asked, entering.

"Yes, sir. I'm looking to pay my debt."

"Good, how's your head? Seein' double, or anything?"

"No, sir."

"Can you ride a horse?"

"I believe so. I don't know how long I could ride. I still tire a bit easily."

"What kind of work did you have in mind?"

"I don't know, I've worked the stables and rode the post roads. I can work with stock."

Dixon listened and while he did, his face worked. He nodded and frowned and looked up from under his brows. He whistled a time, or two. I couldn't tell whether he was impressed, or mocking me. Maybe, he just didn't care.

"How are ya with a revolver?"

The question took me by surprise and I sensed a trap. He was suckering me.

"I don't rightly know. The last time I held one, I got shot a couple of times. That ought to tell you something about it."

"Well, it don't matter any," he said, suddenly busying himself with papers on his desk. "I don't aim to have you mill about town for weeks and weeks. I want to take care of your debt all in one job. We're going into Indian Territory to pick up a Mexican. They have him locked up and waiting for us up at Fort Washita, or what's left of it. There's still a few army tents and they have this Mexican held there for us."

"What happened to the fort?"

"Burnt down, all the buildings destroyed, but the Army can't leave, yet."

"When are we leaving?"

"Now. They're getting your horse ready. You don't own nothing that ain't already on your back."

"I'd like to get a hat. The sun gets pretty rough in August."

"It ain't August, fool."

"What month is it?"

"It's near October. How long you think you were in that bed?"

"Few days, week maybe."

"Lord, boy, we thought you died three, or four times. You been laid up most of a month."

I was shocked. A month? It didn't seem that long and it was still so hot during the day.

"I still need a hat...in case it rains, or something."

Sheriff Dixon took an old hat from a peg and tossed it to me. It was an awful thing and I was loathe to put it on, but I knew it was the best I was going to do. It was too small, to start with, and grimy. I pulled the bandage off my head and felt at the wound. The past month, just when it seemed healed, it'd break open again. I put the hat on, testing it in different positions, so as not to rub the wound. It felt best riding a little low on my forehead. I threw the draw string around my neck and let the hat hang along my back until it was needed.

"That Spencer's quite a rifle," Dixon said, holding the Colt out for me to take. "It's with yur saddle and things."

We started out for Fort Washita with clouds hanging low and heavy. It'd surely rain before we got very far. It depressed me to think of it.

The ride was a silent affair. Dixon wasn't much for random talk, but if he wanted to know something, he wouldn't shut up. We rode north all that day. It started raining a few hours after we left town. We got our slickers out before it started and were dry under them, except for what little rain got in. I was grateful for the filthy hat, though it fell over my eyes with the added weight of the rain.

We made camp, but could find nothing that'd burn. Instead, we wrapped ourselves in the slickers and slept on our saddles to keep them dry. It was miserable, but we slept on the crest of a hill so the rain wouldn't puddle. Around midnight, the rain stopped. I can't say as I got much sleep, but it didn't seem to bother Sheriff Dixon any. I could hear him snoring the whole night through.

It was bright and sunny the next day. The sky was a deep blue and puffy white clouds drifted lazily by. But everything was soaked. We couldn't even make a breakfast fire. I wasted all my matches trying to find one that worked. All the while, my anger grew. Then, we packed up our dripping articles and set out toward Preston and the crossing nearby. When I saw the town lying in the slight distance, I lost my temper.

"I can't believe that we were that close to town and you decided that we should camp in the rain!" I said, figuring the distance at six miles. "Lord knows, it would've been better to sleep in the miserable rain, than to go a few extra miles in the dark."

"I don't ride this horse in the dark," he said. "She's old and she don't see too well anymore, and if you weren't so darned young, you'd take better care of your horse as it is. But, you don't. You'd ride the poor old boy to death if it pleased ya. Just like all you fool younguns. Never a moment's thought, but your own durned comfort. That's all you think about, fightin' and ridin' and whorin'. It ain't no wonder so many of y'all's necks've been stretched."

"We were six lousy miles from town! I've ridden twenty-five, no, thirty miles in the dark, in the rain during the war. It would've been nothing and everything wouldn't be wet, and my horse would have gotten a nice brushing down and some dry straw." I let out a breath to cool my anger. "You old coot!"

"Mind your temper, youngun. I could still find someone to lock you up. That one fella, the Marshal that wanted to cut your cheek, he runs this town. I could let him cut ya and hang ya before lunch."

"Wouldn't surprise me if you did. Here I am, a day out of the sickbed and you try to give me pneumonia. You're still trying to kill me. If it wasn't a sin, I'd shoot you right here and now."

"Keep on talkin', boy. I'm learning more all the time."

I felt my eyes narrow. He was right. He'd gotten me so angry that I'd begun to tell him everything about me. A few more minutes and I'd have told him about the horses I'd ridden and under what circumstances and where.

"If you're so interested in my identity, why didn't you let me go on and talk? Why stop me?"

"Because, I find your squealing anger intolerable to listen to. My ears are more important than my curiosity."

With that, we rode into town. We rode up to the Sheriff's office and tied up the horses.

"You go on in. Tell him you're here on business," Dixon said.

He was pulling something. I could sense it.

"Go on, boy. Do as I tell ya. You working for me?"

I went up to the door and opened it. The other lawman was standing with his back to me, pinning up posters.

"I'm here on business," I said.

The lawman turned around and when he caught sight of me, he threw himself backward and reached down for his gun. I felt my hand move instinctively for the pistol in my waistband. Just then, Dixon burst through the door.

"No, no, wait!"

By the time Dixon stopped it, I had my gun drawn and cocked, but pointed at the floor halfway between myself and the other lawman. The lawman had his revolver out of his holster, but it was pointed down at his foot.

"Lord Jesus, almighty!" the lawman said, putting his free hand to his chest. "Dixon, you sorry old fool! That ain't no way to startle a man and you know it."

"I'm sorry. I'm sorry, please, put your weapons away. He's with me, Fred." Dixon was flustered by what had taken place. Maybe, it seemed like a funny idea, back on the trail with me scolding him like a child for having to sleep in the rain. It might've seemed funny then, but when he saw Fred reach for his gun, he jumped in to stop it.

"You're lucky nobody got killed! That's the most reckless damn thing I've ever seen!" Fred continued.

"I didn't think you'd pull your gun on the boy."

"I thought he'd come to kill me."

"Why would he do that?"

"I don't know, 'cause I wanted to hang him, I guess. I didn't have time to think it through."

"I'm going to have a glass of beer," I said, putting my pistol in my britches. I walked out of the office shaking my head. There was more at play than a game. Dixon was testing me, or trying to get me killed sure enough. He was a vindictive, clever man that demanded attention. I didn't think he'd have jumped in the way he did if I hadn't been beating the lawman at the draw. Or, maybe he knew I'd beat the lawman. Maybe, that's what he wanted to see.

What sort of place was Texas? There was none of the civilization I'd known in Mississippi. Folks didn't shoot each other they way they did in the Frontier. It wasn't heard of. A rare duel happened on occasion, but that was with deliberation. The sort of killing in the Frontier was at will, without much thought to it.

I walked into the saloon and ordered up a glass of beer. It only occurred to me then, that I was eighteen years old. I'd had a birthday while I was asleep for the past month. I could scarcely believe it. A whole month had passed while I lay in bed with wounds received in a gun battle.

It was a wild country, that's for sure. There were Indian attacks, hangings, thievery, midnight gun battles. This is what my father's sent me into? This was the way to make a mark? The only mark I thought I was liable to make, was on the front of a tombstone.

12

I sat at the saloon until Sheriff Dixon stopped by to gather me. I didn't speak to him then, nor did I speak to him as we mounted up for the ride to the ferry. We were into Indian Territory before I could bring myself to talk without fear of forcing some sort of confrontation.

"What are you playing at?"

"I apologize for what I did. It was uncalled for. I agree, now pardon me, but I've apologized enough," Dixon said, in a stubborn, defiant tone.

I shook my head. Did he really think I'd let it die at that?

"Your apology is accepted and appreciated, but that wasn't what I was after. You're a clever one, Sheriff. You've been baiting me since I met you and you've gained a bit of knowledge about me. I grant you that," I said, thinking of how to phrase what I had to say and remained silent for a mile, or more.

"What else have you in mind? Am I to go through a series of tests to satisfy your curiosity? Believe me, Sheriff, I'll not tolerate this sort of reckless behavior."

"'Not tolerate'? You little squirt, who do you think you're talking to? Some servant? I'm Bill Dixon, you little toad. I've fought off Indians, badmen and Mexicans for 35 years near the Red River. You'll tolerate whatever I have to serve ya, or you'll die trying. Now, sit your horse and be quiet. I don't have the time, nor temperament to listen to your aristocratic rambling."

"You have no right to treat me the way you do. I'm a free man. I have no record, and no one has made a complaint against me. But for the debt I owe Mrs. Beaufont, I could ride back to Preston this instant and forget you as quickly as the dust settled. You have no legal right to keep me, nor kill me."

Dixon burst into a heavy laughter. "You're such a blamed fool! You ain't where you used to be, boy. There ain't no law here, except myself, and I'll do just as I please with you, or anyone else I've a mind to. Remember that and you'll be wiser and happier for it." Dixon was quiet for a minute, or two, then he spit into the dirt. "Hell, boy," he said grinning, "you can turn back anytime. You wouldn't make it back to Preston, 'fore you found your scalp on a pole."

"So you say, as if there were less danger with you than without you. But, I don't believe that," I replied, rolling my eyes and taking the opportunity to look around behind us.

"Say what you will, there's Cheyenne and Kiowa about these parts," he said, looking at me with contempt. "You don't even know where you're at. You don't know nothing about this country. And, that's why my curiosity's up like the hair on a dog's back. You don't belong here. You don't fit here. You weren't raised here, but you're here and under some suspicious circumstances, at that."

He stared at me then, with eyes narrowed. Dixon let all of his pretense fall and looked at me as one man naturally looks at another. I was a threat to him until he figured me out. As long as I remained an enigma, he'd respect what he couldn't figure out.

"So, why don't you just forget all of that nonsense of before," he said, "and just tell me exactly who and what you are, how you came to be here and when you plan on leaving and what you plan to do when you leave?"

"No, sir," I said, wanting to do just that to end the constant harassment, testing and suspicion, but something inside told me to keep my distance from the cantankerous old man. Whatever I told him would only serve to lessen his respect for me. As it was, he had a grudging respect for the boy who confounded him so. I felt that there was a thin line to ride with him and the only peace a person could find, would be found somewhere between respect and contempt. The old Sheriff would kill a man too far on one side, or the other.

"What do you mean, 'no, sir'?"

"Just that. I'll tell you nothing. You want to know something about me, you just keep testing me in the bizarre way you have and you'll find all you need to know."

"You'll never know another minute's peace," he said, staring intently.

"I know it, but I've lived that way before. You aren't the first."

We rode on for several miles. Dixon would search the horizon with clear, blue eyes and glance behind him in a casual way that unnerved me.

"We being followed?" I asked.

"Yep," he said, spitting tobacco.

"Who?"

"Injuns. Kiowa probably, Cheyenne, maybe."

"Where?"

"I don't know."

"You don't know?" I asked, suddenly startled and concerned.

"Nope."

"Well, if you don't know where they are, what makes you think they're within a hundred miles of here?"

"Because, you blamed idjit, we're in Indian Territory," he said, shaking his head in frustration and pulling his hat lower on his face.

"That doesn't mean we're being followed."

"No," he said, measuring his words, "but, even if we ain't, we are."

"Now, what's that supposed to mean?"

"In Indian Territory, even if you ain't being followed, you'd better durn well act like you are. You can't imagine how fast these Cheyenne can come up on a man. I've heard tell of men being shot between the eyes while staring directly at the Injun that shot him, 'cept he didn't see him."

I looked all around at the horizon and behind us. I didn't see anyone, but after that, I wasn't comforted by it.

"Why do you think you're here?" he asked. "They'll shoot you first, seeing how lost you are to the proper ways of actin'. Then, I'll have a chance to get away while you lay dying in this God-forsaken country."

"I ought to kill you, old man."

Dixon laughed again at my expense. "That's right, you shoot me. Go ahead and bring out every Injun in the Territory. You wouldn't live a quarter hour longer than me. Only difference is, I'd die fast and you'd die slow."

I was so angry, I was beside myself. The old goat was using me for bait on top of every other injury I'd received at his hands. I'd ridden with the man barely 24 hours and he'd abused me in ways I'd never thought of before. He was cruel and cunning and had every angle figured. I was indeed mad enough to kill him at that moment, but just as before, he had me hog-tied by every limb. I couldn't do a thing, but ride along and ponder how easy it was for him to get the jump on me. What burned worst in my mind, was the idea that I was supposed to be intelligent and I was out-smarted at every turn by a withered old man without sense enough to get out of the snake pit he lived in. I spit in frustration.

From the corner of my eye, I saw the faintest glimmer of a smile in his eyes. He watched me turn the problem over in my mind. He watched as I searched for a rational way out, and when I spit, he knew he had complete command of me.

"All right, you got me. You win. I'll go along with this chore of yours, but when we get back, I'm done. I owe you nothing, I owe Mrs. Beaufont nothing. I'll just walk away from your miserable town and never look back."

"Well," he said, "there ain't nothing says you'll get back, but if'n you do, you can go."

I nodded and put my mind to the trail ahead. At first, I cursed myself for my poor luck. It seemed that since I'd made my way into Texas, I'd found nothing but victimization. I'd been at the mercy of everyone I met. Then, it dawned on me that it was my fear of being alone in such a vast and violent land that caused me to gravitate toward those willing to exploit the weak. Had it not been for my quick reflexes with a gun, I would've been killed many times over.

There came a sense of understanding. I realized that I'd been fighting the ways of the Frontier. I wanted to make it civilized, or expected it to be civilized when I had no cause to believe such a thing. It was for my own comfort that I chose to see the Frontier in this way, instead of how it was.

Then, I understood Sheriff Dixon, Thomas Garfield, Ned Smith and Old Ben back in Port Caddo. They were products of a world in which the legal issues didn't count and where a gun and the will to use it reigned supreme.

Not because they were evil, or even cold men, but because they knew how to survive under the conditions presented to them. It was due to their experience and pain that went beforehand, that a person, such as myself, could enter the Frontier without being killed and robbed immediately. They were the buffer between the savage and the civilized, all except Ned, who was most certainly the evil each of them worked against in their own ways.

I laughed at myself, after I understood it. Did the Indians respect the law? Our law? Did the thief respect the law? Did the desert, or the snake, or the gun? No, and I was wrong to expect it of them.

I thought it out further as we rode toward Fort Washita. We came upon the fort at dusk. There were a number of army tents pitched on the plain next to the burnt out, destroyed buildings.

"In the days of the Confederacy," Dixon said, "this was the headquarters for the Indian Department."

I nodded. Of course, I knew of Fort Washita. My father often spoke of it in passing, but did not describe it in any detail. He only referred to it as the Department Headquarters, but every now and then he'd say something about "that fort on the Washita," which was technically inaccurate, but accurate enough for his discussion.

I wondered, silently, what Bill Dixon would say if he knew how close to the Confederacy I'd been. The thought brought a smile to my lips.

We rode casually up to the structure. It was the first time the Sheriff relaxed his attitude since crossing the Red. He seemed to sag all over, as if some inner supports had been cut. We pulled up to a tent and tied our mounts to a hitching rail hastily thrown up for the purpose.

A sharp looking Union Corporal stood beside the flap of the tent.

"May I state your business?" the Corporal asked.

"I'm Sheriff Bill Dixon, and this here's my deputy for the purpose of escorting Manuel Garza to his prompt hanging in Texas."

The Corporal entered the tent, I heard some conversation, then he came out through the flap and held it back for us. Dixon entered immediately, with me on his heels.

The man sitting behind a table wore the oak leaf insignia on his epaulette. He smoked a big cigar and seemed somewhat at his leisure.

"Major," Dixon said, nodding. "This is my deputy, Jeff."

I nodded, but the Major didn't acknowledge me in any way.

"Sheriff," he said, "I'm glad you've come. We've been issued orders to move out soon. I didn't know if I were going to have to turn him loose, or shoot him."

"I trust shootin' weighed most favorite."

"The Corporal outside will take you to him directly. We have no accommodations to offer, but you're welcome to lay out your bedroll and partake of our mess."

"Thank you for your hospitality, Major. I believe we'll accept."

"Would you like an escort back through the territory to the Red?"

"No, thank you. The less fuss we raise, the less likely we'll find trouble."

The Major nodded his head and puffed on the cigar. He stood then.

"If that will be all, I have preparations to make for our move."

"Thank you, Major," Dixon said, turning to leave. I followed him out and the Corporal took the lead. We came to a tent guarded by four sentries.

"Wait here," Dixon mumbled, and I waited by the entrance with the Corporal.

Inside, there was some speaking, but it was all Dixon. Manuel was saying nothing, but the tone of Dixon's voice was gruff and short. Then, Dixon came through the flap.

"That's him," he said. "Where can we throw our bedrolls?"

"Over there, sir," the Corporal replied, "by the fire, in the space between those tents."

Dixon nodded and instructed me to get my bedroll laid out. When we were all situated, we leaned back on the blankets and waited for dinner to be ready. There was a fire with several pieces of meat being roasted. The grease dripped into the fire, hissing and flaring the flames into a spire.

Around us, the others were growing restless for the food. They began to gather at the edges of the fire and discussions cropped up among them. Dixon and I seemed to be of great interest, but no one would confront us directly. There were whisperings about the Mexican. Everyone seemed to know that we'd come to fetch him back to his death.

"Be careful with that Mexican," one of them said. "He bit the finger off one of the men."

"He didn't bite it clean off," another added, to correct the first.

"Did I say he bit it clean off?"

"That's what you seemed to say."

"Never mind him," the first one said. "That Mexican is a wild one. He shot at us until he ran out of ammunition, then he tried to cut us up. We had a time getting him down and shackled."

"Thank you," Dixon said, diplomatically. "He'll be easier to handle now."

"Yep," the speaker said. "Of course, you have to watch his tongue as well. He tried to bribe some of the men into letting him go. If we weren't in the army he might have succeeded," he said, glancing at me. "He says he has gold buried somewhere."

"Gold, eh?" Dixon asked.

"Yes, sir. A bunch of it, if you believe him. I don't, but some men do."

"No, I don't," the other responded, though he'd not been mentioned.

"I didn't say you."

"That's what you meant. I only listened to him to find out what he was about. I wasn't going to throw in with him. I came right to you with what he said."

"I didn't say you," the first one repeated.

"That's what you meant," the other replied.

Then, there was a ringing of metal against metal and all the men lined up with tin plates held out before them. There was a cook, cutting pieces of the meat off and another dipped a stew out onto the plates. Dixon and I dug around in our saddlebags for plates and lined up behind the others.

"Sure is nice, not having to rustle up my own dinner for a change," Dixon said.

"Got out of it last night, too," I said, needling him, and he shot back a glance of anger that I took for mocking anger. To hell with him, I thought. The rules had changed since I started this journey and they'd change more before we got back to Sherman.

I noticed that before most of them men ate, they bowed their heads in prayer. It seemed like a comfortable time and place, so I did the same.

"You a prayin' man?" Dixon asked.

"I have a strong belief in God and Jesus Christ," I said, plainly.

Dixon shrugged and went about tearing the meat apart and stuffing it into his mouth. "Good luck holding onto that belief, youngun. Their ain't much left of God in this country, what with the cow thieves, pistoleers and murderers roaming about."

I let the remark alone. It seemed to me, that this would be just the sort of place a man could use the faith. It's easy to lose faith when everything seems fine. It's during the worst of times that a man needs to rely on the wisdom of God.

"Anyone in charge of a gun ought to believe in God," I said, finally.

"Well, I've only seen it the other way. In my opinion, it's always the person standing before the gun, or the rope, that believes in God," he said, grinning. "The trouble is, all the real believers don't live very long."

Dixon and I ate in silence. The others, however, joked and prodded each other and tempers flared now and again. All through it, I noticed one man watching me with some curiosity. I first noticed him sitting back, away from the fire, but when he'd finished his meal and sat holding a cup of coffee, I saw him move closer.

"You a reb, ain't ya?" he asked, with coffee dripping from his mustache. He wiped his mouth with the back of his sleeve.

"That business is done with," Dixon interjected.

"Lord, if we ain't feedin' a Johnny Reb," the man said, giving a malevolent grin.

I'd waited for this moment, but no one mentioned the war the whole time. Maybe it was because Texans in general didn't want to bring it up. But, in Indian Territory, a few yards from a Union fort, it was bound to be raised. I dreaded the moment and feared it. I was afraid that I wouldn't lie.

"Last time I seen a Reb, he was hightailing it out of this country." "Listen, we don't need any of this talk," Dixon pleaded, and I realized that he had a stake in trying to keep the peace. I suppose he needed me at the time. I'd come to realize that no one stuck their necks out without just cause.

But, things had changed for me in the past few hours. I'd come to understand the Frontier and I was no longer afraid of killing someone. I no longer worried about it. It was the only language anyone seemed to understand and I was learning to speak it, too.

"Let's hear that good ol' rebel yell, there Deputy."

"Where I've been and what I've done is none of your business, private," I said.

The private's face grew serious and he stared hard.

"It is as long as you sit around this fire. There's a bounty out on men that never took the pledge and you sound like one that never did."

I stared right back at the man. All of the talking had stopped and everyone was alert to whatever might happen.

"This here young man is my deputy," Dixon said, with a firmness to his voice that surprised me. "I hired him and I know his past. If there's any question about him, you can direct it to me, or keep your mouth shut."

"Well, now, Mr. Lawman, you ain't in Texas and you ain't wearing no stripe on yur arm, so you ain't nothing to me," he said. "Understand that?"

"Should I make a complaint to the Major?" Dixon asked. "Is that what you're after? I can do it."

"I ain't done nothing, but ask a question."

"And, this man has...," Dixon began, but I cut him off. I wasn't going to let anyone think they had to take care of me. Not anymore.

"Shut up," I said. "I was in the Confederacy and I was proud to serve."

The private leapt to his feet and I stood to meet him. We were both armed, but neither of us were thinking about shooting. He wanted to fight, not kill. He walked over to me and I found that he was taller and heavier, but I'd assumed that. It didn't matter, I had to start squaring my own troubles, or I'd be left to the mercy of men like Bill Dixon.

I knew one thing, as I watched my rival come, I was going to hit him first. He strutted around the fire to where I stood and the others began to cheer him on. Even those who'd been friendly to me earlier were exhorting him to whip me, to beat that "ol Johnny Reb".

Several hours before, I'd have been afraid to be beaten, but I made up my mind about such matters and I wasn't afraid anymore. I didn't even expect to win. That wasn't the point of the fight. The purpose rested deeper and I couldn't have lied if I'd wanted to. To deny I was a part of the Confederate cause would have been to deny everything I was raised to believe in. I knew whatever beating I was about to take was inspired by differences too vast to be settled by a lie.

Despite my plan, he hit me first. I went backward several steps and wiped the blood from my mouth. The sight of my own blood enraged me. The stupidity of the fight enraged me. Did he think that he could beat me into submission to the Union cause? Did he think it was that easy? Already, men had died on each side in the hundreds of thousands.   It was a number so vast, I couldn't comprehend it, and even after that, the South only surrendered when their defeat was total. Did he think that my resolve was so weak that I could be deterred by a little blood on the mouth?

I came back at him and took a swing with my right. He blocked it and hit me in the temple, sending me to the ground.   And, there, lying on the ground, I felt a tremendous sense of power as if all the injustices I'd been dealt were personified in him, in that one man standing over me with the gloating expression. I rose up and the others, including Bill Dixon, called for me to stay on the ground.

I walked over to the private and he saw that there was something different in my eyes. I saw him literally flinch when he noticed it. But, he regained his confidence and he scowled back. I neared him and he raised a fist. All right, I thought, let's give it a real go, and I kicked him on the side of the knee. His leg buckled and he dropped to his knees. I looked down at him kneeling before me and I grabbed the back of his head. I shoved his face downward as my knee came up to meet his nose. He flopped over backward. As he lay on his back, he coughed from the blood running down his throat and rolled onto his hands and knees. He coughed up some blood, while a stream poured from his nose. Then he stood and turned to look at me with a crooked nose and blood starting down the front of his shirt.

There was a craziness about him. He bent over and charged at me. I did as I was taught and went down just before he reached me, grabbed his shirt and threw him over onto his back. He lay there as long as it took for him to get rolled over and he came at me again. By that time, I was up on my feet and I dodged him. I took a swing at the back of his neck, but I missed and he came around again.

All this time, the crowd around the fire was yelling at increased levels. They'd begun to chant, "kill the Reb". I heard the noises and the words, but they were far away and of no consequence. Caught in the middle was Sheriff Dixon, who looked at me with sympathetic eyes. I couldn't use his sympathy.

"You filthy Reb," the private said. He walked up to me, then and faked a punch with his right and clipped me under the chin with his left. I was stunned by it and felt myself go over backward. In a moment, he was on top of me. He was beating my head from side to side. I reached up and grabbed him by the Adam's Apple. I put my other hand behind his neck to support the pressure I was giving to his throat. He beat me more often, but the blows were growing weaker and weaker. Then, he started pulling on my arms, but his strength was slackening and his eyes were watering. Somebody from the crowd pulled him free and I got back onto my feet. The private was off to the side, coughing for breath with others gathered around him.

I looked at the faces around the campfire. Standing beside Dixon was the Major. He seemed casually interested in the fight and I shook my head. No good commander would let such a thing take place in his presence, much less condone it by taking a spectator's role.

Suddenly, the private broke free of those around him and he came at me again. I stood with my chest heaving, and my mouth dry, waiting for him to get close enough. He kicked at my face and I jumped back and caught his foot. I looked at him over his extended leg and shrugged my shoulders. He was in a bad position and it showed in his eyes. I threw the leg upward as hard as I could and he flipped over backward onto his face. He scrambled to his feet before I could get there. He came up with a knife and I reached for my Colt, but it wasn't there. It must have fallen out in the struggle. I looked quickly around at my feet, but couldn't find it. I pulled my Bowie out and we began to circle each other. As he neared with the knife, I felt my confidence wane. I thought I could still win, but I'd get cut up no matter what the outcome.

"Put the knives away," the Major boomed from the side.

The private looked startled and looked at the Major with a curious glance as if the Major should understand that I was a Confederate. Then, he tossed the knife away and I did too. He came after me again. I stood my ground and he hit me on the jaw. I tried to block it, but he was too fast. I stumbled sideways and he slammed into me, knocking me to the ground. I went onto my belly and felt his hand dig into my hair. He lifted my head up and whispered into my ear.

"If I still had that knife, I'd be cuttin' yur throat right now."

"If I still had my Colt, you'd be dead," I said, through a tight, swollen jaw.

He smashed my face into the ground and bloodied my nose, then raised my head up again.

"I still have mine," he said.

"Then use it," I replied.

He reached for his revolver and I felt him being pulled away from my back.

"That's enough," the Major said. "I'll have no killing in my command. If you want to kill someone, go find some Injuns."

I got up from the ground and dusted myself off. There was blood all over my face and shirt and it hurt to move my eyes. I was hurt, but I wasn't beaten. Yes, the man could have killed me and I could have killed him. The crowd intervened for each of us. I felt no shame. I gave what I had to defend who I was. A man can't be asked to do any more than that.

The crowd dispersed at the order of the Major and I was left looking into the eyes of Bill Dixon.

"Well, you nearly got us tossed out of here by our shirt collars."

"I don't care."

Dixon looked at the ground. "Fought in the war, eh?"

"No, sir, but I was a Confederate. I won't deny that."

"Maybe you should, from here on," he suggested.

"No, sir. I won't, not if it means a thousand such beatings. There's more to it than a little fight. Men died for the cause of the Confederacy. Would I disgrace their names by refusing that I, too, was a Confederate? Did they deny it?"

"It ain't the same thing," Bill said.

"Yes, sir, it's exactly the same thing and it meant their death. Or, are you suggesting that I'm less a man than they were?"

"No," he said, with certainty, "I wouldn't suggest that at all."

"Good. Then let's not hear anymore of it."

Throughout the night, I heard men swear they'd kill me. I heard the curses and disparagements from men hidden deep within the anonymity of an entire camp. I challenged the first few to a fight, but gave it up as no one came to take up the challenge. I then understood that they just wanted to be a part of the beating and to make me afraid. But, I wasn't afraid.

13

We woke early the next morning and gathered Manuel Garza before dawn. The sun was just breaking over the horizon as we left the camp behind.

All that morning I noticed the looks from those we met. Even in the darkness, I could sense the anger and hatred in their faces. I'd never seen hate like that, it was an internal loathing for what I represented. They thought of me as a snake that's best killed than walked around. It might have created a sense of shame in me, but it had the reverse effect and I began to hate them for their short-sighted arrogance. From then on, I'd carry a peculiar dislike for the Yanks that was different from hating the ideology of the Union. It was a more personal hate, a hate for a particular persecutor embodied by Union soldiers.

Manuel rode with his shackles tied to the saddlehorn and his horse tied to mine. Sheriff Dixon rode behind with his rifle resting on his thigh. There was plenty of rope between my horse and Manuel's so that I could drift back to talk to Dixon, if I took a mind to. Manuel was silent most of the time and only spoke to ask for water. Sometimes Dixon would grant this request and sometimes he wouldn't.

The Sheriff kept an eye out for trouble, as did I. We were both a bit edgy and my face hurt from the fight. I didn't think too much of Manuel. I was more concerned about Indians and rattlesnakes that might spook either his horse, or mine. I glanced alternately from the ground to the horizon.

We stopped at noon to boil some coffee and to eat some jerked beef. It was then that I got my first real look at our prisoner. He was in his mid-twenties with a huge mustache and bushy eyebrows. He tried to grow a beard, but it was sort of hit and miss. When he looked at me, it was with dull, brown eyes that showed his weariness of running from the law, or the depression at facing the gallows.

Sitting on the ground, he spoke in a loud voice, addressing the air about him in a general way.

"This es no bueno," he said. "They will not hang the Bandito de la Pampa! Is no bueno, taking him to Techas." He slapped himself on the chest. "Is commandante."

"Silencio, Manuel," Dixon said, "it's as easy to shoot you here as hang you there."

Manuel pulled his threadbare shirt as far open as he could with the shackles on his wrists. "Tirar," he said, defiantly and with pride.

"Death will come soon enough."

Manuel jutted his chin out at me, as if to make the same offer. I lowered my head and ate what was left of my jerky. I saw, out from under my brow that he'd dropped his hands and was looking out into the distance. I glanced over my shoulder to where he was staring to ensure that no one was coming. I could see no dust from horses and looked back at my lap.

It was a sad business taking a man back to die. I think he expected his companions to save him, but I figured they were already fighting over who'd lead them on to more robberies and killings. I doubted they were tearing their hair out over Manuel.

The journey was sad in a number of ways. For me, it was a sadness at realizing the certainty of death that awaits us all. For Manuel, it was the slow realization that no one would rescue him, that he had no loyal men. For Dixon, it was a realization that he could not go on forever, that his career was coming to a close. The weariness showed on him.

We rode on then, and the day slipped away in a cloud of dust. As time went on, Manuel's hopes faded and Dixon grew pale and tired. There was no escape for either of them, not in the end. And, I got caught up in their world and became depressed and sullen. When the sun dipped low toward the horizon, we were all anxious to rest.

We made camp in sight of Preston. Small lights shone from the tiny windows across the river. We ate and drank coffee and when it was over, Dixon tied Manuel to a tree, then he made a place to sit. We made up fake beds and moved out away from the camp to sleep. Dixon kept the first watch.

I woke early in the morning, long before light, and relieved Dixon.

"He's asleep," Dixon said, "but, keep your rifle on him and keep a lookout for others coming out of the darkness. If you hear something, get down on your belly, so you can use the sky to light up a man, or a horse."

"I know how to do it," I replied, feeling insulted.

The Sheriff paid no attention to me, he just walked off.

I knew most of the secrets, thanks to Corporal Donnigan. Now, there was a man for this country. There wasn't much the human race knew about precautions and clever evasions that wasn't known to the lanky, red-headed corporal.

The rest of the evening passed in quiet boredom. I thought I heard movement in the darkness a few times, but it was nothing. There'd be no saving grace for Manuel. He was doomed and alone and he seemed small and pitiful tied to the tree. He lay ten foot away with his head resting against the roots and his shackles tied to the massive trunk.

I'd expected Manuel to tell me of the gold and try to enlist me against the old man, but he didn't. Somewhere, out there in the dark void, was his band. I thought there were those who wished to free him and continue their banditry, but they were obviously in the minority and were probably dead by then.

The Frontier was a cruel place. Loyalty was a game played by those who survived. I worried that if the only people who'd survive were the lying, unfaithful, murdering slobs, what would become of this beautiful new land? Would it always be a land of outlaws and violence? Perhaps, I thought, unless the "good" people became much more cruel and unleashed their healthy evil on the outlaws and drove them out. But, what would happen to those "good" people if they were forced to do so?

I was telling a story of myself and I knew it. I wondered what would happen to me, now that I'd changed enough to survive the Frontier. Would I lose that which was moral within myself? Would I slowly degenerate into Manuel? I looked over at him again. He lay sleeping with his arms stretched toward the tree.

Toward morning, as the sky grew lighter in the East, I built up the fire and boiled water for coffee. I had some salted bacon and fried some in a pan while the sun spread its red fingers across the land. Dixon rose and untied the prisoner.

We ate and moved on to the ferry. After passing back into Texas, the going was smooth and easy. We picked up a few deputies in Preston as escort. Dixon was smart and knew that Manuel would come peacefully while he thought his rescue was imminent, but the last night before the Red River was the only chance his band had of saving him. The extra deputies were to help discourage Manuel from desperate action on the last leg of the trip.

As we neared Sherman, Manuel mentioned the gold and tried to make a break for it, but the rope alerted us to his intent and he was pistol whipped for trying to escape. It was his last act of defiance and he went the rest of the way into town without a word.

We approached the town in the dark. There were lights in the saloon and a few of the houses. We rode directly to the livery and put our horses up. The deputies did the same and agreed to have a drink with the Sheriff. Our small group walked loosely to the hotel. There were several horses tied to the rail. Dixon threw his hands out before the men and grabbed Manuel about the neck, clamping his hand over the prisoner's mouth. In a moment, Dixon had his handkerchief off his neck was stuffing it into Manuel's mouth.

"What's the matter?" one of the deputies asked.

"These horses," he said, "I know the paint."

I looked at the deputies, who glanced at each other and then at the Sheriff.

"You know this caballo, Manuel?" the Sheriff asked.

Manuel shook his head, but he stood straight and looked suddenly emboldened. He was again the defiant commandante of a band.

"Yeah, you know him." Dixon looked around at all of us. "They're in there," he said. "This horse was stolen after the murder. I don't know how many are in there. I guess there's a bunch." He looked around at the street. There were several horses tied up to different hitching rails.

"Jeff, get the prisoner back to the livery and tie him to a stall, then get back here."

I nodded and led Manuel back the way we'd come. He fought and resisted until I hit him in the back of the head with the barrel of the Colt. His knees buckled for a second, then he caught his weight and walked. I tied him up to a stall. I used most of the rope I had. The last thing I wanted, was for Manuel to come up from behind and kill us all.

Just as I got halfway between the livery and Sheriff Dixon, a man came out into the street in his nightshirt. He carried a shotgun.

"They've been in there all day," he said.

"Are they drunk?"

"Probably. They were much louder earlier. It's been somewhat quiet for an hour, or so. They were yelling your name and saying all sorts of vile things."

"Go on back to bed, Jim. We'll handle it."

The deputies and I shot glances at each other. I thought we could use all the guns we could get, and by the way the deputies looked at me, they thought the same. But, we held our tongues.

"Let's go, boys," Dixon said.

"Hey," one of the deputies spoke up, "shouldn't we get some more help? There's probably ten of 'em in there."

"We can't let them run this town. Can we? Preston'd be next, Deke. You want to wait for that, or should we settle it here? Let's go." He could see the hesitation in our eyes. "Well, do you want to take them drunk, or sober?"

Dixon started toward the saloon and we followed with our guns drawn. Just then, a man came flying backward out of the open doors. We stopped short and watched him skid on the boardwalk, fall, and roll into the street beneath the hitching rail. The horses made room for him.

"Nine," Dixon said, over his shoulder.

We entered the saloon like a bomb going off. The minute Sheriff Dixon walked through the doors, he started firing at those inside. We pushed hard on his back and hot lead split the air. In a moment, it was hard to see through the gunsmoke. I tried to pick my shots, but tables were tossed over and men hit the ground to fire from the floor. Sheriff Dixon killed two men and wounded another before they began to return the fire. One of the deputies was hit in the leg and went to the floor, where he continued to fire his pistol until it was empty. I heard him cuss as he fumbled to reload. The first deputy through the door took the opposite side and shot at least one that I knew of. I couldn't get off more than two clear shots, myself.

Everything began to explode. Pieces of wood flew away from walls and door frames. Glass broke and I know for a fact that several of the bandits were shot by their own men. I'd never seen anything like it. One moment there was laughing and hollering and drinking and the next minute, there was a chaos of screaming and dying. Shattered pieces of objects seemed to float up and hang there as if suspended in the smoke filled air.

I saw one of the men dive out a side window and I turned away from the door and charged to the side of the building. I saw a figure receding into the darkness and I leveled my revolver. The powder flash lit up the man's back as the bullet knocked him forward. I ran to him. He spit dirt out of his mouth and tried to crawl away. Then, he saw his revolver laying a few feet away and he tried to get to it. I shot him in the back of the head.

I ran back to the saloon and threw myself into the action with vigor, though there was little left of the battle. A few of the banditos were crawling toward the door. I felt a man pull at my pant leg and I shot him through the chest. The wounded deputy sat in a puddle of blood and shot anything that moved. He was crying. He wiped the tears away to take aim. Dixon stood in the middle of the room reloading and kicking those he suspected of being alive. He shot those who groaned. The other deputy stood with a blank sort of look on his face. Suddenly, he ripped the pinned badge off his shirt and walked out. I heard his horse pounding out across the road a few minutes later.

When the banditos were all dead, Dixon looked at the deputy on the floor.

"What are you crying for?"

"They're gonna cut my leg off, I know it. I don't wanna be without no leg. What am I gonna do?"

"They ain't cut it off, yet," Dixon replied. "Now, shut up, will ya?"

The man sniffled and wiped his eyes. "Sons of bitches," he said, and shot one of the dead men.

There was blood all over the floor and small pieces of wood and glass. A fire burned in the corner of the saloon. Dixon put it out with a blanket. I tied a tourniquet around the wounded deputy's leg.

"Start hauling this trash out into the street," Dixon said, and walked out. I heard him stop at the drunk man in the gutter and shoot once more, then he cussed.

Before long, Mrs. Beaufont was doctoring the wounded deputy across the lobby from the saloon area. Someone was called to clean the floor and I went about pulling bodies into the street with some help from the other townspeople. When I was done, I went into the Sheriff's office and sat down.

Blood was on my hands and my face. My ear had been nicked in the commotion, but I didn't notice it until I saw the puddle of blood on my shoulder. As I reached up to touch my ear, Dixon walked in with Manuel. He pushed him over to the small chair and shackled his hand to the rail. Manuel looked white as death.

"Get out of my chair," he said, to me and I rose. He sat down and put his face in his hands. I started to leave when he called me back. He rose and we locked Manuel in the office.

"Come with me," he said, and I followed him to the saloon where he grabbed a bottle of whiskey. I followed him up the stairs to his room. Once inside, he sat on the bed and pointed to a wooden chair beside the door. I sat down and looked at him.

"Where'd you go?"

"I went outside. I couldn't get a clear shot with everyone firing at the same time, and I saw one of them go out the window."

"You shot him?"

"Yes, sir."

"He's dead?"

"I made sure of it."

"God, I hate this business," he said, and took a long drink from the bottle. "But, what's a man to do?"

He handed me the bottle and I took a drink. I handed it back to him and felt that I'd changed. I felt complete as if I'd accomplished some important task left undone. I tried to feel bad about those I'd killed, but I didn't, I couldn't. I was complete and didn't have enough left of who I was to be ashamed of it. It was the Frontier. I understood it before, and now, I'd become part of it and I'd never be the same. My innocence was gone. I'd become as filthy as Manuel, or Dixon, or Ned Smith. The only regret I had, was that I wasn't ashamed.

"You know a lot about the Bible?" Dixon asked.

"Yes, sir. My father made me study it and talk about it with him."

"Is there any way a man can get to heaven after doing what we've done?"

"It's said that a man can repent all his sins and take Jesus Christ as his Lord and Savior and be born-again and all sins will be forgiven."

"Do you believe that?"

"Yes, sir."

"Do I need a priest, or something?"

"I don't believe so, I think you can just say it."

"Then, what?" he asked. "Do I have to go to church every Sunday and pray and get down on my knees?"

"You should want to go to church, if you've taken Jesus Christ as your savior."

"What's the law? What does the law say about it?"

"There is no law, there's only your heart," I replied as simply as I could.

"Here," he said, handing the bottle to me. "Take this and get out of here."

I leaned forward and took the bottle. I held it up to the light and took a drink, then turned to the door.

"Wait," he said. "If you believe in God and the Bible, how come you're out here? There ain't no God out here and you ain't acted like no Christian."

"No, sir, I haven't," I said, unable to explain my feelings to myself, much less him. "I have no excuse for it. I find myself in the eye of a hurricane and try as I do to fight against it, I feel it sucking me closer and closer to the depths of Hell." I thought for a moment. "What we done down there was murder, plain and simple and God saw it all and he knows that I shot the man in the alley without remorse. It would've been too inconvenient to take him as a prisoner and I killed him instead. That was my choice and God knows it like he knows the dawn and the far mountains. I'll be judged one day for what I took part in and I know my judgment will result in damnation," I said, swallowing hard. "The trouble right here and now is, I don't care."

With that, I walked out of his room and went downstairs to get a room of my own. I found Mrs. Beaufont bent over the wounded man, holding a cool rag against his forehead with bloody hands. She showed me where the keys were and I took one, then climbed the stairs. I fell on the bed and took a drink from the bottle.

I lay there for a long time. I wanted desperately to feel some sense of shame, or pain, but it wouldn't come. I had no feeling in my heart. Everything inside was dead. I took a few more drinks, then felt myself slip from the world of exploding wood, shattering glass and gunsmoke. I drifted into a world without dreams and without rest. Just before I was lost to it all, I remember asking God to wake me up when the time came. I knew my world was gone and would remain so for a long time, but I wanted desperately to awaken some day and feel the pain that was missing.

14

The day following the massacre, the townspeople were busy. If they weren't digging graves, building a scaffold for Manuel, or caring for the wounded deputy, they were preparing food for those who were. There was a strange festival atmosphere about the town.

As soon as I woke, I took a warm bath and went to buy some new clothes. The suit I'd been wearing was dirty and bloody. I stopped at the Sheriff's office to see if he'd help me get some. Surely, after all I'd done, I deserved a new set of clothes.

Dixon wasn't in his office, but stood out on the boardwalk. I came up easily beside him and let him recognize my presence before speaking.

"I hate to ask for anything, but I was sent into the country with one set of clothes. I've pretty much ruined them and would like to get a new set. Do you think it's possible to arrange that for me?"

Dixon turned a vacant stare at me, as if he didn't know who I was.

"Surely," he said, then looked at the ground. "The people of this town'll give you anything you want. We've become heroes to them." He paused, "blamed fools."

I nodded. We'd become heroes, because we slaughtered those who made them afraid. That's all it took. None of the townspeople saw that we'd become monsters ourselves. They saw us as rescuers of the frightened. We provided them a sense of security, false as it may be. They could believe in their safety because they knew the slayers and could identify with them.

"Go down to the general store and get fitted," Dixon said. "They'll charge you nothing."

I stepped off the walk and started across the street.

"Wait," he said, and I returned. I looked at him. The sun was behind him and I squinted against it.

"I'm gonna quit," he said. "I'm old and tired and I doubt that God has any more patience with me. I don't want to die the way I am. I want a chance to prove that I'm a good man." He looked straight into my eyes. "You're probably the only man in the territory that'll understand."

"I understand," I assured him.

"Good, because I'm going to ask 'em to hire you as the new Sheriff."

I shook my head.

"Listen," he said, sweeping his arm in an arc to encompass the whole town, "look at these sheep. They were terrified the other day. I can't quit and leave them terrified again. They don't trust their own men, because no one stood up to the Mexicans. You're the only one who can give them peace. Redeem some of your own soul by giving it to them."

"No," I said, and turned and walked toward the general store. As I crossed the street, I noticed the looks on the faces of the people I met. There were smiles, and nods and handshakes of appreciation. They trusted me, liked me and respected me. But, they did so, because they were decent people who wouldn't have slaughtered men the way we had. The decent people thought I should be respected because I could do what they couldn't. Because I could be brutal to outlaws and kind to them. I should have been run out of town for what I'd done.

It was confusing and comforting. I felt proud of them and their good conscience. I entered the store and was met immediately by the storekeeper. He was a short man, thin and with long sideburns that reached toward his chin.

"What can I do for you, Jeff?"

It struck me odd that he knew my name. I suppose they all knew my name, either from before, or from the past evening.

"I need a set of clothes, though I don't know when I'll be able to pay."

"Never mind that. You paid me all you'll ever have to last night. Did you know that those men had been here since you left? They terrified everyone and took what they wanted. They slapped men and women alike when we refused to give them something. They were a bad lot. Now they're in the graves that should've been dug a long time ago."

"What sort of clothes do you have?"

"The finest," he replied.

"I don't need the finest, I need some durable clothes."

I was fitted with some good clothes and some extras so that I could launder the others. I was given a suit, so that I might go to church with the townsfolk.

"Make up a bill," I told him, when we'd finished.

"No, sir. I'd be hung alongside Manuel if I asked for a dime. The townspeople won't hear of it."

"I need a hat," I said.

When I was done, I stepped out onto the walk and took a deep breath. I went to the livery to check on my horse. The gelding stood in a stall. He smelled me and turned around to greet me with a nuzzle. I slapped him on the neck and rubbed his nose. We were in it together, whatever came of us, we were partners.

By the time I got back out into the street, a crowd had gathered about the hotel. When I neared, the crowd parted as they turned to recognize me. In front of them was Sheriff Dixon. He was trying to explain to the people that he was tired of his office and wanted to settle down quietly. He wanted to go to church and to read from the Bible.

The people groaned and begged him to stay. They protested that there wasn't another man in town as fit for the job as he was.

"Yes, there is," he said, and I tried to make a silent exit. "There he is. Young Jeff, come up here, boy."

I shook my head and walked toward the hotel for a drink of beer. The others grabbed at my arms and begged me to step forward. I resisted, but not very hard. If I'd had any other place to go, I'd have left right then and there, but I didn't. I stayed to listen to what was said and when it seemed inevitable that I'd have to take the job, I took it.

"But," I said, to the crowd, "I'm not interested in staying for a long time, so be looking for another Sheriff. I'll see you through the winter. Come spring, I'll be moving on."

And, so it was settled. My first official act as Sheriff was to oversee the hanging of Manuel. It was on a clear October day. The sun was high and there beside the hotel the same people who hired me came out to watch Manuel Garza drop three feet to his death. It was not a handsome sight.

I was paid quite well and lived in the hotel. I'd become known as J.D. Wilkes as that's how I signed everything official. There wasn't much trouble. All the badmen stayed away from the town that'd wiped out the "Banditos de la Pampa" as Manuel's bunch were known.

Most of the time I spent in Sherman, I felt like a fraud. I was only eighteen and though I no longer looked like a child, I felt like one. There were no times like before in the town. It was peaceful, quiet and boring. I drank more than I should and I gambled with a few men I figured to saddle with the Sheriff's job when the time came. They were older than myself and were more attached to the country. I was like a leaf waiting for a gust of wind. I told the people this, but most failed to believe it. They thought I'd always be happy there.

I must admit, I stayed longer than I'd hoped to. I wanted to leave in April and talked with all the people passing through to find out if there was anything further along that interested me. Some of them were going to the mines in the territories of Colorado and Arizona. Some still believed in the gold of California. Most of them were on their way to die, whether they knew it, or not. Others wanted to be farmers, but that wasn't a life for me.

All in all, I stayed until late May. In the meantime, Bill Dixon became a devout man. He spent the better part of his days studying the Bible and went to talk with our pastor often. They'd become great friends and Dixon rarely showed himself in town. He no longer drank, nor visited the saloon for cards. Then, he died in March. It was a peaceful death and I could only hope that he made his peace with God and would be taken into heaven.

After burying him, I started to look for opportunities with more vigor. I guess I always sensed that Dixon was my only reason for staying. I wanted to fulfill some obligation to him. I don't know why I felt obligated, but I did. Maybe, I reveled in his spirituality. Maybe, I saw the glory of God in him as I watched the change take place. Bill Dixon was an inspiration to more than myself and the balance of church funds raised significantly during the time he went. Dixon was a man who went after what he wanted, be it a man, or salvation. He was tenacious. When he was gone, the town held no attraction for me.

One night, as I sat playing cards, some men entered the saloon. They glanced at us and walked right to the bar. I recognized them, but they were dirty and unshaven. I thought they might be from Preston, or one of the other towns I'd visited, like Station, Bonham, or McKinney.

"There ya go, J.D.," one of my friends, Harold Dobson, said, tossing some coins into the growing pot. "Two bits to ya."

I looked my cards over. I had two pair. My money was diminishing rapidly. Did Jackson have more than two pair? I studied his grinning face.

"I fold," I said, rising from my seat. "I better look in on these two." I walked up to the bar. I didn't look at the men, but ordered a beer. The bartender poured a beer and set it in front of me.

"We're looking for Sheriff Bill Dixon," one of the men said.

"He died back in March," I replied.

"Is that so?"

"Yes, sir," I said, turning to face them.

There was a shocked look of recognition in all our eyes.

"Well, I'll be," Clyde said. "Here's the boy!"

I'd not been referred to as a boy in a long time. It angered me.

"Here I am," I said, pulling the lapel of my jacket back to reveal the star pinned to my vest. "But, I'm not a boy."

The other man was Tom Garfield and we all shook hands. They congratulated me on my job and we talked of old Bill Dixon. It was all small talk until the card game broke up a few hours later. Then, we sat about a table and drank. Toward midnight, when the bartender locked the outside doors and left Tom and Clyde with keys to their rooms, we had a real discussion.

"From cow thief to lawman in less than a year!" Clyde said. "That's pretty impressive."

"I didn't know we were stealing those cows," I protested.

"You knew," Tom said.

"I thought it was possible, but no one stopped us."

"I stopped you," Tom replied.

"Clyde stole more than I did," I pointed out.

"That's how I work," Clyde said. "I get inside and Tom follows my trail and rounds up the owners to take care of the dirty work. Then, we ride on."

"Now, you're a Sheriff. If that doesn't beat all," Tom said.

"I'm Sheriff until I find something better."

"What's better?" Clyde asked.

"Anything that doesn't include farming, or mining."

"You could be a school teacher," Clyde mentioned.

"No, I want to travel. My feet feel planted right here and I don't like the feeling of it."

Tom studied me. "You're looking a gift-horse in the mouth."

"Maybe," I said, in all seriousness, "but, there's things you don't know. I took part in something here and I feel dirty for it. As long as I stay here, I'll feel dirty. I just want to get clean again."

"What you do doesn't belong to a place, it belongs to you," Tom said. "No matter where you go, you'll take it with you."

"Yeah, I suppose you're right."

"We know a man, a cowman," Clyde started, but Tom glared at him and he stopped.

"What man?"

"Nothing," Tom said. "Clyde was just spouting off. What do you say we get some sleep?"

"It's been a long ride," Clyde admitted.

"I have to check the town before bedding down. Will I see you fellows in the morning?"

"We'll be here."

I nodded and they went up to their rooms. I wondered why Tom stopped Clyde from telling me of the cowman. I thought about it for quite a while and decided to ask him in the morning. I unlocked the door to the saloon with my key and walked about to make sure that everyone had locked their doors and that no one had broken in. Everything was quiet, but as I walked the streets, I felt as if I were seeing it for the last time. I hoped it'd be the last time, but there was something about that town.

Sherman was familiar and comfortable. I pondered it a moment and decided that it was the feeling of being wanted. I'd never felt wanted before. As I thought, I walked on out of town to where Bill Dixon was buried and knelt at his grave.

"Well, old man, I hope you made it to heaven. There isn't much left for me to do around here. The town is quiet and the ruckus we made has chased off all of the badmen. I think it's time I was moving on. I don't know if I'll ever get back here, so rest well and enjoy the glory of God." I thought for a moment and added, "that is, if he accepted your soul, and I'm sorry if he didn't."

I got up and went back into town to get some sleep. In my dreams, I saw the massacre all over again, but it gave me no sense of sorrow. Instead, it was like watching a play in the theatre where a person is interested in the outcome, but not affected by it. I was restless and woke often, always with thoughts of the trail.

There was a need within me that cried out for movement. I don't know where it came from. There was a time when I could think of nothing but staying in Mississippi. I missed my home state and wondered about my father. I wondered about the slaves we'd owned and how they made out after the war. But, I had no desire to return. Instead, I thought only of the road ahead and what I'd find on it. Somewhere along that road, I'd make my mark and settle down in the place where I'd die. Somewhere, I'd find the comfort that'd ease my mind and soothe my soul.

The next morning, I found Tom and Clyde arguing with the owner of the general store about the price of supplies. The owner was explaining the dangerous trail of the freight wagons and it all fell on deaf ears.

"Why, this is out and out thievery," Tom shouted as I came in.

I tipped my hat to the owner and looked at the provisions laid out on the counter. It was the typical supplies of men who planned to eat on the prairie.

"Settle down, Tom," I said. "I'd hate to have to put you in jail."

He scowled at me and remarked, "you just go and try it, youngun."

The owner pushed himself back against the shelves, thinking there'd be trouble.

My anger began to surface. I knew that he meant nothing by it, but there was still that edge he thought he had over me. He still thought of me as a boy. Either he'd not heard of the massacre, or put no weight into what he'd heard. I had the edge, but he didn't know it.

"You're speaking to the law, Tom, not some child you found out on the prairie. I have an obligation to these people to make sure they're not harassed. Settle your business in here and do it quietly."

"Get a load of him," Tom remarked to Clyde, who was staring at me with narrowed eyes.

"I am," he said. "Let's finish this business."

Tom studied me, then looked back at Clyde. Suddenly, he dug in his pockets and tossed some gold coins on the counter. They carried their supplies out to their horses and loaded the saddlebags. I spoke with the owner to make sure enough money had been laid out. When I was satisfied, I joined them outside.

"Fellows care for a drink before you leave?"

"That star's weighing heavy on your shirt, boy," Tom said, and I knew the argument was between he and I.

"It's my job, but you know that. I don't know why you think you should get treated any different from any other drifter coming into this town."

"Maybe, because I saved your life."

"No, sir," I shook my head. "Clyde saved my life by sending me out of that snake pit. You tried to take it. I've thought about it a number of times. You sent me into that camp with every expectation that I'd die. You probably thought it was right clever to do it. You used me to kill Ned, with no danger to you, or your rancher friends. I was expendable and you took advantage of me. I don't blame you for anything, Tom. It's just the way things are done out here, but you didn't save my life."

"Who do you think carried you into town?"

"I don't know and it doesn't matter. If you hadn't Clyde would have. I know what I was to both of you and I appreciate your kindness, but let's not play around with it. Clyde used me as much as you did. He wanted me around to kill Ned, because he knew I would when the time came. That's all. I enjoy your company, but don't expect me to mope around as if I owe you something, because I don't."

"Well, now," Clyde said, "maybe we ought to tell him about that cowman after all."

Tom stared at me, trying to make a decision. "Go ahead, I think he can handle it."

"There's a fellow, used to be tracker like us. He's got him some cattle that he's getting ready to drive into Colorado Territory. He's looking for young men who ain't afraid of some hard work and can handle stock. He's over near the Palo Pinto country. I know you can handle stock and you can work, but it looks to be a dry and dangerous trail. I know the way he plans to go and we don't like it. There ain't gonna be many that do, so if you want to see some country you can take up with him."

"Why didn't you tell me about this last night?"

"Well...," Clyde began, but was cut off.

"We didn't think you could handle it. You've done a bit of changing the past few months," Tom said.

"Show me a man that could be in this country for a few months and not be changed by it."

"I could show you lots of 'em," Clyde announced, "but, they're all dead."

"We're headed back that way," Tom said, after moment. "We have some business with a group up near Jacksboro."

It took some time to get the mayor to accept my resignation, but I named a good man to take my place and the mayor acquiesced. Before noon, I was riding out of town following the two men I'd come there with. The only difference being that I was upright in the saddle.

"Seems you could have mentioned to the Sheriff that I wasn't a cow thief, or a wanted man when you brought me into this town," I said, on our way out.

"I did," Tom replied. "I told him you were just a young fellow that got sideways with Ned Smith when he tried to steal your horse. I told him you shot Ned and Butch in self-defense and everything was proper."

We looked at each other in disbelief.

"Why that old snake," I said, shaking my head at how he'd played me just right. He was a wise and thoughtful man, and a conniving old coot for using it against me.

15

We were a few days on the road before we came to the town of Fort Worth. There, Tom and Clyde pointed me toward Palo Pinto River and wrote a note of introduction to Charles Goodnight, a rancher out that way. But, they told me not to mention that I rode with Ned Smith. To endear me to the man, Tom included the information that I'd killed Ned, was a lawman in Sherman and that I'd had a hand in killing the Banditos de la Pampa.

"Goodnight can't stand a cow thief and can just barely tolerate Clyde because he rides with them on occasion," Tom said.

I nodded and turned my horse toward the Palo Pinto. I rode toward Weatherford and only then realized how sparse the country was compared to the thick tree country of Mississippi. I was comforted by it in the way that it was easier to see one's enemies in the open. Where I'd grown up, something, either human, or not, might lurk behind each tree.

I came upon Mr. Goodnight almost by accident. I inquired at Weatherford about the location of his ranch and found that the man was in town at that very moment buying supplies for his trail drive. I went over to the general store where he was loading a sturdy, re-built wagon with iron axles. I'd never seen iron axles on a wagon before and I thought the man was taking precautions that seemed not only sufficient, but extravagant.

I tied my horse and entered the store. Goodnight was talking lively to the owner and making sure that he was getting a good deal on all that he purchased.

"Mr. Goodnight," I said, extending my hand. "I've heard you might be looking for help."

"I know everybody I want on this drive and I don't know you," he said, as a matter of fact, but shook my hand.

"My name is J.D. Wilkes, and I have a note of introduction from Tom Garfield."

Goodnight stopped at the mention of Tom and took the note. "Is he still keeping company with that cow thief, Clyde? I don't know what's the matter with that fella."

"I met up with them in Sherman," I said.

"This note doesn't do me any good. I don't need a lawman and I can't take their word for the fact that you can manage cattle. One man's word about another ain't worth spit."

"I agree, but if this note can persuade you to give me a chance, that's all I'm asking for."

He looked me up and down. "Says here you killed Ned Smith."

"Yes, sir."

"Get this here wagon loaded and follow me."

I finished loading the wagon and tied my horse behind. I followed him southeast of Fort Belknap where they were gathering a herd. We spent a few days preparing for the drive. Another cowman, Oliver Loving, threw in with us and brought several hundred head of his own cattle.

Everytime I looked over my shoulder, Goodnight was watching me. He studied my habits and the way I rode, and what I knew about cattle, which was, admittedly, very little. He came to me the night before the drive.

"I'm inclined to make you stay here," he said. "You can ride well, but I have two things against you. First, I don't think your horse is a good horse. It'll take more than an average horse to make this drive. Second, you don't know enough about cattle to fill a spittoon. I need the best hands I can get and I don't need to be worrying about your side of the herd."

"Those are valid concerns, Mr. Goodnight, and I thank you for being honest with me about it. But, this is a good horse. I've been through a lot with this horse and he's never failed me, nor will he. I admit that I don't know a lot about cattle, though you can see how fast I've picked up what I do know. I'll learn all I need to before we're halfway."

"Well," he said, still wary. "I just don't know."

"If you ever have to tell me anything twice, I'll turn right around and leave."

"It'd be best to leave you here, before we get that far," he said, then shook his head.

"Well, you leave me in quite a position then," I said.

"Can't be helped."

"Do you mind if I ride along for safe passage to Colorado Territory?"

"You're bound and determined to go on this drive, ain't ya?"

"Yes, sir."

"You can come then, but I'm not going to pay you the same as I pay these others. You'll get two-thirds of their pay, but no gambling on the trail. Understand?"

"Yes, sir."

"Go on then, and get your gear together."

The next day was the 6th of June, 1866, and we started out. I rode toward the back of the two-thousand head of cattle of all shapes, ages and sizes. The more experienced riders took the forward positions to guide the herd. My job was to keep the herd from expanding too far out. I had my hands full and blushed at the trouble I had while everyone else seemed to be having a fairly easy time of it. I rode on the dusty side of the trail. I figured Goodnight wanted to discourage me, but he was mistaken in my ability to endure.

We travelled steadily into the arid distance. The first part of the journey was much the same as I'd known in Ned Smith's bunch. It was tiring and dusty and long. We camped and ate from the back of the wagon.

I came to know several of the other hands working for Goodnight. There was a negra and a one-armed man named Bill Wilson. I didn't get along well with many of them. They had their suspicions about me and knew that I wasn't a very good cow hand. They speculated as to what sort of favors I'd done for Goodnight that allowed me on the drive with so little experience. I didn't try to answer their taunts. For the extra money they were making, they could wonder about it.

For the most part, I was left alone. No one cared much for my company and I didn't encourage friendships. When someone deigned to speak to me at all, it was in reference to my inability to handle cattle. I flushed with anger and did what they asked.

Through it all, a good deal of contempt grew for me. But, I looked down at the ground when I ate and looked forward when I worked. I knew I'd have to take some punishment as I learned, I accepted the fact, but prayed every day that I might prove them wrong.

The edge I had over all of them, was that I learned fast, and I was learning the Goodnight way of herding cattle. I figured when I was done with this drive, I'd have enough knowledge to attempt a similar thing on my own. If I could get the money together to buy a herd, I could hire enough good hands to make it work. As long as I knew the route and how to get through to good markets, the men would follow. The first drive would be the worst, but after that, I'd have history to back my plans.

Yet, there was a great deal I needed to know beforehand. I still didn't know where to sell the cattle, or how much a person could get for them.

In the meantime, I watched Goodnight and Loving with great curiosity. These men knew something about cattle and trails. I watched how Goodnight chose the trail ahead. I noticed where the water could be found, which holes were good watering holes and which were laden with alkali. I didn't know what lay to the northwest of Fort Belknap, but it must be a bad piece of ground to force a solid man, like Goodnight, to go away from a direct route.

"Hey, close in that flank," one of the others yelled at me while I was making notes of the route with my pencil and the paper. I put the materials in my shirt pocket and brought the cattle further in toward the herd.

The cattle weren't that far away, but the others felt obligated to yell at me over any slight discrepancy. "Yeah, yeah," I said, under my breath.

It was a long drive to the Concho. When we arrived, Goodnight and Loving started to plan the most treacherous part of the journey. Around camp that night, I heard terrifying stories of one hundred miles of arid land. They told of how the Comanche Indians used to raid the land with frequency.

"There weren't a place in Texas, or Mexico, that didn't suffer from them," I heard one man say.

But, I let it roll off my back. I figured most of them were just saying what they were to get to me and I wouldn't give them the satisfaction. I didn't believe Goodnight would choose a trail that put a hundred miles between us and water.

"We'll see what the tenderfoot's made of in the next few days," I heard one say to another in reference to me. Yeah, I was a tenderfoot. That's why I killed Ned, brought Manuel Garza to justice and fought it out with his band of Banditos. But, these men knew none of this. I felt so alienated from them, they didn't get a chance to know of my virtues and even after I'd learned to be as good a hand as many of them, they still held me in contempt.

It was much the same as it'd been with Gregory and William back in Mississippi. Once these men got something into their heads, it was impossible to remove it. No one understood me. They all had an idea of who I was and let that guide their beliefs. But, none of the cowboys knew me well enough to come to any sort of rational conclusion.

That evening, at camp by the Concho River, we spent a good deal of time filling canteens and water barrels. We drank as much from the river as we could and the next day we kept the cattle on the river until the heat of the day had caused them to drink until they were bloated with water. We left by mid afternoon with bellies sloshing until the sound was almost comical.

The land was vastly different from what I'd known before. Even in Northern Texas it was somewhat humid and bushy. South of the Concho, the land was dry and dusty. What plant life there was, seemed more like irrational and strange devices contrived by wishful imagination. The sun was merciless. It felt like the breath of the devil.

That night as I whispered a prayer of thanks for the absence of the sun, I realized that the cattle, that should have been exhausted and weary, were roaming. Instead of bedding down themselves, the cattle continued to mill about until we were all brought out to hold them from scattering to every point of the compass. Tempers flared among the men and I took a considerable amount of abuse, as if I were the cause of it all. I bit my tongue and went about my business.

From then on, we didn't make camp at night, but continued to let the cattle roam at a slower pace through the dark, desolate, God-forsaken country. The drive became a nightmare. I was so tired, the rhythmic movement of the horse rocked me to sleep. I'd catch myself falling forward in the saddle and wake up.

The next day was no better. My throat was dry and breathing was a chore. My day dreams were delirious and filled with water flowing cool and cold over rocks. I longed for Mississippi and swore if I ever got out of Texas, I'd go back to where water ran from the leaves of trees and all one had to do to drink was tip their head back and open their mouth.

But, even through my own self-pity, I felt most for the cattle that were in no better shape. Their tongues hung from their mouths and they grew increasingly thin over the next few days. At least, I'd been able to choose whether or not to go on the trail. The cattle had no such choice and looked at me with accusatory expressions on their bovine faces. They grew remarkably thin during that stretch and I reluctantly accepted the blame for their condition. I was saddened to think that the only friends I had on the drive were the cattle and they'd turned against me as well.

Loving was kind enough to show me how to put a pebble in my mouth to keep the thirst away. It worked quite well, but no trick could alleviate the affects of thirst. Tempers grew shorter and shorter as the days seemed of infinite cruelty. Even the most experienced hands spoke sullenly and felt abused by Goodnight. Still, there was no water in sight.

The best part of the ordeal was that the others had taken to harassing one another, instead of me. They'd gather together and complain, but since I spoke to no one generally, I kept quiet. This gave the others the impression that the thirst, heat and endless days and nights without sleep didn't bother me as it did them. They started looking for excuses for it.

"He ain't smart enough to be worried," I heard one of the men say.

I grinned and it made the horrid conditions much more tolerable to see their incredulous looks.

"He ain't human," another said. "He must be a snake." They all laughed, but quickly slipped back into bemoaning their current state.

Despite appearances of super-human endurance, I found myself quite busy trying to keep my thoughts clear and dwelt on the concept of water for hours at a time while pushing the stragglers up to the rest of the herd.

Goodnight tied a bell to one of the most forward of the steers and it was my duty to make sure I kept the back of the herd within reasonable hearing distance of the bell. I had my hands full because it wasn't a herd of steers alone, but a mixed herd of cows, calves and steers. The steers could travel much faster than cows and the calves often had to run to keep up.

So, at the tail end of the herd, on the dusty side, I worked harder than ever to keep the cows and calves up with the rest. All the while, my throat burned with thirst and my eyes were heavy with fatigue and sand. I felt that Hell couldn't offer any worse than West Texas.

If that wasn't enough, there were rattlesnakes as abundant as rocks. Those who had spare ammunition shot the snakes when they seemed a threat to the cattle, or horses. The others would stop to kill them with rocks, or by some other method. I had plenty of ammunition and was grateful for it.

Even those of us who weren't particularly religious prayed for water. One or two of the men claimed to see a vast lake off in the distance. Goodnight was quick to deny it and explained it as a false vision.

"You'll die chasing that water," he told us. "It ain't there. I know it ain't, so stop thinkin' you see it."

He told of others who'd believed in the vision and chased it only to find themselves being drawn even further from the real thing. If it weren't for the knowledge and strong character of Goodnight, there would've been a rebellion. To be honest, I'd have been right in the middle of it. But, I trusted in the man and knew that if there were water anywhere near, he'd have gotten his cattle to it at all costs.

We were allowed to sleep for short intervals in the saddle. The cook pushed the wagon ahead on the trail and had coffee waiting for us as we rode by. Goodnight used the last of the water to keep us from dropping out of the saddle.

And yet, through all my weariness and responsibility, I'd periodically find a sense of God in the huge sky above us, with twinkling stars vast and broad from one horizon to the other. Lord, it made one take a breath to see the beauty of it. Before us, we drove the beasts entrusted to man. Yes, I thought, even in that hell, there was evidence of God and where God could be found, there was hope and I drew strength from it.

Mr. Loving rode with us at the back of the herd. I learned a lot from him. He was a strong, reliable man who had a degree of patience with the cattle that I found elusive. He had, in fact, more patience for cattle than men. But, I knew somewhere deep inside, he was my staunchest ally. I'm sure that his words brought Goodnight to change his mind and his attitude toward me.

Though all of us lusted for water, none were prepared for the reaction of the cattle when they got the first whiff of it. Suddenly, there was a rushing toward the Pecos. We tried with all our might to turn them from the steep banks. I rushed into the dusty confusion and fought and yelled until I was hoarse. I slapped at them with my rope, but they were threatening to drag myself and the horse down. We'd been so engulfed by the herd, that I could've stepped onto their backs and run up to the leader. Short of that, I decided to save myself by taking a gentle angle toward one side of the herd. It was that, or die under the smashing, pounding hooves.

The cattle plunged off the bank and several were hurt. We shot the ones that couldn't continue and let the others drink as much as we dared of the poor water. We cut them out after having a bit of the water and kept them away from it for a while. There were places along the Pecos that were so concentrated with alkali that cattle would rarely make more than a few steps before death took them.

There was a sense of accomplishment that night around the campfire. As a group, we'd survived the worst of the journey. For a moment, we could relax and revel in our success. That's when the trouble started. I'd heard enough about myself and after proving that I could take anything they could, I wasn't in a mood to remain silent in the face of their unjust remarks.

A couple of the men, two of the best at what they did, neared me as I ate from a plate of beans and wiped it up with a sourdough biscuit.

"Nearly got yourself killed out there, Tenderfoot," a short, stout, curly-headed man I'd come to know as Henry said.

"That and run all those steers off'n the cliff," the other, Jack, added.

"As for putting myself in danger, that's my business. As for putting the stock in danger, that's Goodnight's and Loving's business. You aren't Goodnight, or Loving and I know for a fact that you aren't me, so what business is it of yours?"

"That fancy talk of yourn ain't gonna get you out of it with me," Jack said, from out of a heavily stubbled chin with a dark streak of tobacco bisecting his jaw.

I'd just plain had enough and I'd come as far as I had a mind to with the whole company of them on my back. So, I threw down the gauntlet. Maybe, they'd all kill me. I didn't care. There's just so much a man can take and when he's had his fill, he'd rather die than take another ounce. I was at that point when I spoke again.

"Well, sir," I said, setting the plate aside and standing up, smacking my hands together. "I'm done talking. Everyone gather around," I hollered into the crowd. "Come on, gather around. Line up there, everybody in single file, just like an Army chow line."

The cowboys stood up slowly and stared at me quizzically. They moved somewhat into a line. "That's it," I encouraged them, then looked back at the two in front of me. "Come on, get in line. Henry, take a step back and get behind Jack there." Henry's eyes narrowed and he slowly took a step back.

Jack started looking about himself in a curious panic.

"What you aimin' to do?" he asked.

Just then, Goodnight strode up to me.

"What's this all about?"

"Well, sir, it seems that all of these men aim to whip me. I've taken their insults as long as I'm going to. Now, I'm going to whip them one at a time and when I'm done, I'll either have peace, or I'll start the killing."

Goodnight chuckled a bit, then brought a serious look to his face. I saw that some of the others, those who were most friendly to me, stepped out of line and sat down by their plates to watch. This left more than half of them in line.

"You think you can whip all these men?" he asked, scratching his head, sounding doubtful.

"There isn't any other way. I can see they have it in their mind to hound me, to nip at my heels, until I go crazy and shoot them all. This is more peaceful."

"If that's the way you want it," he said.

"It's the way it has to be," I replied. "Now, step aside so I can have at the first one, unless you aim to whip me, too."

"No, I think you're fine and if these men would open their eyes, they'd realize that you've turned into quite a hand. But, I'll let you handle this matter," he said, stepping out from in front of me. A few of the others stepped out of line when Goodnight finished speaking, but there were still six left to take their turn. In front of them all was Jack, who'd lost his panic and relished the idea of beating my head into a clot of blood and jagged bone.

As soon as Goodnight was clear, Jack came at me. He was a saloon fighter and not very skilled. I'd been trained by one of the best pugilists around: Corporal Donnigan. Jack waded right in with a looping right hand that was easily ducked. When I went under his swing, I caught his left arm, that was thrown stiffly behind his back as a counter-balance. I grabbed hold of that arm and jerked on it, pulling him backwards and down to the ground. Keeping hold of his arm, I kicked him hard in the back of the head. I kicked again and he leaned over, unconscious.

I looked up at Henry, who was already upon me and knocked me backward with a powerful left hand. He hit me in the stomach with his right, doubling me over, and struck the back of my head. I went to my knees and charged at his legs. He went over the top of me and grabbed hold of my feet. I pushed his legs apart and threw my head backward into his crotch and stood up, leaving him moaning on the ground. I kicked him in the head, too, to keep him down.

I stopped and looked at the others. I took off my shirt, because I was bleeding at the eye and didn't want the blood to stain it. Fighting was getting expensive on clothes. It'd be cheaper and easier on me to shoot them. But, I wasn't out to kill anyone, I wanted to be left alone. I caught my breath and motioned for the next one to near. This man, the negra, waved his hand at me, like swatting at a fly, and sat down. I had no illusions that he was afraid of me. It seemed more that he didn't have the energy to waste on it.

The next man was a tall, skinny kid not much older than I was. His hair was long and stringy and he came at me moving from side to side, putting his hands up like a kangaroo. He took a jab at me, then another. He wasn't trying to hit me, he was measuring me for a hard blow. I moved my head out of the way of the jabs. This fellow was a classical sort of fighter, trained by someone who knew the business of fighting. But, he was fundamentally flawed, because that sort of fighting required that each man knew the rules and played by them. In the current situation, I was prepared to cheat.

I stopped, dropped my hands and stared off to the side. I turned my head to listen with my ear, not looking at him, but seeing him. "Listen," I said and the three of them that were left, looked where I was looking. Then, the fellow I was fighting thought that it was a trick and neared me to take me when I wasn't paying attention. When he got close enough, I reached up and kicked him right in the side of the head. He fell like a deer shot through the heart.

The two that remained lost interest and wandered off. I let them go. I was worn out and had used the majority of my tricks. I was grateful they'd allowed me to take them one at a time. But, the cowboys were generally a peaceful bunch. Some of them could fight pretty well, but their job was to drive cattle. To be honest, if they were determined to kill me there would have been little I could have done about it, but that's just where I took advantage of them. They underestimated me and overestimated their friends. Most of them thought that if they ever did have to fight me, I'd be so beat-up, that I wouldn't be much of an opponent.

Goodnight came up to me as I was putting my shirt back on.

"Where'd you learn to fight like that?"

"I was in the war," I said. "I was in a special unit that moved about at night and often had to go behind the lines. There's special training given to people like me, because the idea is to get far enough away to kill yourself, but you have to be able to make the break, even when vastly outnumbered."

"Pretty smart, getting them to accept your terms of the fight,"

"Yeah, well, they accepted it because they thought I'd be easy. If they weren't so sure of themselves, they'd have thought about it a minute."

"Get some sleep," he said, "you won't have any more trouble from them on this drive."

"I don't need anyone to protect me."

"I'm not protecting you, fool," he said, grinning. "I know these boys and they won't be too anxious to tangle with you again, not without a lot of whiskey in their bellies."

"Oh," I said.

16

Next morning, we commenced to drive the cattle along the Pecos up toward New Mexico. The men stopped giving me looks of disgust. I don't know if they'd come to understand that I was working as well as anyone else, or if they just didn't want to tangle with me over it.

Needless to say, Henry and Jack weren't going to let it go that easy. They rode up to me in the morning.

"This ain't over, Tenderfoot," Jack said, wheeling his horse around to go back up front. Henry looked me over and did the same. As soon as their backs were turned I fired my Colt. Their shoulders hunched and they pulled back on the reins. Each turned slowly to where I held my gun.

"Snakes," I said, then nodded toward the ground.

Jack and Henry looked at each other, then back at me, and rode on up to meet Goodnight. Mr. Loving swung his horse in close to mine.

"You may have whipped them boys last night," he said. "But, don't go to thinkin' you can scare 'em off. It's liable to come back on ya."

"I'm not trying to scare them," I said, looking right into his eyes. "I mean to kill them if they don't leave me alone. I don't ride up front and bother them. Every time we've had a run-in, they've been on my side of this herd."

I heard of Mr. Loving during the war. He was a beef supplier and I knew if I'd mentioned my father's name, he'd know him. A lot of these men would've known of my father. But, there was no reason for him to know who I was and if I wound up doing something infamous out in the Frontier, I'd just as soon my father never hear of it.

I had a great deal of respect for Loving and it was with this in mind that I looked at him and said: "maybe you best go and tell them they aren't going to scare me."

"Tell them yourself," he replied.

"No," I said, shaking my head, "I've told them honest enough already. If they haven't figured it out, they must be stupid."

"Don't put too much past a cowboy," he said. "They ain't hired to add figures."

Loving rode toward the back of the herd and left me to my job. I thought there couldn't be much worse than the ride between the Concho and the Pecos, but trailing up toward New Mexico was as bad. The only difference was the available water. It was so desolate that a man felt sorry for the buzzards.

It was tough going. The calves that were born on the trail were too young to keep up and had to be shot every morning. This made it more difficult to keep the cows moving. They always tried to turn back and bawled all day and night for their calves. After a while, their voices became a din so loud, I thought I'd lose my mind.

If that wasn't enough, the rattlesnakes seemed to multiply as we headed north. Old Cross-Eyed Nath blew lead at them at every opportunity. Between the bawling and the snakes and the banging of Nath's revolver, a man had to fight for sanity.

Several days passed in moving toward Pope's Crossing. During those days, the others had taken to glancing at me now and then, but otherwise let me alone. Even Jack and Henry decided that maybe I wasn't much fun at that. They tried psychology when outright hostility didn't seem to affect me. They moved away when ever I came up to get my grub. They slept away from me and there was always a distinct distance between where I sat and everyone else. They didn't understand that I was so isolated in my own mind, that I only noticed it on rare occasions.

Instead, I thought out all of the things I'd been learning about how to spot a trail, find water and read cattle. I liked to stand close to either Loving, or Goodnight when they talked to pick up whatever scraps of knowledge they might relate.

We reached Pope's Crossing, crossed to the west side of the river and followed it past the rivers; Black and Delaware, then crossed back to the east side to put the Pecos between us and a band of Mescalero Apaches that were known to strike out from the Guadalupe Mountains.

The trail drive was hardest on the cattle. They were thin and their ribs showed well against their hides. There was so little for them to eat on the way, it amazed me that we hadn't lost any more to fatigue than we did. But, I was not prepared for the sight at Fort Sumner. There, the Navaho Indians were in much the same shape as our cattle. They were thin and starving and numbered close to nine, or ten thousand on the reservation. Since coming to the Frontier, I'd learned how to despise the Indians, to fear them and to prepare for them. I'd not learned to pity them and my first taste of their predicament sent shivers down my back.

Up until then, I'd never gotten a good look at an Indian. I was struck by their sunken eyes and hollow, high cheekbones. Of course, I was looking at starved Indians, not the rugged, well-muscled braves that'd present a danger to us. But, even starved, one could see the nobility, the pride and power of the desert warriors.

We held the cattle outside of the fort on good grass while Goodnight and Loving went on in to discuss the sale of the beef to a man named Roberts. The cook was busy rustling up some grub. Then, Jack rode up beside me and stopped his horse. Without looking, I could tell who it was by the smell. To be honest, I had no room to talk. None of us were fit for dinner in a decent place.

"Who in hell are you, anyway?"

"What do you mean, Jack?"

"You know what I mean. You fight like an Injun, work like a dog and talk like a school teacher. On top o' all that, you read that durned Bible too much for me."

"Well, Jack, there's a reason for it."

"What is it? A secret?"

"In a manner of speaking, yes."

"You're the blamed most infuriatin', tenderfooted, smart-mouthed little snake I've ever seen," he said, and spit tobacco into the dirt.

"I killed the last man that called me a 'smart-mouthing little snake', Jack," I said, turning to look him dead in the eyes.

"Who was that?"

"Ned Smith."

"You didn't kill no Ned Smith! What do you take me for?"

"A dead man."

"Now, just hold on. What do you want to kill me for?"

"You remind me a lot of Ned. You look like him in ways, smell like him, too. Your last name isn't Smith, is it?"

"No," he said, but there was a hesitation in his voice. I didn't know if I'd struck a nerve, or if he felt guilty, but the word caught in his throat.

"What's going on here?" Henry asked, riding up.

"This blamed fool thinks I'm Ned Smith's brother, or something. He's crazy; the heat's got to his brain."

"Is that right?" Henry asked, but I kept silent. I didn't owe either of those two a nod of my head. "Is that right?" he asked, again. "Come on, Jack, let this fella alone. Stay away from him."

They rode off together and I looked down at my hand, slightly trembling above the butt of the Colt. I didn't know what was happening to me. I wanted to kill him for nothing, because he'd insulted me, I guess. I was losing perspective, but the isolation of the drive and the feeling of being hated all the way had done something to me. It put my nerves to fraying and an orneriness I'd never known showed itself. I'd always liked the company of men before, but on that drive, I'd learned to hate all men instinctively.

I didn't hate Goodnight, or Loving. No, I couldn't claim to hate them, but they were rare men on the Frontier. Few were as disciplined and well mannered. They were strong and capable men. It seemed to me that too many men were weighted too heavily on one side, or the other, and none were as well balanced as either Goodnight, or Loving.

Men like Jack and Henry couldn't stand me. They wanted to believe they were superior to anyone with an education and it burned them up to know a greenhorn fellow, like myself, could work right along with them. But, I couldn't help the way my life was turning out. Lord knows there was nothing I'd have rather been doing than sitting in a parlor discussing political theory and legislative action. That's what I was raised to do, not crawl around in the desert trying to find food and water enough to stay alive.

Goodnight and Loving came back toward the afternoon with a group of men. They'd sold the greater part of the herd and we set about cutting the one, two and three year old steers out for them. They couldn't sell the rest of the herd made up of cows, calves and older steers.

They made a load of money on that deal, 8 cents a pound on the hoof. Considering that we sold twelve hundred head, that came to quite a sum. We were all paid up to date and moved the remainder of the herd up the Pecos to a place where there was plenty of good grass and water. It was nearly a month since we'd set out from Texas. We passed the Fourth of July right there north of the Las Carretas Creek.

The cook made up a grand meal and we all ate in leisure while Goodnight and Loving decided what to do with the rest of the herd. I hoped that we'd take them on to Colorado Territory as I'd heard a lot about it and wanted to see the mountain range there. I didn't believe the stories that claimed they were much higher and much more rugged than those I'd seen near home. I couldn't imagine mountains higher than those in Georgia. After a trip across the flat, rugged plains, I was sure that it was only the suddenness of the peaks rising out of that oblivion that gave them increased significance.

"Well, boys," Goodnight said, addressing the lot of us, "I'm heading back to Texas. Loving here is going to take what's left of the herd and sell them near Denver. The Wilson boys will accompany me back to get another herd ready to drive before the snow falls. We'll all meet up back here and settle in for the Winter."

We nodded our consent and got ready to move out in the morning. I'd just turned away to tend my duties, when Goodnight called me over to him. He stood alone on the prairie with the rugged wagon as a backdrop and I strolled up to him level-eyed. I thought he was going to fire me right then and there for the trouble I'd caused on the drive.

"J.D.," he began, "I was wrong not to take you on at full pay when we started. You've learnt as fast as you said. But, here's a friendly warning. You leave that gun in your belt there. I've seen enough hide-splittin' younguns in my life to fill a canyon to the top. You hear what I'm tellin' you? All those boys are dead now, spilt out onto the streets with their brains shot out."

"Thank you, Mr. Goodnight, I appreciate your kind thoughts. I've learned a lot from you and Mr. Loving. More than you know. I'll take your advice as good and stay true to it as long as I can, but I can't guarantee that'll be any longer than it takes me to get over that hill. I never meant to cause trouble in your camp, but I'll tolerate no amount of abuse. I've taken more than my share since I've been in this country and I'll have no more."

He waited patiently through my long-winded acceptance, then he smiled. He raised a finger to my chest and poked it hard into my breastbone.

"Read that bible more and talk less," he said, as a final word. I stood there after he'd gone and thought about how little I'd read from the book in my saddlebags. But, it was still there and so was I, so I figured I'd have time to read it.

As I went about my chores of getting everything ready for the rest of the drive, I thought about that elusive "someplace" I was always going to go to and settle. Where would it be? None of the country I'd seen so far would do. It was too exposed, too little grass to raise cattle.

Jack rode up close to me as I led my horse out to graze.

"Looks like we'll be going to Denver, Tenderfoot. What do ya say about that?"

"You'll never see Denver," I replied.

"Now, what's gotten into you? Every time I talk to ya, all I hear is killin' talk."

"You've ridden me hard, Jack. I told you once before that I'd had enough. You keep pushing me and I'll kill you. It's as simple as that."

"I'm not pushin' you. I asked what you thought of..."

"Get away from him," Henry called. "Damnit, Jack, I told you to leave that one alone."

"Lord, I cain't even talk to the boy!" he said, wheeling his horse and trotting off.

At the same time, Henry walked his horse over to me. I had my back to him and when I heard a hoof strike stone, I whirled. Again, I found the revolver in my hand, cocked and aiming square in the middle of Henry's chest. Henry's eyes were wide as saucers.

"You're jittery as an old cat," he said, showing his open palms.

I put the gun away and felt embarrassed. Again, I'd had no intention of pulling iron. Fear, that's all it was. Every time I got startled, the gun came into my hand and it always left me feeling foolish. Every time I'd needed the gun, I'd had plenty of time to pull it. The only ones that needed a fast draw were idiots, who couldn't wait to kill, or to die and they usually did both before long. It wasn't that way with me. I didn't like the killing. I could do it and I knew when I had to. Then, I could push my moral indignation behind and go about business, but this habit of jerking the Colt every time I got frightened brought a flush to my cheeks.

I heard Henry talking, but I was so flustered that I hadn't understood a word of it.

"What?"

"I said," he began again, exhaling through his frustration. "Ease off old Jack, there. He don't mean nothing. You whipped him in a fair fight and it was hard for him to swallow it, but he got 'er down and you don't have to get yur back up whenever he comes around."

I understood they were trying to let bygones be bygones, but I wasn't through with my anger. I had no need of friends and I could handle my enemies better when I didn't consider them friends to begin with. It was fine with me the way it was. At least I knew who to look for. I wouldn't let it be like before with Sheriff Dixon. I wasn't going to trust someone just so they could put a knife in my back.

"Ya hear me that time?" Henry asked, genuinely curious.

"Yeah, I heard you," I said.

"But, it ain't gonna change nothin' is it?"

"No, sir, I like it when I know who my enemies are. I've seen plenty of double-dealing."

"Well, that's all I come to say," he said and rode off shaking his head.

In the morning, we struck out north for the town of Las Vegas. north of there, we headed for the Raton Range and I got a glimpse of the high, sharp peaked mountains that would accompany us into Denver. They rose up out of the plains and grew larger until they seemed as if they'd fill the whole sky, in time.

Aside from admiring the beauty, I noticed that they'd provide plenty of shelter for a band of Indians, or bandits. I kept a close eye on the goings on about those hills as we rode. I hoped we'd veer off away from them before long, but I had no idea how extensive the range of mountains could be. The very thought that it might extend as far as Denver was overwhelming.

There was plenty of water on the drive and a sea of grass for the cattle to graze. The country was so pure, it felt as if every step of the horse brought one to a place untouched by man. It was all clean and beautiful and I got the sense of what living there in peace must have been like for the Indians. I could see how they might fight as they had to keep it. Lord knows, I would've fought for it.

In camp, the night before we reached the Iliff place, where the cows were to be sold under the original agreement, Mr. Loving called me away from the others. We went for a walk under the huge sky. To the west, the still snow lined peaks stood out in the bright, full, moonlight. It was light as day, even away from the fire. The smell of coffee was on the slight breeze and I felt homesick for the first time since Port Caddo. The gentle, friendly smells, the beauty of the mountains and walking with a person I respected, who seemed something like a father to me, all reminded me so much of home, I had to swallow hard.

Back at the fire, we could hear the others making jokes and roaring with laughter. It wrankled me a bit to think they were laughing at me. I didn't know if they were, but they might as well be. It didn't matter, but it added weight to my homesickness.

"You hear them boys laughing?" Loving asked.

"Yes, sir."

"You know why that is?"

"No, sir, not exactly. I know they only laugh when I'm not around. I suppose they're laughing at me," I said, drawing myself up. "It doesn't bother me, if that's what you think. I understand it. I speak with some education, and I was such a greenhorn when I hired on. It's all..."

"That ain't it," he interrupted.

I was at a loss. What did he mean that wasn't it? What else could it be?

"They're laughin' cause you ain't around," Loving said, grinning at the misunderstanding. "You have them boys wound up tight, like a fist," he said, holding his fist out for me to see. "I can't have that anymore," he continued. "When we get to Denver, you're on your own. That's what you wanted anyway, isn't it? To get to Denver?"

"Yes, sir," I said. "But, what do you mean, I have them wound up tight? I thought I'd see Denver and ride back to Texas with your outfit. Catch up to you at Bosque Redondo while you winter."

"I like you," he said, "or, I wouldn't even bother with ya. I'd just tell ya to pack yur things and run you off. So, I'm tellin' you as nicely as I can. You ain't wanted anymore."

There was a huge roar of laughter from the fire and anxious, loud spurts of profanity.

"You hear that? That's how a cow camp's supposed to sound. God, I've missed that sound on this drive," he confided. "You're the one who's put a stop to it."

"How?" I asked, hoping that I could change it all back for him. I felt a bit of the boy I used to be while hoping that I could make it all right. If there was anything I could do, I would.

"It's that temper of yours. Ordinarily, they'd use it against ya and get you all worked up over nothing and watch you fly off the handle. They'd do it for fun, you see. But, then you went and proved that you'd kill 'em for it if they tried. Henry told me you pulled down on him. Is that right?"

"Yes, sir," I admitted in shame.

"Quick as lightening, he said. Faster than a rattlesnake. I'd like to see that sometime," he scoffed.

"It's a reflex," I said, apologetically.

"You're a smart fella, you see what's happened, ain't ya?"

"Yes, sir."

"I know some of what you've been through. Ned Smith, Manuel Garza and his banditos. That's one reason I wanted you on this drive. I know Charlie didn't, but I did. I thought you'd seen enough killin' to make you respect that hog leg of yours. I'm not blaming you for anything. Ya Understand?

"But, these cowboys, their a tough lot, see, but they ain't lawmen, nor badmen. They're just men doing a job. They shoot their pistols in the air and whoop and holler and every once in a while you might get one, or two that want to test out their hand, but usually, they're just men from little towns that find this life under the stars more precious than anything they own and they chase it, like they'd chase a woman.

"I don't know what's happened to you, I know something has. I've seen a lot of this frontier and I've seen a lot of men like you. At heart, you're good and decent the way your momma raised ya, but something happened and you got cold inside. Take what I'm tellin' you now as the Gospel truth. There's two ways for a man like you to go. You can either be a lawman, or a badman. If there was a war, you could go and fight it. You could join up with the cavalry if you weren't a Confederate. But, let that be as it may, you're stuck now and you only have those two ways to go.

"I'm letting you go," he said, taking a deep breath, "because you don't know which way to turn your life. If you go bad, I don't want you around."

Loving finished his speech and turned to go, then stopped and faced me.

"You know, you may not like old Jack for the way he gave it to ya, but if he hadn't, you wouldn't have learned as well, nor as fast. Don't blame him, son, he's a good man down deep."

Then, he left me there on that prairie to think it over. I looked up into the stars and I knew he was right about a lot of it. Maybe not about Jack, but the rest of it was on the mark. Worst of all, I hadn't decided which way to go. I was letting things take their course and was willing to go any way that seemed best.

I glanced over my shoulder at the dark figure of Loving. The fire stood roaring before him and the other men were lit up orange by the flames. The wood popped and sent sparks flying straight up with the smoke. The men let out a loud burst of laughter at that moment and it all became crystal clear to me in an instant.

The game we'd played during the whole drive was no longer a game. They alienated me to punish me and I frightened them with my willingness to kill and now nothing could be done to bring us back together. We'd become different sorts of men as the miles passed beneath us. There was no repairing it now.

I walked back to the camp and loaded up my belongings, then went a mile, or so, and made camp for myself. I'd ride out with them in the morning and drive the cattle to Iliff's. From there, I'd draw my pay and ride into Denver to see what happened.

17

Denver City lay to the west of the trail cut by Capt. J.C. Fremont. It was a city thrown together in the haste of gold and silver mining operations and survived as a base camp for prospectors and a market for local farmers.

After splitting with Loving at Iliff's place, I rode toward town with a sufficient amount of money in my pockets and a desire to sit in a warm tub of water. I rode through the streets crowded with horses, carts and pedestrians. I sought a good hotel with a saloon. It was a busy town and a sense of urgency hung in the air like dust. There were a lot of diversions available to a man in from a long trail drive, but I rode directly to a hotel and livery. I made arrangements for board of the gelding and went into the lobby.

Whatever I might have thought of the integrity of the building by the looks of the outside, the inside offered almost civilized accommodations. I signed in at the desk, bought a bottle of whiskey at the saloon and went up to my room. While I lounged on the bed, a porter brought in a couple of buckets of steaming water and poured them in the tub. I thanked him with a coin and stripped.

As I settled down into the shallow water and began to
soap myself, I thought of the trail, of the words Loving said
the night before and the looks of relief on the men's faces as
I drew my pay and rode out. Strangely enough, their
company had been the most pleasant I'd had in a long time.

Even when I was Sheriff of Sherman, I didn't feel
comfortable. The people there were nice enough, but they
regarded me as something more than human. To them I
was a savior, a war hero and a living legend all rolled into
one. It was flattering at first, but later it became a weight
around my neck. Everyone deferred to me as if I weren't
just a kid, as if my ability to kill somehow provided a sense
of wisdom. It didn't, and I felt ashamed of the treatment. I
saw myself as a murderer and I could never shake the
uneasiness the contradiction produced.

Out there on the trail, however, I felt much more equal
and was treated as well as a greenhorn kid could expect.
That I grew tired of it was my own problem. Loving got it
right when he said that if it hadn't been for the way Jack
and the rest treated me, I wouldn't have learned as quickly,
or as well. Loving was right about everything.

I took the cork out of the bottle and took a drink. It was
hot up there in that room, in that tub, and the whiskey
warmed my stomach. I felt my mouth water and my head
shudder involuntarily.

I tried to think of what to do next. Go down to the
saloon? No, get a good meal for once, then to the saloon.
There, amongst the drunkards and gamblers and miners
I'd hear of something.

All the way to Colorado Territory I'd thought of putting
together a herd and making some money ranching. Maybe,
it was all something to occupy my mind, but sitting in that
tub, with the warm water all around, I thought of easier
money. Mining perhaps, or work on the mail routes.

I liked the look of the mountains. They were comforting in their bounty of minerals and a man could live up there on deer and other game. The mountains offered hope and life. There was water and trees and berries. It was nothing like the barren desert I'd just been through. It seemed like the Garden of Eden compared to the dusty wasteland of the Pecos.

I took another drink of the whiskey and stood up to dry off. I brought up my pack with the extra clothes. I put them on and waited for the barber to come up. I was living pretty well, I thought, standing there in clean clothes. Oh well, it only happened every few months that a man could get cleaned up and there were some pretty bad conditions to live through between.

After dusting off my hat, I looked for a mirror. There was just one small square over the wash basin. I moved quickly to it, holding my hat up, and was startled at the sight that greeted me. In my mind, I was a kid, not yet nineteen, but someone else stared back at me in the looking glass. I lowered my hand that held the hat and leaned closer to the mirror, trying to find the boy in there somewhere.

My face was sunburned to a deep brown, my lips were tough like rawhide and there were scars on my cheekbone and my temple. My ear was a bit deformed from where the bullet nicked me that night in Sherman. There was another on my neck and yet another one at the top of my head in the center, which made a natural part for my hair.

A lot of time had passed and I'd not taken note of how my experiences were etched into my face. There was something completely different about my eyes. They were narrowed and small wrinkles stood at the corners where no wrinkles had ever been. Though I looked at myself with my own eyes, they didn't seem to be mine. They looked distant and clouded and had lost the rapid, shifting nervousness they had before. Now, they lay dead and cold in my face, like marbles. When they did move, they followed a slow, easy pattern.

I stared into the glass for a long time and studied myself, getting to know my reflection again. Then, I drew away and noticed that I moved differently, it was slower and more measured. I realized that I no longer existed as I was, but had been transformed into something unique. It was an alarming revelation and I felt a sense of loss, like a death, a death of myself. Strangely, I felt that someone was to blame, that I should be mad at someone for having changed me. But, there was no one to blame. Whatever I'd been, I wasn't anymore.

I heard a knock on the door and let the barber in. He was a heavy man, sweating profusely from the climb up the stairs with his bag. His eyes looked me over and focused on my long, wet hair.

"I have the right room, at least," he said, dragging the only chair in the room out into the center where he could maneuver around it. "Sit down."

I sat in the chair and felt his hands on my head. He cut swiftly with the scissors and shaved my face and talked. Once, when he came to the big scar down the center of my head, he stopped cutting. Then, he started again without a word about it. He talked of the mines and the treacherous stage routes. He told of Indian attacks and robberies and local politics, that seemed based on corruption and intrigue. I listened and watched clumps of hair fall onto the sheet he'd draped around my neck.

When the barber left, I felt new and clean and a bit wholesome. Some of the trail dog had fallen away with the hair and I felt respectable. I laid down on the soft bed. It was like a cloud compared to the past month of sleeping on the ground with the insects, dust and rocks. I went right to sleep with the daylight streaming through the small window.

It was dark when I woke with a headache. The saloon below was busy and noisy from the gambling and drinking. Gunshots of enthusiasm could be heard randomly in the street at wide intervals. They startled no one, least of all myself.

I rose and went down to see what sort of entertainment the place offered. The saloon was well populated and a heavy layer of smoke hung about the ceiling. Card players and dice throwers were off to one side and conversations were taking place about the tables set in a pattern in front of the bar.

I eased up to the bar and ordered a beer. Toward the middle, a fight broke out and the two participants bloodied the floor with their noses before being thrown out into the night. I'd just watched the last of them go out head first and was returning my attention to the beer when I noticed Henry, Jack and a few of Loving's outfit sitting about a table. They hadn't noticed me, or didn't seem to. Like me, they'd cleaned themselves up and were hardly recognizable.

They looked out of place, as if they belonged on the prairie and were there against their will. When I looked about more thoroughly, I realized they appeared to be much the same as the rest.

Then, Jack looked up and caught my eye. He nudged Henry and they all turned towards me with a steady gaze, waiting for something. I raised my glass of beer to them and they nodded back. There wasn't anyone else for me to talk to, but I didn't want to spoil their fun and stayed at the bar. When I glanced over my shoulder at them later, they were engrossed in conversation.

I thought I'd try my hand at poker and pushed away from the bar with a full glass of beer. I walked by their table and touched my hat as I went. Halfway across the room, I stopped short. I recognized one of the men at the poker table. His profile was so familiar I had to hold onto the glass of beer with both hands to keep from dropping it.

Sitting there in a reasonably good suit, with tie and derby hat, was Gregory Jackson, from Mississippi. I wanted to rush up to him and grab him. I felt my face grin from ear to ear. What was he doing there? To find him in Denver City of all places!

"Gregory," I hollered out over the heads of the players. He looked up at me with greedy, angry eyes. Then, his face lightened and a smile spread over his face, but it was quickly clouded again and a cold stare slid over the dancing eyes. He turned back to his cards without a word.

I gulped and felt the smile on my face freeze into a toothy grimace. So, that's how it was, was it? I shook my head and as I did so, I felt someone move close to my side.

"He holds a grudge," a velvet-smooth voice said in a whisper.

I glanced over and saw William Flout standing beside me. I wasn't as surprised to see him, and I was no longer capable of the genuine excitement I'd known a moment before.

"It's unnecessary and wrong-headed, William. And, how are you these days?"

"Oh, I'm as good as can be expected. We're somewhat of a team, Gregory and me."

"A team? How's that?"

"Well, he cheats at cards and I handle anyone who calls him on it."

"Really, William? That's an enterprising occupation, what's led you to that?"

"Another time, Jeff. Right now, that fellow in the tie sitting next to the dealer is getting wise. I have to do my job," he said, slapping me on the back and strolling in front of me to take a position next to the staircase. I took a drink of my beer and turned around.

Before me, Loving's cowboys sat looking up. They seemed vindictive and knowing, as if they understood why someone would pretend they didn't know me. I glanced at them and went on about my business.

There was an aching in my heart. I guess I'd always thought that Gregory, William and I would be friends. I knew there were some hard feelings after the war and maybe, rightly so, but to hold onto it that long seemed foolish and ridiculous. There we were, childhood friends who'd known each other all of our lives and because of one thing and another, we acted as if we were enemies. It didn't seem right, or just. I simply wanted a chance to explain. I was sure they'd see it all my way if they'd listen, but now Gregory wouldn't even give me a chance to square it. His heart was so consummed with bitterness that he couldn't see past it.

During the drive, when everyone cursed and hated me, I took refuge in the belief that I didn't need them, because I had two of the best friends a man could have. I believed that they'd always be my friends and would see through their initial antagonism towards me. I felt sure that when I saw them again they'd have forgiven me. Or, at least would listen to what I had to say on the matter. Suddenly, that was gone, too.

All right, I thought, I could hate as well as any man alive and if they wanted to be on the wrong side of me, they'd found a way to do it.

I'd just settled that in my mind when I heard a commotion at the poker table. When I looked Gregory was standing up. With a cat-like pounce, William grabbed the man he'd spoken of by the collar, slammed his face into the wall and threw him out of the saloon. Gregory sat back down, eased a knuckle-duster into his vest pocket and pulled a pile of chips towards himself. "Deal," he yelled.

"Real slick," I whispered to myself. I turned my back on the scene and lifted the glass of beer to my lips. I felt somewhat abandoned and angry. I'd only known betrayal in my short life. Even when that betrayal turned out to have a benefit, it was a betrayal all the same. Well, I thought, I'll give no one else a chance.

I glanced over my shoulder at Gregory, who sat plump and self-satisfied in his chair. He'd grown a big mustache and it bushed out thick beneath his reddened cheekbones. His complexion had paled in the time he'd been a gambler and his opulence was beginning to show at his belt line. Yet, there was something solid and muscular about him.

Then, William walked toward me with a smooth, easy motion. He moved like a cat: quick, sure and agile. There was a bit of bored amusement on his face as if he were secretly pleased about something rather ordinary.

"What brings you to Denver," he asked. "Whiskey," he said to the bartender, then turned toward me for the answer.

I kept silent. I didn't want to start a conversation with him. I was afraid of my anger, of his boldness and Gregory's resentment. It was a bad mix all the way around and the whiskey and beer would only inflame whatever hostility remained.

"I didn't quite hear you," he said, in that familiar Mississippi drawl that sounded familiar and distant like something that belonged to a world long forgotten. But, the sound of it took me home again and put us together on the river shooting at Union gunboats.

"This and that," I replied.

"Oh, yes, that does prompt one to travel. Same with Gregory and me."

I felt my eyes narrow as I realized he was mimicking my speech, my breeding and social standing.

"I believe," he continued, "that we are the victim of the same man's desire."

"In what way?"

"Well, your father ran you out of town only a month, or so before running the two of us out." William watched my surprise. "We were a bit surprised ourselves. We'd done nothing to warrant it, you see."

"Okay, knock it off, William. You're mocking me and it's a lot of fun, but I don't like it."

"You don't like it? What a shame," he said, downing the shot-glass of whiskey and motioning for more.

I turned around to face him directly. I took a glance at Gregory. He was losing players quickly and I watched another stand and walk off. Gregory put his arms in the air and I heard him say above the din of the saloon, "What? Where's everyone going? This is an honest game. I'm just lucky."

I looked at the table where the boys from Loving's outfit sat. They had their eyes glued to William and me. They could tell trouble was brewing and I think they wanted to watch me die.

When I turned back to William, he'd just downed the second shot of whiskey.

"Why would my father run you out of town? How could he, even if he wanted to? Vicksburg's been taken over by the Federals. He's poor and probably in danger for his life."

William laughed right in my face. He laughed hard and long. Too long for my taste and I thought about hitting him in the jaw to shut his mouth.

"You underestimate the old man, Jefferson. He's bigger now than he ever was and much more powerful. He's a ruthless old tyrant, as well. He runs Vicksburg and everything that surrounds it. Him and his Yankee friends."

I burnt all over with embarrassment, anger and resentment. My stomach felt weak and while I heard his words, I was shocked that he could say such things. How and why would he make up such nonsense? To goad me into a move? If that was his intent, he was remarkably close to it. It took all my strength to keep my fist out of his face.

"Yes, your father is quite a piece of work. He had all the angles figured and when the war was over, he didn't miss a beat. Which leaves me to wonder why he'd want to bother with the likes of Gregory and me. Why would he? That's what I ask myself," he said, then paused as if in thought. "Listen, Jefferson, while you're here, why don't you tell me. Surely, you know what he has against us, that he'd sully our names, frame us for murder and run us out of town with a lynch mob on our tails. Why would he? You know why, don't you?"

"I've no idea," I said, honestly.

"Ahhh, I see," he said, with a sardonic grin. "I'd forgotten that other aspect of your character. Well, I don't blame you, under the circumstances. I mean, a regular man would just say it, he wouldn't be afraid, but you...oh, you, it's your cowardice that holds your tongue. You're afraid I might hurt you if you told me. Well, I understand perfectly."

I knew I was going to kill him. I knew that he wanted the confrontation. He wanted to be justified in killing me and he wanted to kill me to vent whatever frustrations he had about my father. I didn't know what happened back in Vicksburg, but I was sure that my father had done nothing to him. William blamed him for his own bad luck and he wanted to kill to set it right in his mind.

I looked at the table full of men. I could use their help about then, but there was such a distance between us. They sat and listened, though I didn't think they could hear what was being said. They listened as hard as they could and they could tell there was trouble, but they wouldn't help. They might even give William a hand when it came to it.

I was surrounded by enemies. But, there was some comfort in it. I didn't have to worry about someone cutting my throat in the night, or using me as bait. This time, I knew who my enemies were and where they were. I decided to go at it headlong. Bill Dixon taught me the value of wading right in with guns blazing. It was clean and simple. All a person had to do was kill.

"You don't even have the guts to stand up to me, Jefferson. You sit there like a wounded child, weeping over the memory of your corrupt father. You don't deserve the good name of Jefferson. You should give it back to the man it belongs to. He's in jail now, and I'm sure he bears it with more pride and dignity than you ever could."

"I'm going up to my room," I said, setting the empty glass on the bar. I looked at him once more and pushed away from the counter. The hairs on the back of my neck stood up. The smoke was thick as molasses and the piano plinked away, sounding as if it were underneath a washtub. I saw, in vivid detail, the astonished looks of the men at the table. Jack and Henry both let their jaws hang slack as their eyes followed me. Jack spit at my boot as I walked past.

I was almost to the bannister when I heard the booming sound of Gregory's voice. "Slink off, little coward," he yelled. "Slink off and hide."

I turned the corner and found myself halfway between William and Gregory. Gregory took it into his mind to rise up out of the chair. I saw from the corner of my eye that he was reaching into his vest. I had them on each side of me and behind as I faced the wall that ran up the staircase. I whirled around toward William, knowing he'd be the one to shoot first.   Gregory's motion for the derringer was to provide the excuse. If I went after Gregory, William would be in his legal right to shoot me down. If I hadn't seen what I had in the past year, I'd have fallen for it easily. If I hadn't known the men I'd known, I'd have thought Gregory was the only real threat. He was the one who seemed to hate me the most. But, it wasn't so often the ones that expressed hate, but the ones that could fake forgiveness that were serious. People like that were free with the tongue, because they were intent on murder. They'd say anything to help their plot along.

I found the Colt in my hand as I turned toward William. Like always before, it was just there. I shot across the tables. He saw it coming soon enough to have pulled his gun swiftly from his holster, raised it and even had time to lean away from the path of the first bullet.

Men scattered to the floor and pulled their own guns. They tipped the tables over and pushed themselves away from the action in whatever direction they found clear.

William was bent over from dodging the initial shot and my second shot took him in the upper left corner of his chest. His pistol came up and discharged at the same instant that my second shot entered his body. I didn't see it. I was already turning to shoot Gregory, who also fired before I could train my pistol on him.

Missing my first shot slowed everything down. I was caught trying to catch up with movements and firing angles. I had the gun cocked and was swinging it to bear, when William's shot struck the wallpaper just behind my head. It was at such an angle that I saw the paper rip with my left eye, now that my head was turned directly away from the path of the bullet.

Gregory's first shot hit me in the upper left thigh just as I was squeezing the trigger. It threw my shot off and the bullet entered his lower left side. William fired again from the ground and I heard it thud heavily into the ceiling above me. I knew then, that he was dying.

I was shocked by the sudden, massive pressure of Gregory's bullet. It seemed as if it pressed dully through my skin. I didn't feel the pain, but rather an area of considerable pressure. My second shot at Gregory caught him looking out the door of the saloon. Even as I fired, I wondered what he was looking at.

The gun jumped in my hand and he was knocked to the floor when the piece of lead slammed into his jaw, just below the ear and travelled upward, exiting his head in a bloody explosion.

Then, the pain started to come. There was a burning and a wetness that I didn't want to look at. Not until I found William. I searched the room for him with dazed and wandering eyes. I suddenly felt nauseous and could feel myself drifting out of consciousness. I fought for control.

Then, I saw him. He was dragging himself along the floor with his gun in his left hand. He was leaving a bloody trail and a gurgling emitted from his chest. Bubbles of blood were blown and burst as he struggled to get a clear shot. I felt so sorry for him that I shot him in the forehead to end it.

Shooting William was all I had energy for and I sat down heavily on the steps. I knew I had to get up to my room and lie down. I didn't want to vomit right there in front of the people who'd not been able to escape. I turned over on the stairs and raised my head. They were steep and rugged. Fortunately, my leg wasn't broken. I didn't know how bad of shape it was in, but it wasn't broken.

I kept the gun in my hand as I put it against the wall for leverage. I gripped the banister with the other and raised myself to my feet, but remained bent at the waist. I took the steps slowly and stopped to rest a couple of times. I tried to concentrate on one step at a time. My hand slipped off the wall and my shoulder was driven solidly against the wood.

I continued to struggle up the stairs until I reached the top. Then, I crawled along the carpet, dragging my bad leg. I realized then, that my key was missing, or in one of the pockets I didn't think I could reach. I decided to just lay there on the carpet for a minute. It seemed like a good plan. I'd just lay there a minute and catch my breath.

I rolled over and put my back against the wall. I looked down at the hand that carried the pistol. The gun was an unnatural part of my hand, it seemed. I looked at my feet. All parts of my body seemed disconnected, though I knew they were mine.

I closed my eyes. My throat was dry. I wanted a beer, but couldn't call for one. Where was everyone? I no longer heard the piano and only hushed voices could be heard downstairs. It felt good to have my eyes closed and I thought I could sleep for a minute before trying to get the door open. I let myself sink into the dark depths of sleep. I promised myself that it'd be only for a minute. I still had to get the door open and crawl into bed.

18

When I woke, I found myself being lifted from the floor and carried to a bed. I assumed it was my bed, but I didn't come around well enough to open my eyes. When my britches came off, I tried my best to protest, but made only a moaning sound. I heard the murmurings of men and felt their hands on the whole length of my body. They pushed hard. Then, it felt as if someone had stuck my leg with a needle. I jumped and they pushed harder. I tried to scream, but my words didn't go beyond my lips. There was more probing around with the sharp instrument. I felt pressure of a bandage as it was being evenly wrapped about my upper thigh. Then, all was quiet and I drifted off again.

The doctor was there when I woke. The sun was easing away in the western sky and it cast orange shadows across the small window. Coal-oil lamps burned above the bed. The doctor was a young man, not at all old enough for me to trust. He was short and had curly, dark hair and glasses. His effeminate hands were busy fiddling with his bag.

"Where's the real doctor?" I asked, hoping he'd know.

"Perhaps, I should put this bullet back into your leg. Maybe, I should just cut the leg off and stop worrying about gangrene." He looked at me with a strange expression of severity and humor. "Fortunately, the bullet didn't penetrate far enough to break the leg, but you lost a considerable amount of blood. Why didn't you just stay where you were? What made you climb the stairs?"

"Seemed like the thing to do," I said.

"Lord, I hate it when you cowboys come to town. Everyone else has a sense of society, of behaving properly in public."

"Like the gamblers I shot," I said, though it cost me some energy to join the argument.

"Gamblers aren't citizens, not in the true sense. They're often cowboys, too. In fact," he went on, "if it weren't for cowboys, we'd have no gamblers here."

"Prospectors," I said, but it was the only word I could manage.

"Okay, prospectors as well. But, you see, it's only those who use this city as a supply station that cause the trouble."

"Poli," I started, swallowed, "ticians."

"Look, no more talking," he said, flustered. "You rest some more. I'll be by tomorrow to check on the wound. Stay off your feet and eat and drink as much as you can. I've left instructions for your medicine with the bartender."

"Colt?" I asked.

"No shooting, either."

"Where's revol...?"

"Oh, it's on the chair."

"Bring it."

"No."

I started to raise up. Pushing back against the bed, I rose to a sitting position and swung my leg off the side of the bed.

"All right, all right, I'll get it," he said, moving to the chair and lifting the gun.

"Load it."

"No, I can't," he replied.

I pointed to the saddlebags in the corner. He brought them to me and I loaded the revolver. I put it under the sheet and went back to sleep.

The next day the doctor came in the afternoon. With him was a lawman. The lawman was big, over six feet with long sideburns and a mustache. He wore a suit and derby like a businessman. He had keen eyes and a stubbed out cigar was jammed between two fingers of his left hand, from which a copy of the local newspaper dangled. To his right side he wore a holster. The butt of a revolver thrust forward, so he could make his pull with his left hand.

"There he is, Marshal," the doctor said.

"How you doing?"

"Fine. I feel much better today. I suppose you're here to arrest me, or to run me out of town."

"To the contrary," the doctor said, "he's here to thank you on behalf of the citizens of Denver."

The Marshal stared angrily at the doctor, who decided that he should go about his doctoring business. When he pulled back the sheet, the Marshal saw the gun.

"Expecting someone?"

"I don't know," I said.

"That's a Colt, ain't it?"

"Yes, sir," I said. "It's a fine firearm."

"I brought you the paper." He opened it and showed me the story about the gunfight in the saloon. "You might want to read it later. It seems that your identity is somewhat in question, but that you were known in Texas. Says you were a Texas lawman."

"Yes, sir, in Sherman, Texas up close to the border with Indian Territory."

"Were those men wanted in Texas?"

"I don't believe so."

"If you don't mind, what was the nature of the disagreement?"

"Well," I said, "I do mind. It was personal."

"According to the paper, you've single-handedly abolished the town of evil. Now, I'm sure you can understand how angry I am about the assumption," he said, raising his voice.

I nodded.

"This town has been plagued by the poor and worthless since the gold tapered off. We're trying to build a town and all we've been able to accomplish, so far, is to attract the kind of filth that you killed a few days ago." The Marshal paced back and forth and the doctor looked at my wound and re-wrapped it while the Marshal talked.

"The men of this town, like Larimer and the newspaperman, Byers, who prints this rag, and a few others are gonna offer you my job. So, I've come to ask if you want to come to work for me, instead."

"Why would I do that, Marshal? Why would I be a deputy instead of a marshal?"

"I don't know. It's the only way I can see to keep my job," he said, plainly, honestly.

"Don't worry about your job, I don't want it."

"Thank you," he said, shaking my hand. He stumbled out of the room and closed the door.

"You should've taken the job," the doctor remarked. "That man's a drunk and whether they give the job to you, or someone else, he won't have it for long."

"Yeah," I said, "but, I've made enough enemies. Don't you think?"

"You've made nothing, but friends here. Flout and Jackson were notorious for dishonest gambling, and treachery."

"Tell me about them," I said.

"They came to town a few months ago. In a few days the other gamblers in this hotel, the good ones, either left town, moved over, or were killed. They didn't have everything their way, but enough so they were content with their little game. The Marshal was under a lot of pressure to get rid of them, but every time he went into the place, they bought him so much whiskey that he usually left sideways," he said, sighing. "Then, you came in and shot them both."

The doctor packed his things into his case.

"I'll have a crutch sent up. You're going to have to start putting some weight on that leg. Get it used to walking. You're fortunate that I didn't have to cut it off. I won't be coming back, but if you'd like to stop in, my office is above the general store down the street from here."

"Thanks," I said, and lifted the paper. There was a big headline at the top that read: TEXAS RANGER LIBERATES TOWN.

I wasn't a Texas Ranger. Newspapers always got the facts wrong and it seemed particularly disturbing to me because they were supposed to be scrupulous in their investigation of the facts. I read the story to find out what I could about the town and my poor dead friends.

The rest of the article read: "Yesterday evening the notorious gamblers and ruffians, William Flout and Gregory "Slickhand" Jackson, were gunned down single-handed by a Texas Ranger, a Mr. Jefferson, who had come to our fine city only hours before.

"In the tradition of the name Jefferson, we have found liberty at his hand. Those who witnessed the event, recalled a gun that spoke with the eloquence of our great forefather of the Union, Thomas Jefferson.

"Witnesses say that the evening began in normal fashion. Slickhand Jackson was practicing his peculiar form of card tricks and Flout had accosted two, or three patrons before events began to turn against them.

"Mr. Jefferson was drinking at the bar in all privacy when Flout stepped up to him and began to question him. Those close enough to the conversation remarked that Flout called the man by name, saying: 'Jefferson, this, or that' implying that each of the combatants knew each other quite well. Jefferson replied to these statements in kind fashion, but Flout pressed his inquiry to the point that Jefferson could take it no longer. Then, just as a peace-loving man would, Jefferson left the bar for his quarters upstairs when he noticed Jackson reaching into that infamous vest for the small instrument of death he carried there.

"It has been speculated by some that Jefferson had intimate knowledge of the workings of the gambling team as he drew his pistol and shot, not Jackson as one might assume, but in the direction of Flout as he was raising his revolver. The first shot missed, but the second shot struck Flout's chest."

The story went on to tell of the whole battle, of my "infinite courage" and the apparent incompetency of the local Marshal. It was all a fallacy. The story alluded to the fact that I may have tracked them across Texas.

I tossed the paper onto the floor. Only minutes later, I heard a knock. I gripped the revolver under the sheets.

"Come in," I yelled.

The door opened and a smallish sort of man entered and announced himself as a reporter for the paper. He saw the paper on the floor.

"I see you've been reading. How did you like the story?" he asked with a wry grin, thinking I'd be delighted that I was shown in such a favorable light.

"Aside from being somewhat fallacious, it was passable."

"Fallacious?" he said, "in what way?"

"My first name is Jefferson, not my last. I go by the name of J. D. Wilkes and I'm not a Texas Ranger." I knew I was telling him more than I should, but his inaccuracy infuriated me and I was taking revenge for his shoddy work.

"Well, Mr. Wilkes, would you like to tell me the story yourself?" he asked, readying his paper and pencil.

"No, I wouldn't. I simply don't want to be associated with Thomas Jefferson in that way. I also don't think the Texas Rangers would appreciate anyone taking such liberties as to call oneself a Ranger who was not. I'd like a retraction in these areas."

"Tell me," he said, writing, "did you know the men you killed? How did you hear of them? Where have you met before?"

"I want a retraction. That's all."

"Well," he said, looking at me and lowering the pencil. "You see, we're the only paper in this city. What we say is the truth to one degree, or another. In other words, you have no recourse besides the News. If you want us to take something out, you have to replace it with something."

"Well," I said, after a long silence, "we were friends. That was a long time ago. After I left home to come out West, they had some confrontation with my father. I don't know what it was about. When I showed up here, they thought they'd get even with my father through me. So, I shot them."

"Where are you from?"

"That's not important," I said.

"They were from the Southern states. Mississippi, I believe."

"Is that what they said?"

"Isn't it true?"

"No."

"They spoke as if they were from Mississippi."

"If a person chooses a place to be from, they'll probably do what they have to, to make it believable."

"But, you have the same manner of speaking," he objected.

I stared hard at him and my breathing came shallow.

"Why did you shoot William Flout first?"

"I saw the way they handled things. It was obvious."

"Where were you a lawman?"

"In Sherman, Texas. I was a Sheriff, not a Ranger."

"What did they say to you that started the fight?"

"I won't answer that. It was personal."

"Were they wanted for murder in Mississippi?"

"As far as I know, they were never in Mississippi."

"The men at the saloon said you were a quick-draw expert."

"That's nonsense."

"You shot four times before they got off more than two."

"I started sooner," I replied.

"No, you didn't," he said, smiling. "Everyone clearly saw both men reach for their guns long before you did. You're lying to me," he said.

"See, I'm the one and only undeniable source of information you've got. What I say is the truth, to one degree, or another, because there's no one else to ask. Unless you'd like to speak to Jackson, or Flout in hopes of getting a different story."

"What brings you to Denver?"

"No. No more questions. If you want to speak to me in a few days, I'll talk to you. First, print the retraction and the correct story before I give you any more answers."

When I could get around, I went down to the livery and paid my bill. I talked to a man who worked with the stage company. I asked him about supplies headed south into New Mexico.

"We have three wagons headed to Santa Fe in a week. I keep the livestock, but the owner of the goods is at the general store. He owns the store, too."

I went down Market Street to the general store and entered. It was a dark, gloomy place stacked high with mining supplies, flour, sugar and the like. I made my way back to the small office. Behind a desk was a large man. Receipts and bills were scattered all over his desk. Paperweights came in every variety and were placed on several piles of paper.

"Pardon me," I said, looking in.

"What?"

"You have a load of goods for New Mexico?"

"Yeah, so what?"

"I'd like to provide security for the wagons."

"I've got security. You think I send three wagons full of goods without rifles and men?" He said all of it without looking up. He sat there marking receipts and noting things and looking into his ledger.

"Do you mind if I tag along with the wagons?"

"Do what you want, but I won't pay you for it."

"When do they leave?"

"Next Wednesday morning. It'll be an early start, before daybreak."

"Thank you," I said, and left.

I looked down at my britches. There was a hole in my chaps and the trousers. The thigh and the bandage showed through the hole. Down the front of the chaps, a blackened, dry patch of blood stood out for all to see, but it was the stiff leg of the drawers that bothered me most. I went back into the store and started looking at the racks of clothes.

I picked out a pair that looked like they'd fit and called back into the small room.

"Hey, can I buy these?"

"If you have money," the fat man's voice came. It sounded as if he were in a hole.

"I have money," I yelled.

The man came waddling up front. He looked at my face, then at my pants and then back at my face.

"You're the one," he said, when he'd made it to my side.

"Yeah, I just spoke to you about riding security."

"No, I mean, you're the one from the saloon the other night."

"Oh, yes, sir."

"You want to ride security for me?"

"I did, but that's okay, I'll go along for free. A man can't just ride out across the country alone. A lot of people have died that way."

"Do you know how many times we've had our wagons looted, burnt and stolen outright? Plenty, I'll tell you. I've often wondered how many times the very men I'd hired to provide security had stolen the items themselves."

"Well, if that's true, you'd better find someone else to provide it."

"Who?"

"I don't know. I don't live here. I just came through with some cattle."

"I thought you were a Ranger."

"No, I'm not. I told that newspaperman to retract that story."

"I only saw the one."

"How much for the britches?" I asked, getting frustrated at the way the public mind worked. Once something was printed, it took on a life of its own and grew into the most ridiculous of stories. Everyone had to add a piece of their own information until the truth was dropped outright, in favor of a more interesting version.

"Seventy cents."

I laid the money on the counter.

"What do you think?" the storekeeper asked.

"About what?"

"Well, won't you try to hire some men and provide security for the wagons?"

"Look, Mister, I asked if I could ride along and give you another gun. I don't know anyone to hire around here and I'm not sure I'd want to if I did."

"I'd give ten percent of the load each way."

"No," I said, and walked out. But, I didn't get very far until I realized that I'd be riding along with a bunch that might kill me and take the load. Was there no end to the treachery? Could anyone be trusted? No, I said to myself, they couldn't. I decided to look the men over and if I didn't like it, I'd stay in Denver a little while.

I went back to the saloon. I was still hobbled by the recent wound, but I could walk without the crutch. I was glad to be rid of it. When I'd used it before, everyone knew who I was and they continued to ask questions about Texas and the Rangers. Without the crutch, I was less obvious, though I still got bothered by the questions.

At the saloon, I sat down and was served up a beer. I didn't have to pay anything for it. The saloon owners felt they owed me a debt of some sort. Whatever money I laid down remained on the bar. I wouldn't pick it up and the bartender was getting rich on tips.

"Hey, Slim," I said, calling the bartender over. "Do you know anyone who might ride security for some wagons? Not the usual bunch, but maybe a few others with some fighting experience behind them? Some cowboys, or some prospectors with some grit?"

He shook his long-faced head.

"Just a thought," I said. It'd be a pretty good occupation. If I could find enough men I trusted.

"Hey," I said, calling him back. "Let some of the men know that I'm looking for some help, but they need to be good with their guns."

"I'll do it," he said.

"But, be discreet, I don't want anyone getting wind of it. And, cull out the worthless, or greedy."

He nodded, but glanced at me with humorous dismay.

I didn't know what I was getting into, but I felt that a man ought to be able to send his shipments out without having them stolen by those expected to defend it. All of the lines of propriety were smudged on the Frontier. The gun was the only law.

I drank some beer and went up to my room to rest. It'd been a hard week. I lay down on the bed and looked at the

new britches on my legs. I was asking to get shot wearing
the new clothes.

19

All that night, I got secret tappings at my door and visits from several men willing to take on the duties of riding security. Most of them thought I was a Ranger, that I was sent to recruit men. Finally, I had to go down and tell the bartender to tell them that I wasn't hiring Rangers.

Of the twenty, or so, applicants, I needed somewhere between seven and nine. I could use more, but I figured those would do. Depending on the price of the load, it could mean a bit of change in everyone's pocket.

I worked out all of the details with the storekeeper and told him I could provide the men. We settled on moving the wagons out before daylight on Tuesday. I was counting on the change in plans to avoid any confrontation with the group who used to provide security. I kept my men in the dark until the time came.

Of all that came to offer their assistance, I only trusted six. I told all of them that I'd wake them when it was time to go and asked directions to their rooms. If I'd had to put it all together in Sherman, I'd have known who to choose. But, in Denver, I couldn't take chances, though I recognized that no amount of precautions could stop the inevitable. Men on the Frontier were treacherous, greedy, violent and temperamental. It didn't take much to get stabbed in the back, or shot from cover. The best a man could do, was try.

Monday night, well after midnight, I gathered those I thought were the most trustworthy at the livery. The oxen that'd pull the loads and the teamsters were already there getting things ready. I was nervous. I pulled the men aside.

"Look, this could be very dangerous. If the other outfit gets wind of this before we get very far, they'll come after us. In that case, I'll have the wagons draw up nose to tail in the form of a triangle with the oxen inside. It'll be crowded, so you'll have to fire from under the wagons, or from on top. If I can, I'll put our back to a wall and draw the wagons in an arc. I've loaded as much ammunition as we can fire into the lead wagon. If trouble starts, get close to that and hand some to your partners further down.

"So," I said, "this is what we'll do if there's any trouble, either from the other outfit, or from Indians, or other robbers. We've got our work cut out for us, gentlemen, but I can assure you that if we get a toe-hold in this business, we can make our mark."

I don't think they understood what I meant about making a mark. It was a private thing between my father and I. Most of the men just wanted to make some fast money. Maybe, they had a grudge against the old outfit, or were just poor prospectors left in Denver after the last drop of gold was panned, or maybe, they just had nothing left to lose.

"Have you ever heard of a 'T' formation?" one of the men asked.

"What's that?"

"Well," he said, kneeling and drawing in the dirt of the stables, "when you know which direction an attack is coming from, you draw the last two wagons in opposite directions and let the first one stay in the line. That way, you have a good barricade thrown up against the attack."

"And," I asked, "what if they split forces and come at the flanks?"

"If you see them try that, you can turn both wagons ahead again and move them alongside the first."

"Humm," I said, thinking. "We may have to try that. It sounds faster."

"It is," he said, beaming. "The bad part is that you may have to move the wagons under fire and risk confusion."

"I'll keep it in mind," I said. The man's name was Howard. He was about the same height as I was, clean shaven. It was said that he fought on the side of the Union and received a wound in battle. He'd come out West after his discharge to open a store, but the first one he built was burnt in a fire in '63. The second one was built on credit and was washed away in the flood of '64. Since then, he'd been a gambler and hired hand on some of the larger ranches in the area. Most everyone called him "Bad Luck" Howard.

I could tell that some of the men weren't at all happy that Howard was coming along. But, he was a soldier and a good one. He knew a bit of tactics and was proven under fire, which meant a lot to me.

We moved out of town in the still and darkness of early morning. First, three of us rode out and down the street, then came the wagons and the last four men came out later. I rode with the first group so I could pick out the route I'd followed into town. I wanted to take Loving's trail back down into New Mexico. It was a fairly straight route and we'd had little trouble. There was grass and water along that trail.

Once out of town, we formed the separate pieces of the company back together for best defense out in the open.

The sun rose in the east just as the city was out of sight. The mountains turned orange as rays of light hit the tops and eased down the slope until it spread wide over the plains.

I kept an eye out for dangers and scouted the trail ahead, the way I'd seen Goodnight and Loving do. At noon, I picked a spot to camp that provided protection from whomever might want to attack. We pulled the wagons in an arc against a bank that allowed us cover from the front. The men could also gain position above the wagon by climbing the bank and shooting from behind trees and rocks. It seemed like a good place, but I wondered what a tactician would think of it. I compared my reasonings to those of General Bedford Forrest and others. I wished I could have learned more from them. I couldn't help but feel totally inadequate.

I gathered the men around at that moment and explained that I was open to suggestions, that others had more experience with warfare than I did. I told them I'd be willing to listen to suggestions, but that the final say was up to me and what I said would be the end of it. They nodded and kept silent.

"Most of you have heard of me. I'm more inclined to fight head-on. I don't like taking defensive measures and therefore, have learned little of it. But, I must fight my nature at this point and protect these goods. Finish your coffee and let's get back on the trail. Every mile we make today, the less we have to worry from those who might follow us," I said, looking about at the men.

When we were rolling again, I studied the men who rode with me. They were nervous and continually scouted to their left and right. While I watched the mountains for signs of ambush, they watched the plains. I figured that I was missing something and fell in with one of the men at the rear.

"Why's everyone watching the plains? The best source of cover is from the mountains."

"Injuns like to hide in hollows and attack from level ground. Bandits like the mountains. Injuns are more likely to be afoot, bandits have horses. Bandits like the goods in the wagons, Injuns like to scalp and take horses."

"What does that mean?"

"It means," he said, spitting tobacco, "that we're more afraid of Injuns than bandits."

We made the first day without incident and put up camp. My fears were lessening for a bandit attack. I was sure that if bandits were going to attack, it would be close to Denver, where they could turn the wagons around, drive them close to town, empty them and set them on fire.

Some of the men I'd picked didn't get along with each other. It was obvious before we started out, but I didn't think too much of it. By the time we made camp, the tempers were rising. I felt obliged to make another speech.

"Listen," I said, moving into the circle as they sat about drinking coffee. "I know there's some problems with some of you men. I don't expect you to dance with each other, but for God's sake, let's behave ourselves until we get these wagons through. Then you can shoot each other as far as I'm concerned. The first man that makes trouble will hear from me," I said, letting the threat hang in the air.

The men respected my Colt. I thought a lot of what was said about me was garbage. I was fast with a gun, I knew that, but it'd been taken almost to a mystical level by the newspapers and rumor mongers. But, if those men feared my gun enough, regardless of what caused it, I knew I could keep the lid on boiling tempers.

I walked away into the darkness and had to smile. I was bluffing. Oh, I'd shoot someone I thought was trying to kill another, that was true enough, but I felt like a fraud using my imaginary status as a "quick-draw" to intimidate them.

While I enjoyed the clean, cool air of that wonderful elevation, I looked up into the star-filled sky and felt suddenly as if I didn't have control of the situation. The men would get tired of threats and speeches before the journey was complete. I needed to take one of them into my confidence to act as a window into the feelings of the others.

"Howard," I called into the group.

Howard came out, with his rifle in both hands, ready to throw it to his shoulder.

"I want to talk to you," I said, and watched him let one hand fall from the rifle.

"What is it?"

"You know all these men, or most of them, right?"

"Yep."

"Look, I don't know what's going on with them. I don't know who's causing trouble and who's fighting back. I need you to let me know what's happening."

"Well," he began, "that old Joe Hawkins, he's a miserable cuss and tries to make it miserable for everyone else. He keeps talking about how we're goin' to be kilt and strung up and have our skin pulled off by Injuns. And, Billy Walters," he continued, "that's the fella with the big feather stickin' out of his hat, he's scared to death of Injuns cause his family was attacked by 'em in Kansas."

"Is that all?"

"No, there's other squabbles."

"All right," I said, "let me know if any of it gets close to a shooting."

"I don't know, it might be that close now."

"I just warned them, let them know I was serious."

"They know you was serious," he said, fidgeting. "First time there's any gambling, they'll use that as an excuse to go at each other."

"I don't want any gambling going on."

"Well, they're gettin' a game up now."

I wanted to be a good supervisor, like I'd wanted to be a good overseer at my father's plantation. Why couldn't men just follow some rules and avoid all the trouble. It was easy enough to see how the trouble started.

I went over to the fire and put a stop to the game.

"Gamble in Santa Fe," I said, with a stern face.

I realized then, that I didn't want the job. I wanted to be free and wander about. I wanted to herd cattle and do a job. I didn't like pushing men, I wanted them to go along voluntarily and do the job out of pride.

We'd just extinguished the fire, put our heads to the saddles and had fallen asleep when the first arrow stuck in the side of one of the wagons. I'd left some watches out, but heard nothing from them.

"Don't let the horses get away," I yelled at Howard, who was watching them.

"They're okay," he said, from out of the darkness.

I pulled the Spencer from my scabbard and crawled along the ground, trying to use the sky to spot the Indians. I heard a shot ring out to the right side of my position, then the left. The men had gotten into the free ammunition already.

"Stay out of that," I yelled, but didn't expect to be obeyed.

There were more shots fired into the darkness, but I couldn't find a single Indian.

"Hey, do you see anything?"

"No," a man replied and fired his weapon at the seeming source of the arrow.

"Then what are you shooting at?"

"Indians," he said.

"Where?"

The man shrugged his shoulders and kept on firing. Young Billy Walters was standing in front of the wagons screaming for the Indians to come and get him. Then, he shot into the night and reloaded.

"Check behind us," I said, to Joe Hawkins. Then, I asked if the horses were still there.

"Yeah," Howard replied, "they're getting jumpy with all of the shootin' going on, though."

"Hold your fire," I yelled. There was a dead silence, except for the ringing in my ears. Then two, or three arrows arced into the pack of men from different directions. Shots went in every direction like an explosion set off by the arrows.

"Don't shoot the horses," I screamed, hoping it'd be heard above the noise.

"Don't shoot me," Howard yelled back.

"Has anyone seen an Indian, yet?" I asked, and wasn't surprised to find out that none of them had. As soon as they all replied in the negative, another volley of gunfire erupted from the group. Then, far off, there was a flash and the sound of a rifle. Everyone emptied their weapons in the direction of the report.

"They've got guns," someone screamed in terror.

"Stop shootin'," Howard said, then yelled out to the voice. "Come on in."

One of the sentries came in dragging the body of a young Cheyenne warrior.

"There's a couple of others out there, but I think they took off for home," Lefty Rangle announced. "I saw them sneaking up on the horses and got to the right of them before they starting firing arrows. I don't think they meant any real harm. Hard to tell with an Injun," he said.

"We ought to bury him," I suggested.

"Damned if I will," Lefty replied and went back out to keep watch.

None of the others would help dig the hole. I didn't understand their attitudes, nor them mine. I got out a shovel from one of the wagons and dug a grave. It was after midnight by the time I dropped the little body into it and covered it up. The others watched with great curiosity and not a little cussing and spitting. But, I felt bad about the boy being killed.

They'd stoked the fire up again. No one felt much like sleeping after that, and I sent out more sentries and asked the men who were going to sleep, to sleep away from the fire so they'd have a better chance of seeing whoever decided to attack us. We were caught with our pants down and it wasn't very flattering to have all of those shots being fired into the air.

I went to the fire and brought back a torch. I pulled the Bible out of my saddlebag and read a passage over the grave. It was the 20th Psalm and it seemed fitting, under the circumstances. I finished with a flourish and closed the Bible. It seemed strange in my hand, in that place. Though, I don't know what other place would inspire one to think of God as much, or understand Him as well. There was beauty, power, grass and streams and death.

The night passed with anxiety. Each man looked well beyond the campfire. Several men were now standing watch, circling our position to ensure that we weren't attacked again. Some slept fitfully and were glad to wake and take up a post outside the campfire.

I sat down, after the burial, and had a cup of coffee. There'd be no sleeping for me.

"Why'd you go and bury that little Injun? And, why on earth did you read the good book over his grave?" one of the men asked. "They's all savages. They don't believe in God anyways."

"Maybe, God believes in them," I replied.

"Now, I've seen it all. I could die right now and be happy, 'cause I've seen a preachin' pistoleer," Joe Hawkins said, smiling at me with contempt.

"Don't let it worry you, Joe," I replied. "I'll read the Bible over your grave, too."

"That's impossible," he said, "'cause I ain't gonna die." He rolled over and pulled his blanket up around his shoulders and tried to get some sleep.

We had no more trouble on the trail. A band of Indians, probably the boy's tribe of Cheyenne, trailed us for the next day, but they were far off and we moved as fast as the oxen would go. It wasn't very fast. I decided that the Cheyenne were just seeing that we didn't stay too long. There was plenty of them and if they wanted to take us, they could have. Of course, they'd have only gotten the wagons. We already had plans to leave them and drive our horses to death if we had to, to escape.

It was a fine August day when we pulled into Santa Fe. There was some sort of Celebration going on. None of us knew what it was about. We drove the supplies up to Fort Marcy. It seems that the real value of the shipment had been disguised from us so as to secure the transfer of fifty Winchester repeating rifles. All of the ammunition for them had been likewise disguised under sacks of flour, sugar, vegetables and the like. Except for a rocking chair, almost the whole of the shipment was subterfuge for the real items.

In all, the load was worth some two thousand dollars. Which made our cut two hundred. I went into the paymaster's office to get the complete sum to take back to Denver.

The sergeant behind the desk made me sign for the money and brought forth a cable recently sent from Denver. I took the paper and the money and walked out into the sunshine. I divided up the two hundred dollars, keeping fifty for myself as the one who'd had the most responsibility. No one seemed to object to receiving twenty-five dollars for a week's work. The teamsters were paid by their boss back in Denver.

The others had dispersed, except the teamsters, who were busy unloading the cargo with help from the soldiers. I stood on the boardwalk and read the cable.

STORE BURNED

OWNER DEAD

FAMILY SOLD THE WAGONS

TEAMSTERS TO BRING PROCEEDS

Well, if that wasn't something. That's why no one came after us the first day. They were burning the fat man out. I suppose that was the end of that. I showed the drivers the cable, handed them the owner's money to take back to the widow and went out to find a cold beer.

My fortunes had come and gone so quickly. Everything was at a fast pace in the Frontier. A man could win, lose and win, again, all in the same day. This time, I had plenty of money in my pocket and I could spend some time in Santa Fe. It was a nice town and the Army kept things fairly peaceful.

I untied my horse from the hitching post and walked down the center of the main street. I could already smell beer from a saloon up the street. Then, I thought of the Bible and the words in it. They were beautiful words to me and I'd not been paying much attention to them the past couple of months. I hadn't even been to church, except when old Bill Dixon died. It wouldn't hurt me to spend some time thanking the good Lord for saving my life as many times as he had.

I found a small Catholic church called San Miguel and tied the faithful gelding up outside. I took the Bible from my saddlebags and went in. A Catholic church was not my first choice, but I didn't think there'd be any other kind in Santa Fe.

The priest was not there at the time and I sat down on one of the rickety pews. Surely, somewhere, there had to be a much grander church. But, it didn't matter to me. I wasn't there as a critic, but as a sinner. I opened the book on my lap and began to read.

20

After praying and reading the Bible, I went back out into the sunshine. It was incredibly hot and dusty. I untied the gelding, put the Bible back into the saddlebags and walked down to the hotel for a room. I stopped in the saloon for a beer.

All, or most, of the buildings, including the San Miguel Church, were made of adobe. I'd seen some of it in Texas, and on the way up to Denver, but it seemed a curious building material to be used so extensively. I walked the streets feeling that I'd passed into Mexico itself.

When I entered the saloon, it was almost empty. There were a few New Mexicans, if that's what Mexicans in New Mexico were called. It was different from Texas in the way that many of the businessmen and community leaders, aside from the military, were of Mexican origin. At least, it wasn't that way in Northern Texas.

I was feeling quite out of place in the saloon. I drank my beer and decided to get a room. I wondered if a bath would be available and was told that the barber had the only facilities for taking baths. My whiskers were becoming something to deal with as I approached nineteen. As usual, I thought of buying clothes. I wanted to be true to my father's prediction that if I looked like a gentleman, that I might be treated as such. But, then, every time I bought new clothes, I got shot. I was tired of being shot and laid up. The leg had not quite healed from the last wound and I walked with a noticeable limp. When I rode, there was pain, but I could disguise my weakness on horseback.

I locked my valuables in my room, turned the horse over to the livery and went to the barbershop. I stepped into the place and removed my hat. I placed it on the hat rack and took a seat in the chair.

"Que Pasa, Senor?" the barber asked.

I stared at him with a blank expression, hit suddenly with a panic of inability to communicate and fearful of what the man might do without specific guidance.

"What would you like, Mister?"

I exhaled loudly and told him what I wanted. His English was thick and accented, but understandable. I told him that I needed a bath, to which he agreed quite emphatically. I didn't know if I smelled that poorly, or if he just wanted to sell the accommodation.

It occurred to me, as I sat, feeling my face being scraped by the sharp razor, that I should learn a bit of Spanish if I intended to make my home in the Southwest, away from the Reconstruction policies of the Union.

When the barber finished with my shave, he wrapped a hot towel around my face.

"Cigarro?" he asked, and I opened my eyes to see a cigar being extended. Why not? I thought, reaching for it. He brought me a flaming stick from out of the fire that was used to heat water and towels.

While I sat with my face in the towel, he prepared a hot bath. I took the cigar with me to the bath tub. I hung up my clothes, revealing pale white skin under them. Any part of me exposed to the sun was dark brown and weathered.

Everything beneath was white. I looked strange to myself, standing behind a curtain with different colored parts.

I stepped into the hot water and slid halfway to my chest. I soaped my various body parts, whether white, or brown and relaxed with the cigar. I wanted a bottle of whiskey to soothe my mind as well. I opened my eyes and looked toward the curtain. I jerked in surprise and the water made an abrupt sloshing sound.

"Welcome to our city," the local priest said, beaming with a strangely familiar face.

"Father," I replied, staring at him.

"You needn't be so formal, lad," Donnigan replied, his face missing the beard that was always in my recollections of him.

"Donnigan? Is that you? What...what?" I tried to ask, but was so astonished that I was speechless. He boomed with a great roar of laughter.

"Aye," he said, "I'm a priest. There's so much you didn't know about me. And, to be sure, I was as astonished to see you in my church this morning looking as strange to me as I do to you, now."

"A lot has happened since then," I said.

"To be sure, but this isn't the time to speak of it. Come to the church this evening and we'll have a meal and then some discussion."

I nodded my head. Donnigan turned and left me to my cigar and to soak. I thought of him often since we'd parted, but mostly when I was put in a position of danger. He was the greatest teacher of pugilism, and now he was a priest? It didn't make sense any way I turned it. Obviously, I hadn't known him as well as I thought. What could have turned a religious man into a killer and back again?

I looked forward to the conversation. I was grateful to find someone who knew me for who I was, who could understand the world I'd known and what I'd been forced to endure on the Frontier. Mostly, I wanted a chance to go back in time, to remember what it was like to be a kid hoping to see some action. I'd seen plenty of action since then.

I spent the rest of the day replenishing my supplies that'd been diminished over the past several months. I bought a few cigars for Donnigan and some whiskey as a present. Then, when the sun was losing force and edging toward the horizon, I walked to the church. In the back, there were quarters for the priest and I went to the outside door and knocked.

"Welcome," Donnigan said, and I entered.

The room was small. A cot lay to one side and a table set against a wall beneath the lone window. The table was covered with plates of bean mush, vegetables, meat and a bottle of wine set in the middle. It was quite lavish accommodations and much more than I'd expected.

"I hope you still take whiskey now and again," I said.

"Aye, though drunkeness is not tolerated as it used to be. We'll save it for later."

"Cigars?"

"Aye, a good cigar is always welcome," he said, smiling in a benevolent way that didn't fit with his character as I'd known him.

Meeting Donnigan again was like meeting an old friend and a new acquaintance. I was a little unsure of how to act, or what might offend him. Every time I began to broach an old issue, his priestly dress confused me and kept me silent. We ate and spoke in the most polite terms. It was a superficial exchange of words that alluded to nothing deeper than the bountiful food and the humble quarters.

When we'd finished dinner, I helped him with the dishes and we sat around the clean table. I placed the whiskey on top and he turned and brought out two glasses from a wooden cupboard. He stuck a piece of wood into the small stove and pulled out fire for us to light the cigars.

"You've grown," he said, settling back into his chair, puffing on the cigar and sipping the whiskey.

"Yes," I said, blushing.

"Have you gotten used to it, yet?"

"What?"

"Seeing me as a priest?"

"No."

He laughed a good-hearted laugh. "It's not as strange as you might believe. I was in the Seminary when the Rebellion started. From what I'd studied about the Constitution, I believed that the Rebellion was legal and proper and I placed most of the blame for the fighting on the Union. They should've simply let the Southern States secede." He smiled, "what good is it to have a 'free' nation if the people are kept from pursuing life on their terms, with their own form of government?"

I nodded. "My sentiments exactly."

"So," he said, "I took leave from the Seminary and went to fight for freedom. There were some conflicts within my heart, but I was not yet a priest and felt it was my duty."

"But, you're such a good fighter," I said.

"I'm Irish," he replied, as if that should answer all questions. "My brothers were all excellent wrestlers and fighters. There are some priests who are quite good fighters, lad."

"I'll keep that in mind for the future," I replied.

Donnigan roared with laughter.

"Why New Mexico?" I asked.

"I'm a new priest and this part of the country is seen as fertile ground for the training of priests. Hardships, diverse cultures, humility, chastity, opportunities for good works, everything a priest should learn be here. There be plenty of temptations toward evil. The bishops practice a divining of the soul here, assuming that one survives the trip out from civilization."

We looked at each other in silence. I'd overlooked his good heart during the war. What a man Donnigan was, what a complete and complex individual.

"And, what of you, Jeff? What have you been up to?"

I laughed. He didn't want to know how I'd drifted so easily toward evil.

"You name it," I said. "I've done some awful things and only a few good."

"And, yet, the first thing you do when you come to my city, is pray."

"Yeah," I said, "don't take it the wrong way. It's been such a long time since I've opened the Bible. A few nights ago, I pulled it out of my saddlebags and read over the body of a young Cheyenne warrior. He was no older than 14. That was the first time I'd thought of the bible in a long time."

"But, you came here to pray before anything else."

"That's not entirely true," I said. "I squared my accounts with the man I worked for."

"And, yet, you came to pray."

I wished he'd let it go. What was he trying to get at? So, I prayed. I should've been praying more. Again, people were trying to reward me for a misunderstanding.

"Yeah, I did."

"I must confess, lad," he said, leaning forward to pour more whiskey into our glasses. "I've heard of you in the past months."

"Oh?" I asked, shocked that there was anything to say about me. I wondered who'd been talking and what he'd heard.

"Aye." He winked and smiled. "There were more stories this morning. The others be telling whopping stories of you."

"Well, I don't know what I've done to warrant such talk."

"Your modesty aside, won't you tell me of it?"

"I've made out the best I could. I've done some things that I'm not particularly proud of in the meantime, but I've done as well as I'm able."

Donnigan's smile was both pious and smug. He puffed on the cigar.

"Tell me of Ned Smith," he said.

I was shocked, dumbfounded and my head reeled from the mention of his name. I narrowed my eyes in suspicion.

"How do you know about Ned?"

Donnigan laughed.

"I thought that'd shake you up." He laughed again, "Aye, it had a wonderful effect on you. You must lose consistently at poker," he remarked.

"No, at poker I'm quite good," I said. "Now, how do you know about Ned?"

"Well, I'd have to start all the way back. As far back as the war."

"I've got time," I said, anxious to hear it. If he knew about Ned, he might know about everything I'd done.

"You won't be liking my story," he said, judging me, thinking about me and puffing on the cigar.

"I've grown up a bit."

"Aye, that you have, Jeff. That you have." He leaned forward to rest his elbows on the table, and I felt myself lean forward in conspiratorial interest.

"What do you think about the activities surrounding your father?"

"My father? What's this got to do with him?"

"Everything, my boy. I told you it went back to the war," he said, grinning and testing my resolve.

My chest was tight, the way it was when I talked to William. I didn't want to hear anything critical, or false about my father. I battled with myself over the issue. I thought I should leave before any illusions were shattered, or I was forced to hate Donnigan for what he was about to say.

"Are you man enough to handle the truth? That's what you're asking yourself, isn't it?"

"I'm cautious," I said.

"Well, I'll not tell you a word unless you'll receive it as the truth. I wouldn't wish to become your enemy." He took a drink of the whiskey. "Know this," he said, "your father isn't what you think. He isn't what any of us thought. Don't feel betrayed, because you were deceived like the rest. Beware that what I have to say is only slightly complimentary of the man."

"I thought you were going to tell me how you heard of Ned. I don't know why this has to go through my father and the war."

"They be connected," he said. "As inextricable as light is from day. To answer you, is to reveal the whole operation of your father. Oh, I could say, 'so and so told me', but that wouldn't answer how I know about Ned."

My palms were growing sweaty and I could feel the perspiration under my arms. My head was numb and I had difficulty thinking things through. I seemed poised on the edge of disaster and struggled to put things back the way they were, but it was useless. Even if I'd left right then, I'd have come back to find out the horrible truth, whatever it was.

"It's a sign of your ultimate goodness that you struggle with this decision. If I'd not seen you pray this morning, I'd not brought it up. But, you must agree, lad, that all righteousness begins with the truth. Surely, the lie is easier to live with sometimes, but a lie won't pass through the door of righteousness. If you seek Heaven, you know that it's only through purity of the heart that it may be obtained. Even if you were not aware of the falsity of yourself, God would surely know and punish you on Judgment Day."

"But," I countered, "I've not been false."

Donnigan smiled broadly. "Nay, you've not. Not until this moment have you had to choose whether to become false, or not. But, now, with the facts available and what you heard from the mouth of William Flout, you must either discover the truth, or be faithful to the lie. Isn't that what tortures you?"

"How do you know about William? How do you know what was said?"

"Nay, I'll not tell you the pleasant half of what you want to know."

In the end, when I thought about it, there was no other choice. However it may hurt, I had to know.

"Begin," I said, taking a long drink of the whiskey.

"Your father ran quite an organization. He had people everywhere. Everywhere. In the bedrooms of Union generals and political appointees. A lot of his people be the likes of prostitutes and barkeeps. In a week, he could tell what Lincoln had for breakfast, what medicines he took, what he wrote about in his diaries. He knew when Lincoln doubted the abilities of his generals, which was often. Who he trusted, everything. The war was fought as much in Washington backrooms as it was on the skirmish lines. The soldiers in the war of the backrooms were called, Silent Soldiers.

"Aye, your father was a brilliant man. He never failed to exploit an opening.   Lord," he said, in whistful recollection, "he exerted himself in his attempts to have Grant dismissed. He knew a capable man, he did. All of the horrible things that were said about him were right out of your father's mouth. Not that some of them weren't true, but he had friends in the newspapers, Congress and the White House.

"If you recall, and only as proof that what I'm saying is true, how harassed Grant was when he was close to Vicksburg? Don't you recall the stories printed that said he was often drunk, and more often, incompetent? That be your father's doing. I can see by the look on your face that you're beginning to believe."

I nodded. I did recall the stories and how my father delighted in them. I remembered him saying that he wanted to see him dismissed from command. A lot of it made sense in retrospect.

"Yes, I believe you. I've distinct memories of what you're saying. But, all of this was his duty."

"Aye. I agree completely, but you've not heard all of it."

"Continue," I said.

"So, this is how it began, with Silent Soldiers. This is how and why he built such a complicated and far-reaching organization. Then, something happened. You remember it, don't you?" he asked, staring deep into my eyes.

"I don't know what you're talking about."

"The murder in the cabin."

I shook my head. What murder?

"Oh," I said, remembering. "That was no murder, it was a suicide."

"Aye, you said that at the time, but we thought you murdered the man for one reason, or another."

"But, I didn't!" I insisted.

"It matters not," he said, waving off my determination. "I believe you, but at the time we didn't. We thought he might have said something against the Cause, or your father, or you'd unfortunately said something you shouldn't have and were covering your tracks.

"The point is," he continued, "your father thought it was a murder and he had to cover it up, or it might lead the Union soldiers to his doorstep. By the way," he interrupted himself, "we had orders to hunt you down and kill you if you went to confess the crime. That's why he moved you away from that route and sent you elsewhere."

"My father was going to have me killed?"

"It be war, lad. I forgave him, for even that, under the circumstances. In fact, I was afraid I'd be the one to kill you."

I ran my fingers through my hair and exhaled. I was being overwhelmed and wanted to put a stop to it.

"Anyway," he said, "you didn't. I'm grateful for that, lad. But, what happened as a result of covering up the murder..."

"Suicide."

"Suicide, as you prefer. After the suicide, he realized how easily some things could be manipulated and he took on a darker side of himself. He developed another army in his war against the Washington bunch. These men became known as Shadow Soldiers. The Shadow Soldier would act on passive information provided by the Silent Soldier. The Shadow Soldier carried out assassinations, planted evidence, the physical side of things. Your father was brilliant at this side of the war effort. He came up with complicated schemes to bring about the downfall of key personnel in Congress. He blackmailed, threatened, offered information, whatever it took.

Then, he started to realize the Confederacy wasn't going to win and he went on a campaign to save himself. Of course, I didn't know about any of that until much later."

"What do you mean?"

"He offered information both ways. He'd take Confederate secrets and leak them to endear himself to the Union. He be responsible for bringing about the final taking of Atlanta. It was inevitable, lad, but the Union was wasting so many lives in the taking that your father expedited it to secure himself as a worthy source of information.

"You see, your father was changing this whole time. He was slowly becoming someone else, indeed. He was interested only in himself and to secure his power beyond the war. He kept up with the events of the day and used them to blackmail. He gave out Confederate secrets to ensure his place in Reconstruction.

"Then, came the final betrayal. He helped them to capture Jefferson Davis..."

Donnigan had barely spoken the words, when I jumped from my seat and held the Colt in my hand. His eyes grew large and I saw the barrel waver. I couldn't catch my breath. Who was Donnigan? How could he say that my father would help the Union capture the President?

Donnigan dropped his gaze to the table and played with the whiskey glass.

"You be ready to kill me, now. I like the thought of it in you. To protect your beloved father. You've proven that you can do it. But, you know I be speaking the truth. Who else knew where the President would be? Are you telling me your father couldn't protect him right there in the heart of the South?"

My anger began to lessen. I knew he was right, but it left me shaken. If my father wasn't who I thought he was, who did that make me? I could accept being the son of someone who was a traitor to the Union, but not one who was a traitor to both the Union and the Confederacy.

"Put the gun away, lad, and sit down."

I did as he asked. I felt empty and dirty. I was ashamed and the guilt of killing William and Gregory came to me in full force. They had every right to tell me of the dealings my father'd taken part in. They were honest and good and I shot them down for it. No, that wasn't right either. They victimized others. They weren't clean, but they were right.

"Well, I can see the rumors be true about the speed of your pull. It's becoming a legend in these parts and all the way to Texas. That incident in Denver is well known hereabouts."

"Tell me the rest of it," I said, suddenly tired, soul weary.

"Aye, there's more to tell. After making the capture of the President easy for the Federals, your father was in. We didn't learn of it right away."

"Who's we?"

"I'm getting to that. Be patient, lad. We didn't learn of it right away," he continued, "not until some of us started getting arrested and shot for treason. Your father gave testimony against those in the Union White House. Later, others were shot, or hung. It became obvious that your father was feeding us to the Union for favors. One by one. That's when people started telling others all the things they knew he'd been involved in. He may kill us, but we refused to take our secrets to our graves. So, to protect ourselves, we set up an organization of our own.

"We watch everything he does and whoever he's with. That's how I know all that you've done, except for certain times. When we discovered his association with the Federals and saw people dying, we organized ourselves. We found you in Sherman while you were a lawman. We lost you again until you showed up in Fort Sumner. When we knew your destination, we contacted someone there. You see, most of us have fled to the Frontier to escape his tyranny. There are scores of us hiding out here."

"Who were these people? They weren't the same ones. How'd you know where to put them?"

"We be not gypsies, lad. We can't divine where you're going. We wait to see where you can be found and hope we have someone there to look in on you. You must understand the brilliance of your father. We all have certain names and reach each other through only two other people. No one, not to this day, know who, or how many people are involved, except your father. But, he's lost track of us and searches with all means to root us out."

"This is ridiculous, you can't keep living like this. How long do you think you can keep it all together? This secret society of yours?"

"Nay, we can't. Already, people are being tortured to reveal the locations of our people. He's still eliminating us, but at a slower pace."

Donnigan took another drink of the whiskey and re-lit his cigar. He took a deep pull and blew smoke into a cloud.

"We have to kill him," he said, calmly, clearly and without regret, or remorse.

"When?"

"Soon," he said, watching me. "Aye, now you're beginning to see it. You see the havoc he's wreaking, you can understand the carnage he's responsible for. He'll kill everyone who can prove his part in the capture of Jefferson

Davis. That's the secret he's most afraid will come to light.
It'd ruin him in the South and he knows it. So far, there are
only rumors."

"Okay, but what have I got to do with it? Why have you
been watching me? How do I present a danger to you? I
didn't even know about this."

"Well," he said, swallowing hard. "You're his only
weakness, lad."

"What are you saying?" I asked, my eyes narrowing.

"You be the only one who can get to him. We've tried to
kill him already. He's alerted now and has guards
constantly around. He's awfully powerful. No amount of
Reconstruction policy is undertaken in Mississippi that
doesn't receive his approval. He's building a virtual
empire."

"You want me to get someone inside so they can kill
him?"

"Nay, nothing as easy as that. We want you to be our
Shadow Soldier. We want you to kill him."

I leapt from the chair, but didn't draw the Colt. I went
for the door. I opened it and looked out into the darkness. I
took a deep breath.

"What if I won't do it?" I asked, over my shoulder.

"Then, more of us will die and his dark secrets will be
safe. Do you want me to threaten you? It's not that easy,
lad. This be no gunfight you can pretend is self-defense.
You have to take a moral stand against a man who's become
a monster. You have to be able to recognize it and lust for
his death as much as we do. You have to do it because you
see the evil in him and all that he does. It be your God he
has betrayed as well as ours. It be your Cause as well as
ours. We're counting on your goodness of heart to make you
do the right thing."

"How did you know I'd wind up here in Santa Fe? You must have known that I'd only listen to this from someone like yourself, someone I knew back then. I killed William and Gregory, my childhood friends, for less than what I've heard tonight."

"Aye, we knew that well. When we were sure of your heart, we'd have found a way. But, the fact that we happened to find each other, like this, is proof that it's God's will that's to be done."

"Don't use God's name to legitimize your filthy plan," I protested.

"Do you know a better reason for your appearance on my step, in my church, of all places, just when you did? Could it be the work of any other? Nay, it's not."

I left then. I walked out into the night and felt a cool breeze. It was still hot, even with the sun down, but a cool wind rose off the desert floor and blew through the streets of Santa Fe.

I felt as if I were in prison. I was trapped by the thoughts that were planted in my brain by Donnigan. What a filthy business all of it was. And, my father. What sort of twisted old man had be become? How could I face him, let alone kill him? It was too much to ask of a son.

I went back to the hotel and went to bed. I lay on the soft mattress and stared up at the dark ceiling. Below, I could hear the carefree sounds of the saloon. I realized then, that my life had been one of strife and struggle and far from the aristocratic wonderland I'd dreamed of as a child. All the important things I'd wanted to do. What misspent youth. Even before I was nineteen, I'd been ruined.

I fought and struggled with my conscience. I drifted to sleep only when the sun began to pale the eastern sky.

21

The next day I sat in my room and thought. I thought until I had a headache. How could I put all of those childhood memories behind me and hate the man I'd loved with such devotion? Regardless of what he'd become in life, no matter how he'd blackened his own soul, how was I to walk in and kill him? I didn't see a way to do it. Finally, after I could think no more, I decided to tell Donnigan to find someone else.

I walked into his shabby church and sat down on the wooden bench. I had no Bible and sat quietly. Before long, Donnigan appeared with a pleasant smile. He walked up to me, his hand extended. I stood and greeted him.

"Come into the back," he said, "unless you'd prefer to make a confession."

"It'd take too long," I replied, and walked with him.

When we were settled, I saw the half empty bottle of whiskey on a shelf. I noticed that his hands were shaking a bit.

"I can't do it," I said, knowing this was neither the time, nor the place for such a discussion.

He nodded in silent understanding.

"Aye, it's your goodness. I should've known, but don't despise me for the suggestion. We be desperate as all who face certain death." He sat in deep contemplation. "But, could you do me one wee favor?"

"If I can," I said.

"Go see your father in Mississippi. Pay the man a visit. It's the only way you can understand the nature of the thing we ask." He looked over his shoulder as if not wanting to be overheard.

"I've been sent here to make my own mark in the world. It's what he asked of me."

Donnigan roared with laughter.

"Aye, you've done that, me boy. You've done that already. See how many have heard of you as you travel back through Texas. Your name is well known there."

"They don't even know my name," I said.

"Aye, that's true, but they know the name J.D. Wilkes. You be fancied a pistoleer and a lawman."

"How could they know?"

A twinkle came to his eye and a broad grin drew slowly across his face.

"Your men?"

"Aye," he replied. "We do what we can."

"Why?"

"Now, you be respected and feared. Your whereabouts are easier to track. News of your arrival appears everywhere in the newspapers, lad. Your coming to town is an event to be noted by the community."

I thought it through. They had me coming and going.

"Clyde's one of your people, isn't he?"

This time, it was Donnigan's turn to be startled.

"Nay, I know no one by that name."

"It's a sin to lie, Father," I said, smirking. He smiled. "If I go back, see my father, and still don't kill him, are you going to kill me, or have me killed?"

"Nay, lad, that's none of my affair. I'd certainly have no hand in it. What others do is none of my concern. I be a man of God, but some of them are not."

"I'm leaving town today. I say that so you can rest easy. You don't have to send anyone to find me. I imagine you'll hear of my movements from now on in any case. I've enjoyed our conversations, though I don't care for the outcome. I have a great respect for you and hope to see you again on friendly terms."

"Aye, lad. You've nothing to fear from me."

"That's a comfort," I said, walking out. I went directly to the general store, bought more ammunition for my rifle and revolver and gathered my horse. It was going to be a lonely ride from then on. I hoped to find Loving at the Bosque Redondo. Perhaps some of Loving's men would be itching to get back to Texas and I could trail along with them. I didn't know, but I wasn't relishing a ride back all alone. If there were two of us, one could stand guard while the other slept.

I tied the horse up at the hotel and went in to wait for morning. Wherever I went, I wasn't about to start out halfway through the day. In anticipation of the long wait, I brought up the bible. I thought I'd read from it a bit. I flipped through the pages, now worn and dirty. I read until the light faded in the room and I put it aside.

My reading had been mechanical, functional, but I realized that the messages within were not geared to a land such as the Frontier, where killing was the only way to survive. Did God separate killing a white man from killing an Indian? Though, I'd done more killing of white men than Indians, I wondered if there could be a difference. I pondered such spiritual questions until dark. The saloon below grew lively and I could hear the laughter and sounds of Mexican voices.

I lay down on the bed and slept for several hours. I was tortured by thoughts of my father. When had I decided to go to Mississippi? I didn't recall making the decision, but that was my intent. I thought about that for a while, deciding that I'd made the decision simultaneous to deciding that I wouldn't kill him.

I'd previously felt that I'd been consigned to the Frontier for a period of time, a duration that would come and then I'd be free to return to my lovely state. After talking with Donnigan, I realized that there were no such restrictions. Yet, I liked the West with all of its opportunities. If my father were doing as well as they said, perhaps he'd loan me the capital to buy some cattle.

Whatever my father'd done, or was in the process of doing was none of my business. I'd have to deal with whomever came after me when they came. It was simply too much to ask that I kill my own father. But, I'd return to Vicksburg to see for myself what had become of the great man I admired.

That morning, I rode for the Bosque Redondo. I met up with a branch of the Pecos and followed it down. I was making pretty good time in comparison to what I could accomplish pushing cattle, or wagons. I stayed clear of people, animals and any sort of life, as all life presented a danger. In a few days, I found myself within earshot of Loving's outfit cutting trees and building a barracks. Goodnight had brought the other herd up and was also at the barracks when I rode in.

I kept my face forward and eased into camp. The boys stopped their work and stared at me as if I were an Indian riding into their fort. I didn't acknowledge them, but rode right up to the barracks. Jack stood by the door with his rifle cradled in his arm.

"What's on yur mind?"

"I mean to speak with Mr. Loving," I replied.

"He's inside."

"That's where I'm going," I said, stepping up to the door. Inside, Loving and Goodnight sat at a table. They were visibly affected by my entrance. To one side of the large hall, with cots scattered about, One-Armed Bill stood holding a coffee pot. He paused for a moment and poured himself a cup.

"Coffee?" he asked.

"I'd appreciate that, Bill," I said.

Loving and Goodnight extended their hands. I shook with them and they offered me a seat. I pulled up a wooden chair and sat down.

"What's brought you here?" Loving asked.

"Well, I'm headed back through Texas. I ain't staying, I'm going back to Mississippi."

They nodded and Bill set a cup of coffee before me.

"Thank you," I said, and looked back at the two men.

"We ain't moving this outfit until Spring," Goodnight said.

"I figured that," I replied, "but, I was wondering if you knew of a more direct route to Texas from here. I don't want to follow that God-forsaken Pecos all the way back."

The two men laughed, understanding my sentiments.

"Well," Goodnight said, "you can try your luck across the Staked Plains. That's the way I took last July. It's a treacherous route. You'll have to ride at night and hide out during the day. Get your horse fed up before you head out and take as much water as you can hold. We'll see if we can't find a few extra canteens for ya. There's a lot more Injuns and snakes that way."

"Can't be more snakes," I replied.

The group of them broke into a good-hearted ream of laughter.

"You may be right," Loving replied.

I left that afternoon. I hoped to travel as far as I could during the day and keep it going during the night, then hole up in the morning. In following Goodnight's hastily drawn map, I made it deep into the Staked Plains by dawn. As the sun was rising in the East, I looked for a spot to hole up. There was a small dip in the landscape off to the left and I went toward it.

When I topped the crest of the small rise, I looked into the hollow. There was an old wagon, long forgotten and charred. The belongings, what could be carried on a horse, were gone. The other things, furniture and farming equipment were left in the wagon, which was now partially consumed by sand. Two of the oxen had been left in the yokes and their carcasses were withered and picked to the bone by vultures.

I rode slowly around the edge of the wagon and found the bodies. There were four. A man, a woman and two children. Arrows stuck out from between their bones that had likewise been picked over by vultures, coyotes and other scavengers of the sand.

I dismounted and knelt beside them. The skin left on the bones seemed as a mere covering, like upholstery of the body. It was tough as rawhide and left only a half mask of terror. The man's mouth was opened as if in silent scream. Their skulls had been broken. Their clothes were tattered sheets flapping in the breezes that came across the desert and funnelled through the gully.

I thought of all the tragedies that filled the land of the Frontier. Death, torture, starvation, thirst and illness stood guard over the plains and dealt harshly with those who tried to tame it. Here, before me, was proof that civilization breeds abundant prey for the misfortunes of the Frontier.

I thought of the Sheppards, whom I followed into this wasteland. Were these bones and scattered articles all that was left of them? And, if not them, surely someone very much like them. Families seeking relatives, or a place to make a home and begin a legacy, were scattered in the sands of that time, lost forever to the world from which they came.

I shook my head and tied the gelding up to the wagon. I pulled supplies from the saddlebags and sat down to eat as the desert warmed. Later, I hung the blanket to the wagon for shade. I left the horse saddled for emergency use, but loosened the cinch. There, in the hot silence of the desert, I slept with the bones of fellow travellers.

In four days, I rode into Cook, Texas. It was a large town with all of the amenities one becomes accustomed to. I remembered what Donnigan said about my name. Surely, these people would have heard of me, but that didn't mean I had to tell them who I was. I rode up to the livery to allow my horse some of the graces of civilization as well, and I went to the saloon. A beer would be just the thing.

I thought if I replenished my supplies in Cook, I could make it to the railhead at Marshall in a week without having to stop in too many towns along the way. I wanted to avoid any confrontations and I wasn't comfortable with the knowledge that people were keeping an eye out for me.

I hauled my gear over to the hotel and got a room on the same floor as the saloon. I thought at first that I wouldn't go to the saloon. I didn't want to, but thoughts of my father and Donnigan weighed heavy on my mind. Finally, I sought solace in a bottle of whiskey. Even if I only brought it to my room to enjoy in peace.

In the evening, I walked down the hall that emptied into the lobby. The saloon was off to one side. There were several of the town's influential men and others: cowboys and ranchers for the most part. I kept my hat low across my brow. I stepped up to the bar. The man standing behind the mahogany surface was a tall, heavy-set man with long sideburns that turned into a mustache. It was often the style of such men to wear whiskers.

After the discussion with Donnigan, I'd never look at a bartender the same way. It seemed as if all of them were watching me.

"What'll you have?"

"Whiskey," I replied, determined not to talk to him any more than I had to.

The man slapped the bar and went for a bottle. He plunked it down on the bar and I tossed a coin in his direction. He took the coin and stared at me.

"You from around here?"

"No," I said, hoping he'd understand that I didn't care to converse.

He went away and stood at the back of the bar, as if guarding the bottles lining the shelf. I poured myself a drink and wondered how long I could enjoy the atmosphere of people without risking recognition.

A chair fell over with a crash and I whirled, my gun drawn and cocked. No one seemed to pay any attention and I put it back in my waistband. I looked up at the bartender, who stood with a knowing smile on his lips.

"Kind of jumpy, ain't ya?"

"What if I am?"

He shrugged.

I could tell that sooner, or later he'd have the marshal in to have a look at me. I must have seemed like a wanted man. I took the bottle and glass and turned away from the bar. I stopped short and found myself staring into the eyes of Tom Garfield.

"Howdy, J.D.!" he said.

I looked over his shoulder for Clyde.

"Where's your partner?"

"He'll be in. Where you going?"

"To my room," I said.

"Stay here. Have a drink with us. Tell me how it went with Goodnight. Quite a man, isn't he?"

"He's a considerable man," I replied.

"You seem a bit edgy."

"I'm all right."

Tom clapped me on the back and turned me toward the bar.

"Two more glasses," he said to the bartender. "Still riding that old gelding, I see."

"Good horse," I replied.

"Must be, if he survived that hell-ride Goodnight was planning."

The bartender set the glasses on the bar. Tom grabbed the bottle from my hand and poured out two drinks.

"You don't mind, do you?"

"Not at all," I said, sarcastically. "Anything for my friends."

"That's the spirit," he said, as Clyde walked in. Clyde didn't seem surprised to see me. Clyde looked at me with some loathing. It seemed to me that he'd heard that I wouldn't do their bidding.

"Where'd you find this cur?" Clyde asked.

I hit old Clyde right in the teeth. He fell back against a table and straightened up. He wiped his mouth. Tom grabbed me around the shoulders, pinning my arms down to the sides. It seemed strange that the bartender wasn't objecting to the scuffle in his place, but he remained silent. They're all in it, I thought.

"Let him go, Tom," Clyde said, with a note of resignation in his voice.

I shook free of Tom's grasp and turned to look at him. He could tell I thought he was out of line. He shot back a look of apology. I grabbed my bottle of whiskey and walked down the hall to my room.

I set the bottle on the dresser and sat down in the chair beside it. I wasn't going to let them rile me up. There'd been too many fights and too much killing over nothing. I'd seen too much senseless murder in the Frontier. Besides, I genuinely liked the men, but they didn't know me like they used to. I was different and they didn't have time to realize it.

There was a tapping at my door.

"Go away," I said.

"Let us in, J.D.," Tom said. "We just want to talk."

"I don't have anything to say."

"Be reasonable, Wilkes," Clyde said, his voice coming softly through the door.

"Don't make me come through the window," Tom said, in jest, but I didn't put it past him. Tom had always been the one I found it difficult to resist. I was attracted to his manners, his speech, his reason. He was like I used to be. We could communicate in a way I'd never been able to with the likes of Clyde.

"Come in," I said, preferring to hash it all out in private.

They came into my room. Tom grabbed the bottle of whiskey immediately and poured himself a glass. Then he poured some into the empty glass in Clyde's hand.

"Now, where were we?"

"Clyde had just called me a 'cur'," I said.

"Oh, he's sorry for that."

"No, I ain't," Clyde protested. "And, you had no right punchin' me in the face over it neither."

"Look, what do you want? I can tell there's something on your minds."

"Easy there, J.D.," Tom said. "Tell us about the Goodnight trip. That fellow's something isn't he? Can you imagine driving cattle to Denver via Horsehead Crossing?" Tom shook his head. "When Goodnight goes to Denver, he doesn't go north, or west, but south. Imagine that."

"It's a good thing he did. The direct route west is tough enough without dragging cattle through it."

"There," Tom said, in triumph, "you can be civil."

"We ain't never done nothin' to you, J.D.," Clyde said, wiping his mouth and checking his hand for blood. His glass was empty again.

"It isn't what you've done, Clyde. It's what I know you've come for that's bothering me."

"Are you suggesting that our meeting is somehow contrived?" Tom asked, with an evil innocence.

"Just say what's on your mind and get out," I said, only to Clyde. He was the one. Another messenger, more evidence of some secret evil that tainted my soul as well as his. As hard as I tried to deny it, we were all in it up to our necks and the knowledge of it, that I had to face it, sickened me.

"You've got to do it," Clyde implored. He held a steady gaze on me and said it as a matter of fact.

"Well, now, there you've done it, Clyde. Now we have to get serious and I was just getting J.D. comfortable and easy to handle," Tom said. His eyes emptied what mirth were in them and he stared hard, cold and direct. "But, since that's where we're at, let's get down to it. You have a moral obligation to snuff this thing out. You understand me?"

"He's my father," I said. "What kind of human being could ask another to kill his own father? Could you kill your father? Could any of you? And, why do I have to do it? Why can't you?"

"It's your mess," Clyde said. "Clean up your own mess, boy."

I leapt from my seat, teeth clenched, trying to keep from hitting him again. But, Clyde stood firm, waiting for the blow. I could see that it wouldn't matter.

"Don't push me, Clyde. I'm not one to take much pushing."

"Sit down," Tom commanded. "Sit down and take this like a man. I believe you're a man. You were man enough to kill Ned and Butch and who were they? A couple of no-account rustlers. You didn't have such a conscience then."

"I should've killed Clyde, too," I said, taking my seat.

"I'd have shot you dead before you thought of it. I covered your back, which meant I could've shot you anytime I wanted."

"I know it. I didn't at the time, but I know it like I know the sunrise." I looked at each of them. "You can't know what it'd do to me to kill that old man. No matter what he's done, I couldn't kill him for it."

"That's it," Tom said, as if suddenly pushed beyond a secret barrier. "Tell him the story, Clyde. Clyde's got a story," he said and winked at me, but there was no comfort in it. It was an icy wink like the sting of a scorpion.

I rolled my head back to loosen the neck muscles. I knew what was coming. It'd be some sentimental tale of some black deed of my father's. I wanted to skip it, but refusing the story would've solved nothing.

"I worked for your father durin' the war, in a way. I was in a Union camp, but I wanted to help the Confederacy. My family's from South Carolina, but I happened to be in Pennsylvania at the time the war broke out. My brother was with me and we were tryin' to get a business goin' makin' saddles..."

"He's good with leather," Tom interjected. Clyde nodded.

"Anyways, we's in the Union camp and decided that we'd help the Confederacy by tellin' where we was goin' and where we planned to be and the like. We worked it all through letters and it was hard, but we done it. Then, the war ended and we went back to doin' what we was doin' before. Everything was fine for a long time, then Jed, my brother, he got a letter tellin' him to meet a man, James something, or other..."

"Jameson," Tom said.

"Yeah, that's him. Jameson," Clyde began again, but my heart began to thump. This was no stranger doing things to strangers, this was Jameson, someone I knew and someone close to my father.

"So, this Jameson, he comes up to my brother and wants to know where I'm at. See, he says it like we should've come together. In fact, they thought we'd both be there. But, when I wasn't there, they tried to get him to tell where I was. See, none of us knew too much and all they had was a way to contact Jed. That's all the further they'd gotten. But, Jed, he was no fool. He saw somethin' wasn't right, so he tells 'em that we got separated and he doesn't know where I am."

Clyde's eyes began to mist over and his chin quivered. Tom put his hand on his shoulder. Clyde composed himself.

"He was such a good, boy," he said, and began to sob silently, standing there with slumped shoulders heaving up and down. Then, he pulled himself together and wiped at his eyes. He stared at me. I felt myself getting choked up and could feel the pain he felt. I could almost see Jed in my mind.

"They peeled his damn skin off!" Clyde said, in a lurch of emotion. "While he was alive! My God," he said, sobbing violently. Then he drew himself up, as if sucking the tears back into his eyes. He stared at me soberly.

"And, if you think for one damned minute that I wouldn't like to kill that man, Jameson, and your father with him, you're wrong! If I could get them in my hands, I'd crush them and I'd swim through a river of blood to do it."

I felt a chill run through my body and took some time before I spoke. I ran my hand through my hair.

"I'm sorry for your brother, Clyde. I didn't know," I said, but could tell that my sympathy wasn't what he wanted. "But, don't you see? Asking me to kill my father is like asking you to kill Jed. Blood's a powerful thing, more powerful than justice."

A fearsome look came into Clyde's eyes and he pointed a trembling finger at me.

"If you come back from Vicksburg, if you get anywhere near me without that man's blood on your hands, I'll kill you, myself. Comprende?" he asked, Then, he stormed out of the room, slamming the door so hard that it bounced open again.

Tom got up, moved to the door and closed it.

"Clyde's a bit sentimental, but he means what he says, and that goes for the both of us, but for different reasons," Tom said, pouring himself another glass of my whiskey. "Clyde just wants him dead and he knows you're the only one who can get close enough. But, I'll kill you for a more sophisticated reason that I know you can understand. I don't have any sad story to tell, just a simple statement of fact.

"You see, your father's evil. You don't know that about him, yet. But, you will and when you look into those eyes and see the self-serving, traitorous intent and the ease and contempt with which he dispatches human beings, you'll see it. If you can see all of that and still don't have the honor to put him down quietly and be done with this shameful episode in the Confederacy, I'll kill you. As long as he lives, he's a disgrace and if you can't kill him, you must be with him. I won't have you taking his place. People like your father need to be removed, obliterated from the face of the earth. They're a scourge. Go back and prove you're above it. Go back and kill that man."

With that, Tom left and I sat there on the chair. I threw my glass across the room and bowed my head. I put my face in my hands and realized how complicated it was. It wasn't just a man and his son. It was an ideal, a belief. My father had abandoned it, destroyed it for us all. He'd stolen the honorable beliefs we had. He'd made the Cause a joke, a self-serving, dirty joke. But, could I kill him? Could I do it?

22

The next morning I gathered my things, saddled the horse and set out for Marshall, Texas. It was a long, dry ride that took me through Alton, Stewartsville and Quitman. I travelled through much of the country I'd been through as a rustler. I could say it then, I could allow myself to acknowledge the fact that I'd been a cow thief. I didn't know it at the time and wouldn't have been if there'd been a choice, but I didn't regret it. It was a necessary experience, an enlightening period in which I came to realize that no man could be trusted and only a few relied upon.

The whole Texas adventure taught me things I'd never forget. But, I felt I was out of it, or on the way out. I'd survived the assaults from friend and foe alike. The only thing I hadn't been exposed to was attack by Indians, and they were supposed to be the dangerous element of the country.

The only Indians I'd seen were starving on a reservation in New Mexico, or firing insignificant arrows at our wagons. No, it was white men that were the scourge of the Frontier. Their thievery, butchery, gambling, drinking, shooting, stabbing, lying, cheating, stealing. You name the vice, and the white men had it perfected. The

Indians killed and stole meat to feed their families. Their only crime was that they'd lived at peace too long. If they'd been better warriors, more technical about killing, more ingenious at it, they'd have developed better forms of fighting the white man. Instead, they were overwhelmed and subjugated and fought out from a position of inferiority, and therefore, ferocity was left to make up the difference.

As I rode and thought of such things, I looked about at the landscape. It was a comfortable feeling to see country I'd seen before. The whole first year I'd spent on the Frontier, I hardly crossed the same path twice. But then, as I went back through it, I felt as if I were taking a familiar path home.

The last town I had to stop at before arriving at Marshall was a small farming community called Quitman. It was in the civilized part of Texas where robberies happened infrequently, as did Indian raids and murders. It was more like my home town of Vicksburg, but much smaller and less sophisticated. I rode into town on the main street. There weren't many to choose from.

The town was quiet and peaceful. It seemed that people cared more about how their places looked. It was a place where city council meetings were the hot topic of conversation, where lives were spent in gradual degrees. Unlike the cow towns, border towns, boom towns and ghost towns I'd been through lately, the people of Quitman seemed eager to spend their lives slowly, not to squander them on the slightest impulse. Moreover, Quitman was the kind of place the people I'd kept company with avoided at all costs. It was civilized, by God, and that wouldn't please the scoundrels I'd known.

I tied up the horse and stepped up onto the boardwalk. I went into the saloon, crossed the floor to the bar and put my foot on the brass rail. A spittoon sat neatly to my left. A fat little man came out from a room and asked what I'd have. I told him whiskey.

"Fine town you have here," I remarked, sipping at the glass.

"Lot of work to be done, yet," he replied. The bartender's face was red with exertion. "Do I know you, friend?"

"Not likely," I replied. "Name's J.D. Wilkes, and yours?"

The man seemed to hesitate, then stuck his hand out. He said his name was George Washburn. "After the first President," he said. "Only, it's Washburn, not Washington."

"Glad to meet, you," I returned, raising my glass in his direction.

"You know, we don't like men to wear firearms in town. There ain't much need of them here and it scares the womenfolk."

"Oh," I replied. "Well, there aren't a lot of womenfolk in here, are there?"

"No," he said, blushing.

"That's good." I stepped back from the bar. "Because, you can see by the way I dress, I'm recently from the Frontier and I won't be without my six-shooter. It makes a man feel, well, a bit vulnerable without it."

"Well," he said, thinking and spreading his arms wide to encompass the bar. "As you can see, we're not in the Frontier and we don't like men to have firearms."

I looked at him with frustration showing on my face.

"Are you telling me that you don't have a shotgun behind that bar, or a six-shooter yourself?"

The man blushed. "There have been some dangerous types in here."

"There you go," I said, slapping my hand on the bar. "But, you won't need it for me, so you can put it outside. You put your shotgun, or whatever, outside with my horse, and I'll put up this revolver."

"That's all right for just the two of us, but what if some other fella comes in wantin' to start some trouble? What good would my shotgun do out there?"

"Now, that's exactly my point," I said. "If I knew who'd come through that door next, I wouldn't need a revolver. I could just leave before the badmen show up."

"Let me buy you a drink," the man said, pulling a bottle out from behind the bar. "That's a fair bit of arguing."

"Here's to you," I said, raising the glass. Then I said: "if you don't mind, I'll sit over there at that table. Do you have anyone that can play the piano?"

"Some of the boys can, but they won't be in until later tonight."

"Sorry I'll miss it," I said, and sat down.

I sat there thinking that Quitman was what the world should be about. A leisurely discussion with a bartender, a shot of whiskey and time to put my feet up. I didn't have to worry about killers and Indians. I could look outside, feel the fresh air on my face. It was a bit humid and cool, being October, or it seemed like it should be. I'd forgotten about calendars by then.

Then, some young men walked in. They seemed very young to be in the saloon. They were a bit rowdy, probably horribly bad mannered for Quitman, but quite reasonable for the places I'd been. They were just young and feeling their oats. I looked at them as if admiring youth, and it shocked me to think I might very well be their age. But, it wasn't the same kind of age. There was one kind, that went along with years, and another, that went along with experiences. By that reasoning, we weren't the same age at all.

They were fun to watch. They talked loud and pushed each other in a friendly way, the way the boys on the Goodnight trail did when I wasn't around. I smiled at them behind their backs. They started playing a game of billiards and swaggered about the table.

One of the boys, a short squat fellow with blonde hair and brilliant blue eyes seemed to be the leader. He was very good at billiards. All of these fellows wore guns and it bothered me that the bartender wanted to have mine removed. I guess the rule only applied to strangers, or strangers that looked like they'd be trouble. No one asked the boys to remove their weapons.

I suddenly felt like having a cigar, so I walked up to the bartender and asked if he had any. He opened a decorative box that held a number of fine looking cigars. I chose one.

"By the way," I said, "why didn't you ask these boys to take their guns off?"

He blushed again. "Well, I know all of these fellas," he said.

"I thought so," I replied and went back to my table. I put my foot up on one of the chairs.

The sun would soon be down and I thought I might stay the night in Quitman. It was still a good day and a half to Marshall and I could use at least one night in a bed. Maybe a bath, too. I rolled the cigar in my hand and thought about a bath. The warm, soapy water and the relaxing effect that it had.

I poured some more whiskey into the glass and stared out the doorway at the growing shadows. My head was starting to feel numb and I floated pleasantly in the glow of alcohol.

Another one of the boys, a tall fellow, bumped the chair where my foot rested. We pardoned ourselves in unison and he made his way around the table for a shot. I pulled the chair out of the way and put my foot back up. I'd seen people get shot for less than that, and here, in Quitman, a little civility washed the whole incident away, as if nothing had happened. And, that was the thing about it. Nothing significant had happened. A minor mistake on both our parts, that's all. It was certainly not worth dying, or killing for.

I heard the voices of the boys talking to each other. It was a rhythmic sort of sound. I drifted lazily in thought, admiring the appearance of the street. There'd been a concerted effort to plant trees. It was going well. It was a small town project of beautification, a simple pleasure of civilization. Every small town was interested in proving its sophistication, though the fact that they had to prove it, denied it. But, on that lazy afternoon, it was all charming and decent and wholesome.

I thought back on the trail. I thought of the snakes, the heat, the thirst, the sand and rocks and sour water when there was water at all. I thought of that wagon stuck in the sand with the skeletons lying about half clothed with skin, the arrow shafts stuck uselessly between the bones, suggesting that there'd been flesh there when they landed. I thought of Ned and Butch lying face down by the fire, blood oozing from fresh bullet holes. There were so many souls left to dry in the sun, it seemed amazing that one didn't stumble over them every mile.

In Quitman, life was easy. So, why were these boys wearing guns? What did it say about their thoughts? Were they anxious to die? Did they enjoy the thought of killing? Did they thirst for the action of the Frontier from their comfortable homes in Quitman? I didn't want the Frontier. I was thrown into it by my father, and then further by circumstance. I wanted to find a place like Quitman when I set out. I wasn't looking for Sherman, Santa Fe, Denver or Cook. I wanted Quitman. Did these boys, then, want those other places? Is that what they sought? I hoped not. The Frontier was already full of ambitious children packing iron. It didn't need any more.

"Hey, fella," the blonde boy called to me, drawing me out of my reverie.

"Yeah?"

"Care to play a game?"

"No, thank you. I don't play well."

"All the more reason to get in some practice," he said.

"True enough," I said, "but, I think I'll sit here and sip this whiskey a while longer."

It was growing dark by that time and my eyes felt heavy. My mind was considerably dulled by the beauty of the town and the effect of the alcohol. I took another drink. As in most places, the saloon was part of the hotel and I planned to take a room soon.

The boys went back to their game and I stood up. I yawned and stretched and lifted the whiskey bottle and glass. I walked over to the bar and set the glass down.

"Who do I see about a room?"

"You see me," the man said.

I tossed some money on the bar.

"That cover it? I want a bath, too. Is there one in the room, or is there a barbershop about?"

"We have a tub in the room. I'll bring up some hot water. Here's your key," he said, extending it out toward me.

I took the key and went outside for my gear. I put my things in the room along with the whiskey. I walked the horse over to the livery. On the way back, a breeze blew through the streets, shaking the leaves on the trees, causing a whispering sound. The hair on the back of my neck stood up and I whirled around in the middle of the street, holding my Colt. For a moment, I didn't know where I was. I sensed an ambush, maybe the wind, maybe a distant voice blown toward me. It was like a spirit brushed by.

I realized how foolish I looked, standing in the street with the revolver drawn on a ghost. I put it away and walked back toward the hotel. What was it? Was I missing something? Those boys with the guns. Why did they need them? I shouldn't have had so much to drink. It was hard for me to think.

I went into the saloon. Only the bartender was left. He stood away from the bar. He smiled at me and I tipped my hat on my way to the room. I went in and waited for the water to show up. I heard a tapping on my door. I reached for my Colt.

"Come in," I said.

The bartender entered, carrying two buckets full of hot water. He poured them into an oblong metal tub. They filled it a fourth of the way up.

"Who were those young men at the saloon?" I asked.

"Oh, those were just boys from around here. They act tough, but they're nothing to worry about, really. They have good, strict parents. But, they've outgrown them and spend some time in here now, and again."

"Why do they wear guns?"

"Snakes, for the most part. Indians, too. We still get the odd raid now and again. We're not as far as we seem from Indian Territory. It was worse during the war, when there were no troops to speak of. It's better now that the soldiers have come."

I nodded. It was hard to let old habits die. Once a man gets used to a certain way of life, he doesn't trust anyone.

He's afraid to and rightfully so. Too often, the last person a man trusts is the last person he should.

The man left and I undressed. I felt better about the boys, but I kept my Colt handy in case it was needed.

I sat in the warm water, washing my various body parts. I studied my hands, worn, leathery, scarred. And yet, such a delicate hand on the trigger, such quick efficient movement that allowed me to draw and aim in a fraction of a second. Even when I didn't want to, it worked without my direction.

I slept well that night. It was a welcome, deep sleep like I'd rarely known these past years. Only when I was wounded had I slept that well. I woke long before daybreak. Another habit of the Frontier. I gathered up my gear and left the room. I dropped the key off at the bar and was walking through the lobby with my saddlebags over my shoulder.

"I thought you'd sleep the whole day away," a voice said from the far side of the room.

But, I didn't hear all of that. I heard the first utterance, the first sound and I drew the Colt. I pointed it at a moonlit profile of a person.

"Who's there?"

"Merton Fredrickson," the voice said.

"Who are you? What're you doing in the dark. Move out here."

The figure rose up out of a chair and walked toward me. I could see his revolver still holstered at his side and I eased the hammer back into place. As the figure reached me, I realized it was one of the boys from earlier that evening.

"I nearly shot you," I scolded. "That's not a very smart thing to do."

"You didn't want me to wait out in the livery did ya?"

"I didn't want you to wait at all," I replied.

"I know who you are," the boy said.

"Yeah?"

"Yeah."

"Well," I said, "that makes two of us."

"The whole country knows of J.D. Wilkes, lawman, pistoleer, cow puncher. Some even say you've been a cow thief, but I don't believe 'em."

"Well, that's nice. I appreciate that, but I have to be moving on," I said, picking up the saddlebags that'd fallen off my shoulder when I drew.

"I want to come with you. I'm nearly as old as you are."

"And, how old is that?"

"I'm seventeen. My pa was killed by a horse this year and I need to make some money for my ma. I need to go out to the Frontier and earn some money."

"Why the Frontier? Who ever said a man could make money out there?"

"Everyone knows it. There's money for the takin'. Gold, silver, cattle, sheep and even settin' up store somewhere."

"Everything, but farmin' huh?"

"Yep. That ain't for me."

"Let me tell you something about the Frontier. There's only one thing easy about it and that's dying. Everything else is hard and none of it's worth the trip."

"Let me see for myself. Take me along and let me see."

"Well, I might just do that," I said, knowing that I wouldn't. "But, I'm headed the other way. You see, I just came from over about Cook. So, I'm going east and you want to go west."

"I know which way Cook is."

"Well, then you know more than I did when I went that way. Look," I said, "I'm not your father, so I can't tell you what to do..."

"My father ain't my father anymore," the boy interrupted.

"No, I suppose not, but like I was telling you. I'm not him either and I can't tell you what to do, but if you want some good advice, stay here and live a long, well developed life. Sit in an old rocking chair and tell your grandson of the times you lived through. If you go out there, looking for easy money, you won't see eighteen."

"Well, how old are you?"

"Nineteen," I said, and it sounded wrong. I wanted to take it back and say an age much older.

"So, what makes you so much different from me?"

"I didn't have anything to lose. If you have a ma, you have more than I did. Don't lose that in search of something that won't ever be as dear."

The boy grew silent and rigid. He seemed to back away from me.

"I thought you might understand. Now, I can see you're just like the rest of 'em. You want to tell me what to do, like I ain't a man. But, I am and I aim to prove it, even if it kills me."

"It will," I said, and walked out the door.

23

I got on the train in Marshall. I put the gelding back in one of the stock cars with several other horses along for the ride. I'd come to love that horse, the poor trustworthy soul. Any other being would've cursed me and died peacefully before they'd have tolerated the hardships of my trail.

After I took my seat on the train, I dug through my saddlebags and brought out the Bible. I noticed queer glances from the others as I sat down to read. I suppose my appearance and the sight of my revolver along with the bible, seemed a contradiction to them. But, soon I was afloat in the passages of scripture and lost to the world around me.

The train would go only as far as Shreveport, then I'd have to get off and ride through most of Louisiana until I reached Monroe. Then, I'd get on another train and take it to Vicksburg.

I heard men talking behind me. They spoke of the Reconstruction with distaste. They were engaged in a discussion of business in the New South and it didn't sound good.

"Pardon me," one of them said, over the back of the seat. "You look as if you've been in the West. What manner of business thrives there?"

"There are a number," I replied, not about to tell him my plan to build a herd and drive them to New Mexico, or Colorado. "The security business pays well."

"What do you mean, 'security'?"

"Providing men to guard shipments of valuables from one community to the next. I wouldn't hire anyone I liked, however."

"Why is that?"

"Because, they'll probably be killed the first trip. Fortunately for the owner of the business, there are plenty of men out of work."

"Do all men in the West speak as rudely as you?"

"The ones I know," I replied, turning back to the Bible, wondering where the men had been. They'd gotten on the train in Marshall, as there were no tracks further west. But then, Marshall wasn't exactly the Frontier. It was a bustling, busy town made important by the railroad.

I rode along the rest of the trip in silence. I'd look out the window at the gradually changing landscape, that didn't change that much on horseback, but on a train, one could see it slowly develop more vegetation and could feel the humidity grow.

By the time I disembarked at Shreveport, I was impressed by the gentry strolling about in the light rain with umbrellas, paper collars and tall hats. Some wore spectacles with vest pockets and watch chains. The look of the town was quite sophisticated compared to the hastily thrown together walls of most Frontier towns. Even Denver had only a few buildings made of brick.

I threw the saddlebags over the back of the horse and mounted up. I'd have to find someplace to sleep outside for a few nights. My resources were growing scarce and I still had a ways to go. I didn't mind sleeping out in Louisiana. At least, I could build a fire without worry of attracting Indians and bandits. A man could stay warm in the civilized confines of the state.

I rode the horse east. I figured I could make Monroe in a day and a half. I could go a lot faster than when I'd passed through before. For one thing, I wasn't afraid of the darkened woods any longer, and I didn't have to push a wagon along at the pace of an ox.

I thought of Sheppard then, as I took the ferry across the Red River. Where was that family? Where had they gone when they left Port Caddo? Were their bones lying in the Staked Plains? I hoped the Sheppards had survived it and were living somewhere like Quitman, where the children would have a chance to grow and learn to live.

The rain was coming heavier in the late afternoon and I dipped my head to let rain run off the front of my hat. I pushed the slicker out away from my body and checked that my revolver was dry. It'd be worthless if the paper cartridges got wet and soaked the powder.

I disembarked the ferry wondering what I intended to use the Colt for. Just in case, I said to myself. In case of what? In case civilization wasn't so civilized. The poverty of rural areas had grown in the time I'd been away. There were many more free-negras, in fact, they were all free these days and it astonished me. What would all the slaves do for work in the South, now that their employers had been wiped out by the war, or the Reconstruction?

Reconstruction was a curious word. To reconstruct what? To reconstruct our loyalty? Our status as citizens of the Union? Or, simply to reconstruct our dependence on the North? I knew what the North thought it meant, but what did it mean on the ground level? All reality is vastly different from theory.

Riding across Louisiana with the dim shadows growing slowly longer and wider until they became the darkness that surrounded the trail. With the rain running off my slicker, I felt a familiar feeling and lost the present in the past.

I scouted foolishly for Union soldiers plodding through the woods. It was an unreal feeling of reminiscence. Thoughts of the North and South flooded my brain, leaving an angry churning in my stomach. The old feelings of injustice that had been washed away by the common injustice of early death, arose again in my thoughts. Ideologies, theories and the subjection of the South again revived anger and resentment in my mind.

To the right of the trail was an abandoned shack. It stood dark and empty beside the path of the railroad. Perhaps, it served as slave quarters for the builders of the railroad at one time. I dismounted and led the horse inside. There was a hole in the roof that flooded one uneven corner of the building and the gelding bent to drink. I removed the saddle and threw the slicker in place of it. It was cold inside. I unrolled the bedroll and threw the blanket over my body. The blanket was wet in patches, but it kept me warm as I slept.

I woke the next morning to the smell of fresh horse droppings and rubbed my nose. Outside, it was damp and foggy. I packed up the horse and we headed on toward Monroe. Shortly after dawn, the sun broke through puffy clouds and set the area to steaming, fueling the fog that gathered.

I rode all that day and well into the evening. I put up outside Monroe, knowing that the town would be dark and could offer few, if any accommodations. I built a fire and relaxed beside it, drinking coffee.

I took advantage of the opportunity to dissemble the Colt and recharge the cylinders. Once again comfortable that the thing would fire, I stuck it back in my belt.

From out of the darkness, a man walked up to the fire cautiously, stopping outside the light and calling in.

"Halloo the camp," he yelled.

"Welcome," I said, pushing some sticks into the fire.

As he neared, I could see that he was old and disheveled. His hair was white and stringy and hung to his shoulders. I absently checked the length of my own hair, which was growing quickly, but still just resting on the top of the collar.

"Pardon me, sir. If you might happen to have some bread, I'd be most obliged," he said, his voice quivering in grateful anticipation.

"Well, sir," I said, digging into to my saddlebags. "I have some hardtack, you can have that and some of this coffee."

"Oh, thank you," he said, his eyes leaping to life.

The man ate greedily and I remained silent until he'd had his fill. I hated hardtack. No one liked it, but it was handy and didn't spoil. When the fellow had finished what I'd given him, he looked more robust and healthy for it.

"What brings you out here in the middle of the night?" I asked.

"Here? I live here," he said. "This is all my land. Well, it used to be before the railroad bought it. Stole it, I say."

"How much did they pay?"

"Ten dollars, but I didn't want to sell. They told me I could have ten dollars, or a hole in my head. I should've let 'em kill me."

"Ten dollars isn't much," I said, sympathizing. I'd heard of such things before. His story wasn't a new one, or even particularly sad. I'd heard of others who were killed outright. No one could stand between business and profits.

"No, sir, it ain't much."

"Well, you're welcome to my fire. I've got some whiskey if you're a drinking man."

"God bless you," he said, holding out the empty coffee cup.

I poured him some whiskey and took a drink from the bottle.

"What time do they start running the trains in Monroe?"

"Trains!" he said, spitting. "Oh, that's some awful whiskey. There's folks around here make much better than that."

"Without doubt," I conceded. "This here's Frontier whiskey. There isn't any worse in the world, but it keeps the bones warm."

"That it does," he said.

"About them trains..." I said.

"Trains!" he screamed as if in pain. "Don't make me talk of 'em. They're evil, I tell you."

I grinned at his apparent simplicity and spoke in a soothing tone.

"I'll grant you that some of the folks involved in pushing the railroad through are crooked and even evil, to an extent. But, the trains themselves aren't evil. They're just pieces of machinery, like a plow."

"They're evil, I tell you. I've seen the devil in 'em. Where do you think that fire comes from? It's the devil's own fire, I say."

I couldn't help but to chuckle. The man was obsessed with it. The ordeal had twisted his mind, even if only a gentle twist.

"Come now," I tried to reason with him, "it's nothing of the sort. They put coal in, burn it and the fire heats up the water and the steam drives pistons, which turns the wheels. There's nothing evil about the object. The people, I grant you, are unscrupulous and very likely evil, but not the mechanical thing."

The old man looked about quickly, perhaps to see if anyone were listening.

"I've been in one," he said. "I've heard them stories before and I went in to check and they had coal, that's for sure, but the pit burned with a fire hotter than any fire coal could make. Look," he said, pulling up his sleeve to reveal a big, ugly scar.

"That's certainly a bad looking burn," I said. "But, any fire could make a burn like that."

The man leapt upon me, screeching hysterically. I fended of his first attack, by rolling out of the way, but he jumped on top of me and battered the back of my skull with his gnarled fists. I rose up on my hands and knees and felt his arm come around my neck. I threw myself backward and he landed on the fire. I lay on my back, on top of him, pressing him there as hard as I could, while his clothes caught fire. There was a big "whuump" and he burst into flames. I rolled off of him and burnt my forearm in the coals.

The man kicked and rolled and screamed. His body was aflame and he fought with all he had to get it out. Then, he slowed his fight and finally, his movements drew tight as he slowly died, crackling and hissing. I kicked dirt onto his body to put him out. There was a terrible smell of burnt flesh and hair. Enough that I choked and gagged while kicking dirt.

"Jesus, God almighty!" I said. What was the matter with him? He was crazy with grief and anger. But, why me? What had I done? I wiped my hands against my face and broke camp. I'd ride into Monroe to have a doctor look at my arm. A doctor might have some salve for it, or something.

I shook my head as I rode away from the place. It seemed inconceivable to me that this man had been wandering aimless and crazy through the woods. Perhaps, I thought, civilization caused its own form of insanity. Progress, fine goods, convenience, style. Perhaps they all worked against the human brain as much as the heat and thirst of the desert.

I found a doctor in Monroe. It was dawn by the time I got there. I asked at the train depot, while buying a ticket to Vicksburg, where I could find one. I told the doctor the tale of the old man while he wiped a greasy mass onto my forearm.

"You say this man was old, with long, white hair?"

"Yes, sir."

"I know of him. He's been a lunatic since before the war. He was from a family of lunatics. He never owned any land, though."

"Well, you might want to send the Sheriff out there to have a look at him. It was a pure accident. He attacked me and I was forced to fight him."

"I don't think there'll be any trouble," he said. "Here, keep putting this on your arm until it heals. If this doesn't work, it may have to be amputated."

"Thank you, sir," I said, taking the small can of salve.

"What was your name? In case the Sheriff has any questions."

"J.D. Wilkes," I said, rolling my burnt sleeve down over the greasy spot.

"Wilkes? Any kin to Horatio, in Vicksburg?" he asked, as if in jest.

"I'm his son," I replied. "Jefferson Doddridge Wilkes."

The doctor's face turned pale with suppressed anger. He straightened his posture a bit.

"Get out!" he demanded, throwing his office door open and stepping out into the street. "If you'd told me that before, I'd not have treated you. Get out, you filthy traitor. I'll have nothing to do with you, or your murderous father."

I turned an icy stare at him and walked out. Several groups of people had stopped to stare and point. I ignored them, placed my hat on my head and raised myself up into the saddle. So, it was true. I felt a sinking in my heart. The whole trip, I'd hoped that when I got back home, none of it would be as Donnigan and Clyde had made it out to be. But, it was true. This is how my father was thought of, even as far away from Vicksburg as Monroe, Louisiana. What did that mean? How far did his treachery extend?

I felt a sudden shock to my pride. Are these the emotions my name raises in my countrymen? Has the name "Wilkes" come to mean something akin to the crazy man's? Was I seen as one of a bunch of lying, cheating, traitorous butchers?

Is this what my father intended when he taught me lessons of honor and pride? To sell it for the price of riches? I thought, maybe in a degree of naivete, that we were rich because we were virtuous, that even if the money were gone, we'd still be virtuous and proud. But, that wasn't the case, or at least, it wasn't for my father. I felt the deepest shame I'd ever known. My father had ruined our name, and I had nothing else, but my name and my word. Now, he'd taken the one from me. Could he take the other? How much of myself was of my own design and how much of it was merely instilled by his will? If he no longer believed in what he'd taught me, should I?

I got on the train with my hat pulled low. I didn't want anyone to recognize me as a Wilkes. I didn't want to talk to anyone. But, when I arrived in Vicksburg, I'd have to face people I'd known all my life and they'd know me for who my father'd become. Would they think the same of me as they did him? Would I be forever painted by the same brush?

Then, I felt a shiver of self-revulsion. My father's name was good enough when I took the favors society had to offer because of it. I didn't shun the name when I worked for the President, nor when we travelled about during the war. The name was good enough when I spoke to men such as Nathan Bedford Forrest, General Pemberton and the like. Was I the traitor?

I opened the Bible to read. And, there in Proverbs 22 it began, "A good name is rather to be chosen than great riches..." But, what of my good name? What happens when a good name, and a good man turn to evil? What is a man to do with his name then? Must I be cursed, though I've done nothing to deserve it? Or, have I? God sees all. Am I then, being punished for my actions on the Frontier?

I thought of these things as the train rolled squeaking and bumping along the track, taking me inexorably to Vicksburg and the place of my infamous father. I'd soon be thrust face to face with all that tortured me. Would I be met with fear and hatred? I scoured the Bible for some way out of feeling that I must endure the scorn of others.

I wanted to get off the train and not go there at all. I wanted to vanish and start over. Yes, I wanted to do the easy things. Hadn't I learned anything on the Frontier? Hadn't I learned to stand up for myself and take my troubles head on? Wasn't that the most important lesson?

I looked out the window and saw the greenery flash past. How could the world be so beautiful, and yet contain such filthiness? What was left of purity? Of honesty? Was there nothing left that escaped the dirty hand of man?

But, it wasn't all men. It was my father, that wretch. So terrified of poverty that he'd destroy himself to avoid it.

To destroy not only himself, but all previous generations and all subsequent. All of that destruction in the name of gold.

I was his son. I couldn't deny that by changing my name, or avoiding Vicksburg. Tom Garfield was right. It was a matter of honor and if I didn't have the honor to stand up to my father, I deserved to be killed. That didn't mean I had to kill my father, though. I could stand up to him like no one else would and tell him that what he'd done was shameful. I'd tell him...what?

My mind became fuddled. A lot of things were wearing on me. The ride was long, the crazy old man, my arm, the look of the doctor. I closed the Bible that I'd not looked at in a considerable amount of time and nodded off to sleep.

An hour later, I woke with one thought in my head. I had to kill him. As Tom put it, I had to "put it down quietly." As long as my father lived, there'd be the ghost of shame weighing on my shoulders.

24

When the train pulled into Vicksburg, I felt a great
sense of foreboding. My heart was heavy with the conflict
of loving my father and knowing that I had to kill him. If I
didn't, I couldn't live with the shame. One of us would have
to die before I left.

As I descended the platform, I was not prepared for
what I saw. There was a brass band playing Dixie and
crowds of people, at least fifty of them. A banner stood at
the back of the crowd and read: Welcome Home, Jeff.

I was completely taken aback and slowly made my way
down the steps of the car. Suddenly, I was swarmed by well
wishers. They shook my hand and clapped me on the back.
Sgt. Jameson's short, thin frame was dressed in a finely
tailored suit. He walked up to greet me with a quick, agile
countenance.

But, as I walked down the long gauntlet of the crowd, I
noticed something in their faces. Hidden behind the forced
smiles were looks of hatred, loathing and contempt.
Though they spoke anxiously and complimentary, there
was a darkness, a dread in their eyes.

So, my father had that kind of pull? He could get this
many people to greet me, the son of the man they feared

and despised? I felt like running through the gauntlet to get away from the masks of smiles and feigned compliments. Even before I got to the end, I began to have great contempt for them. It was their weakness and fear that brought them out and they hated me for the fact that they'd been coerced to do it. I thought they should look inward if they wanted to see what they hated.

When we were finally free of them Jameson and I stepped up into a fine carriage pulled by two white stallions.

"How is he?" I asked.

"Fine. He's wantin' to see you. There's plenty news."

"How did he know I was on the train, that I'd be on that train?"

"Your father knows everything," Jameson said, with a bit of sorrow. "Always has."

I nodded. It went with what I'd found out. But, how much did he know of my exploits on the Frontier? I wanted to lash out at Jameson, but I held my tongue. There'd be better times.

"I have my horse on that train," I said, suddenly remembering.

"Someone's takin' care of him," he replied, refusing to look at me. Was it out of shame? Fear? Contempt? "Ye look bad. We'll get you some proper clothes tomorrow. The son of Horatio Wilkes cain't be seen in public lookin' like a lunatic beggar. You're important now, Jeff."

"I've always been important," I replied. "I've enjoyed being unimportant for a change."

"Them days is over."

Jameson's certainty caused me to feel decidedly uncertain. I was no longer a boy who could be bullied into decisions. Of course, I always liked the feel of fine clothes and enjoyed the respect I'd always received.

The first glimpse of my boyhood home took the breath from my lungs. It was beautifully restored and negras still worked the place. I saw Old Ezra standing proudly in a fine stableman's suit.

"Old Ezra," I said, surprised and pleased.

"Yes, sir. He come back on his own. Seems he had no where else to go. We pay him now, of course, but it ain't much. Same with the rest of the negras, all paid a wage. But, your father still believes that negras should do the work, so he pays 'em enough to keep 'em in the fields."

Jameson pulled back on the reins and the stallions came to an abrupt halt. We stepped out, but before I could grab my saddlebags, one of the negras, a boy I didn't know, had it in his hand. I tipped my hat to him and smiled. The negra remained stolid and quiet. He followed behind as we walked to the front door.

As I neared the stately columns, I noticed a man with a gun standing at one corner of the building. He looked me over once and returned his gaze to the surrounding area. I looked upward toward the trees and saw another man. The place was well guarded, they were right about that.

I stepped on the porch and the door opened. Behind the door, I saw a black hand and white eyes tucked into a dark-skinned face. Just inside, my father waited and I'd no more than passed through the door when he smothered me in his huge arms and pulled me tight to his massive chest. The embrace pushed my hat up to one side as my face was forced into his neck. I felt like a child again and slowly put my arms around him.

"My it's good to see you, son," he whispered through emotion.

"Father," I said.

He pushed me far enough away to have a look. His greedy eyes looked at my face and there was a wince of paternal pain when he noticed the scars.

"You look as if you've had a hard time in Texas. Why didn't you cable me? I could've done something to help you."

"I didn't need any help. It's the price of the adventure."

"And, now you've come home to me. I'm so glad to see you. There's a lot we need to talk about. But, first, you must find some better clothes. I'll have the tailor over immediately."

Without even a nod of his head, Jameson left on the errand.

"You must be hungry. You eat, clean up some, then come to my study," he said, then he turned and left.

A negra I didn't know showed me to the dining table that was set for one person. He stopped and offered his hand.

"Your hat, sir," he said.

I handed him my hat and a cloud of dust rose from it as I laid it into his hand. He seemed a bit offended by it, but said nothing and took it away. I walked over to the chair and sat down.

I could hear whispering from the kitchen and a moment later, a young negra girl came out and put a fancy, gold-trimmed china plate before me. There were chicken parts on it and potatoes and gravy. On another plate was cornbread and cold butter. I grabbed the chicken leg with my dirty hands and ate eagerly. The girl's face registered shock and dismay, but only for an instant. Then, she walked quickly to the kitchen and I heard a rush of urgent whispers and saw the kitchen door open a crack, then close on more whispers.

It was a marvelous meal and the pie for dessert was the sweetest I'd tasted in a while. I wiped my mouth with a white linen cloth when I was done and was somewhat chagrined by the fact that it was dirtier where I put my hand than where I'd wiped my mouth.

The girl came out to clear my place and the man came back to show me to the bath that was ready and waiting. My Spencer was already in my room and stood in the corner. My saddlebags were sitting on the chair. I pulled my revolver out of my pants and placed it noisily on the dresser. I unloaded my knife as well and slipped my shirt over my head. I hung the chaps up on the bedpost and pulled my riding boots off. When I was completely naked, I looked down at the pile of clothes and they looked pathetic and filthy on the shining wood floor. I stepped into the water and slid down to my chest. The man picked up my clothes and walked to the door.

"I's be burnin' these'ns, sir," he said, with a haughty air.

I wanted a cigar and some whiskey. I bet my father had some good whiskey and the best cigars. I closed my eyes and it was as if the Frontier was a distant memory, a bad dream that lasted too long.

I scrubbed myself with the soap and watched the water turn a filthy brown before my very eyes. Still there were the lines of dark and white skin around my wrists. I knew my neck looked the same. While I bathed, the man brought in a robe and some of my old clothes. They looked strange and only vaguely familiar.

When I was done with the bath, I got out and dressed. The clothes were tight all over and a bit short at the cuffs. I couldn't wear the jacket at all and the shoes wouldn't fit, so I put my boots on over expensive stockings.

The tailor came and went. As I was about to go to my father's study, I looked at the Colt. I thought about leaving it there, but it would've felt unusual and I thrust it into the waistband of the pants.

I stepped out into the hall and found Jameson back from his errand and standing beside my door. He noticed the revolver.

"Ye ain't needin' that Colt," he said.

"I've grown used to it," I replied.

"What kind of saddle is that you brought back?"

"I traded for it in Port Caddo, Texas. It's a cattleman's saddle."

Jameson nodded and pointed downstairs. I went ahead of him and walked the familiar route to my father's study. It seemed like a long walk and I was quite self-conscious by then. Everyone seemed a bit disdained at my appearance. But, I felt fresh and well-dressed, even in the old boots.

Jameson moved ahead of me and opened the door. I walked through and he closed it. He stayed outside the room. Guarding it, I supposed. But, from what?

My father was busy with his papers and looked every bit the same man I'd known as a child. He motioned for me to sit down and I did. He made some marks on a few of the papers and shook his head at others.

"Jameson," he hollered.

Jameson came in and looked at my father.

"Get down to the store and tell them they're paying way too much for flour. What are they doing? Buying it from England? And tell that skunk, Wilson, that I see through his scheme and if I catch him at it, I'll...fire him!"

Jameson nodded and pulled the door shut behind him. A moment later I heard a carriage squeak and rattle out of the yard. In the distance I could hear the crack of a whip.

"Blamed fools," my father said to himself. "When will they learn?" Then he looked at me. "You can't trust anyone that draws a wage. Remember that."

I felt myself nod, though I knew it wasn't true. When my father finished with his business he looked up at me with tired eyes.

"We have some matters to discuss, you and I. I'm glad you came back. I wasn't sure if you would. The lure and excitement of the Frontier can be a powerful draw on a young heart. Did you make a mark out there? Do you need some money to get things going?"

"Well, I was going to bring that up, in time," I said. "But, now that you mention it, the cattle business seems as good a place as any to put together a few head and drive them to market. They're all driving cattle to market these days."

"Well, good. I'm glad you've found your business sense. I hoped it would have transferred through the bloodlines. It doesn't in some families." He paused in thought. "Would you like something to drink? Or, smoke. Do you smoke?"

"Yes, sir, thank you. I'd like a glass of whiskey and a cigar if you have one."

"Of course," he said, pushing a box toward the edge of the desk. "The whiskey is over there, bring me a glass as well. This is a moment of celebration."

I drew the whiskey and handed him a glass. I took one of the big cigars from his box and a match. Matches, I thought, I hadn't seen a match in ages. A flint provided all the fire I'd seen. I lit the cigar and puffed deeply to get it going. I swirled the amber liquid in the glass and took a sip. It was good.

"Now," he said, in a direct tone, "if we're all settled, let's get down to it."

I nodded.

"As you can see, I've gained all that I'd lost and more. With the grace of God and a few connections, I've turned it all around for you. I have a piece of everything: railroads, stores, land, riverboats, all of it. Do you see how well I've fixed the place up?"

"Yes, sir. It's just as I remembered."

"Better," he said, "and, the best is yet to come. I've gotten to know the officials in the Union and they agree that it's better to let one of us, Southerners that is, run things. It provides for better security and they don't have to watch out for saboteurs. I can handle any sort of trouble like that." He paused and looked up and spoke again with an air of philosophy. "People here are slow to recognize their positions and some harbor ill will toward the Union. They destroy things out of spite.

"Be that as it may, I've been chosen to take over a lot of the property. There were reasons for this, but I won't bore you with them. Needless to say, some of our fellow citizens have it in their minds that I've done something untoward in order to gain special privileges, which I assure you is untrue.

"But, people will think what they will. I endure their insults and go about the business of putting this town back together. It's much more important that the culture prevail, than the prosecution of a war that's been settled the honorable way, on the battlefield.

"Of course, it singes my soul to know that we lost the war, but a man can't fight facts and a businessman can't afford sentimentality to rule his decisions."

He leaned back then and lit one of the cigars. He'd hardly taken a breath since he began. It seemed to me that he tried to rush through the lies as quickly as he could. In that moment, I could see the evil Tom Garfield spoke about. What's worse, I think my father saw what I was thinking, but seemed determined that his will would prove stronger than mine and I'd not ask any questions. He was smug in his lies and challenged me to refute a single word. It was useless at the time and I let the moment pass.

"So," he said, "I'm in a perfect position to offer you whatever you like. The way I have it worked out, even public office isn't out of the question, not for you. Life at the University, you name it."

"Is this what you thought I wanted?"

"Didn't you? Tell me honestly. Isn't this exactly what you wanted for both of us?"

"Yes," I said, thinking that I wanted it, but not the way he'd obtained it.

"I don't know what more I can do to please you. I know how much you wished to go to the University. All right, it's come a few years late. That's why you seem to hold a grudge against me? Because there was a lapse in time? It was a war. It couldn't be avoided.

"No," he said, "I'll not apologize for what's happened over the past few years. You're a man, you know things don't go according to plan every time. You have to accept some deviations. If you don't want what I have to offer, then you're free to go your own way. I just felt that I had an obligation. I made a promise that you'd have a certain kind of life and I've made that possible again."

He looked at me with a disappointment and an anger that was starting to grow stronger as he thought about it.

"You know what? Get out of my sight. I'll not beg you to take these things."

I set the glass of whiskey down and stubbed out the cigar. I turned to walk away.

"You're not out on the Frontier, Jeff. You needn't wear that gun in the house."

"I'm comfortable with it. I've carried it a long time."

"Take that gun out of your pants and put it on the desk."

I turned to look at him. His face was red and he was the demanding father I'd known as a child. I took the gun out of my waistband and set it down on his desk.

"Thank you."

I nodded and walked out of his study. I went upstairs to the bedroom. There were a number of books in my room, books that I'd read, or wanted to read in my youth. I pulled down a volume of Shakespeare. I sat by the window and read about Hamlet. I'd read the tale before and enjoyed it, but somehow, I felt a kinship with Hamlet this time. There was an evil king in my kingdom as well, and the ghost of my father seemed to haunt the halls of our home.

I couldn't decide if he'd changed, or I had. Was my father always willing to do any dirty deal in order to secure power and wealth? I didn't think so. The townspeople respected him before and during the war. That respect didn't come from dirty deals. Or, was their respect actually fear, even then? I didn't know the answers to any of these questions, because I couldn't look through the eyes of a child and find them. I could only judge from what I saw in the present.

As I sat beside the window, I heard the buggy come back in. A man was with Jameson. They stepped out of the buggy and walked toward the house. I gauged where they'd be and just as I assumed they were walking into my father's study, a great roar of his voice erupted. I couldn't make out the words, except for a few, but I didn't need to hear them. I knew what was being said.

I read more from the story. The light at the window waned and I lit a coal oil lamp. I moved close to it and continued to read. It was at a crucial moment in the play where Hamlet had just seen proof that his step-father and uncle had murdered Hamlet's father and became king. He knew it, the way I knew that my father had done all that was reported. Moreover, Hamlet was as tortured as I was about what to do about it. That particular part made a great impression on me that night. Especially when I read: "Whether 'tis nobler in the mind to suffer slings and arrows of outrageous fortune, Or to take arms against a sea of troubles..."

That was my dilemma exactly. Should I take what my father offered and remain obediently silent, all the while being tortured by knowledge of his shameful deeds? Was it more noble to withstand the disgrace of it? Or, to take up arms against him and risk death and disgrace, not to mention hell. The Bible had informed me, as I rode the train, that it was completely immoral to do what I had in mind. There was no justification for it.

I put down my book of Shakespeare and paced the floor. Suddenly, there was a knock.

"Come in,"

My father walked in with a wooden case under his arm.

"I noticed that your revolver, the old Colt, was quite worn and there are so many better models available now. To be quite honest, I felt a bit ashamed of myself for making a scene about the weapon. Do as you please in this house. It's as much yours as mine. Forgive your father, I've not had much practice at it of late."

He extended the case and I took it. I thanked him and when he left, I opened it. There, in a bed of velvet, was a model 1860 .44 caliber Army Colt Revolver, modified to take metal cartridges rather than the paper. I thumbed open the loading door and saw that it was loaded. I tipped the revolver up and one of the heavy, metallic .44 caliber cartridges dropped into my palm. It was much bigger than the Navy model, a .36 caliber.

I'm glad that he'd left. I didn't want him to see the boyish admiration on my face. It was quite a six-shooter, though I had no plans of letting the old one get away. That one had a special significance to it, because I'd gotten it on my own.

I set the case aside and thrust the Colt into my waistband. It was heavier than the other one, too. At least, it felt heavier. I quickly thought of an advantage of the new Colt. If I could get my hands on a Winchester Repeating Rifle, like those I'd taken to Fort Marcy, I could use the same ammunition. Then, I'd be set, I thought, and only then realized that I may never use such things again.

Long after I'd blown out the lamp and crawled into bed, I tossed and turned, wondering what I should do. My father, for all that was said about him, past all of his lies, was heaping gifts on me and the most precious one of all was the gift of life the way I'd seen it as a boy. I had endless possibilities. All I had to do to get them was keep quiet and go about my business.

25

The next morning, I rose to find my tailored suit waiting on me. Actually, there were a number of suits being made and the one waiting was an altered suit. But, I threw it on and looked quite in style. A new pair of riding boots were also present. I dressed, and stuffed the new Colt into my waistband. I went downstairs to eat and asked that my horse be saddled and brought around for a morning ride.

My father was not to be found. I was glad of it. He would've made comments about my dress and made me feel further obligated to him. I wanted none of that. I just wanted to retrace the path of my youth and get reacquainted with my home town. I expected to get reprisals from the townspeople. I could take it.

I rode into town on a very nice saddle, with the gelding looking well fed and slick and clean. He looked as changed as I did. The people I met either tipped their hats politely, or ignored me all together. It wasn't as bad as I thought it'd be.

"Jeff!" a woman called to me. I looked around and saw a stunning brunette that I only vaguely remembered as Mary. She was an awkward young girl of fourteen then. It shocked me. Women? I hadn't thought of women, not like her anyway. The only women I'd seen in years were either pioneer wives, hotel owners, or prostitutes. But, there stood Mary and she was wearing a lovely dress. I tipped my new hat to her and flashed a broad smile. I stopped the horse and swung down.

"My, what a difference a day makes," she said, blushing.

"Yes, ma'am."

"You're back for good?"

"Well," I said, hesitating. "I'm back."

"Aren't you enjoying civilization after your years in the Frontier?"

"Quite," I replied.

"Do come around," she said.

"Would I miss having tea with the most beautiful woman in Vicksburg?" I asked, playing it up.

"You're a charmer, Jefferson Wilkes," she said.

"Adieu."

"Adieu."

I looked up from her face and saw Jameson standing on the sidewalk looking directly at me. He flushed and turned away. I mounted the horse and rode. The horses hooves pounded down the street and out of town. I rode as hard and fast as I could. The gelding wanted to run, and I let the reins sag so he could pick his own pace.

Before I knew it, I found myself just outside of Milldale. I pulled up at the little place where William, Gregory and I had changed the money. I didn't go in, I simply sat staring and thinking about that time. I thought of how that moment had changed all our lives. I thought of how I'd killed them both and how I hadn't felt sorry about it. Not sorry enough.

I pulled the horse around and rode slowly back toward Vicksburg. I looked at my clothing and felt ashamed. I pulled the Colt out of my waistband and looked at it. It was beautiful. Mary was beautiful. My home was beautiful. But, at the core of it all, something was rotten. I could forget shame in a day, but how about a week? How about six months? And, if I let it go long enough, would I ever be without shame?

The horse walked slow and I didn't get back into Vicksburg until after dark. I rode into the streets and pulled up at the saloon. But, it was not the sort of saloon they had on the Frontier. It was in the lobby of the best hotel in Vicksburg. It was plush and grand and only gentlemen went in. I walked right into the expensive and luxurious room and ordered a whiskey. Jameson sat at a table. He rose and started to leave.

"Jameson," I called, and he stopped. "Come here. Have a drink with me."

"I ain't interested," he said, moving closer to the door.

"Nonsense, friend."

Jameson came to the bar. He was angry. I'd seen the look on his face during the war.

"Get him whatever he wants," I said to the bartender.

"I don't want nothing," he said.

"Have a drink," I said, sternly as if it were an order and in fact, I was testing my ability to give him an order. I wondered if he'd obey it.

"I'll have what he's having."

His gaze could have burnt a hole right through me, if that sort of thing was possible. The glass came and he drank. He gulped the liquor and slammed the glass down hard on the bar.

"If there's something on your mind, Sergeant, spit it out."

"I ain't in the Army no more," he said.

"Well, regardless of the fact, tell me what's bothering you."

He leaned real close to me, so close that I could smell the dinner on his breath. His eyes were red and steady.

"That's my girl."

"Who?"

"Mary."

"Oh."

Jameson glanced at the bartender, who was eavesdropping on the conversation.

"Mind yur own business," Jameson said.

"I am," the bartender replied.

"I'm needin' to talk to ye," he said to me and walked out the door. I followed, keeping my hand close to the new Colt.

Once outside, I followed him into an alley. It was dark. A light shone from one of the second floor rooms and plastered the opposite wall with a square glow.

"Ever since you come back to town, you've taken everythin' that's mine. That Colt ye have, is mine. Your father's mine. I helped to build him back up and he's mine. Mary's mine," he said, breathing hard. "Don't get in my way, boy."

"I am in your way. My father and I are blood. Don't underestimate the power of that," I said. "I have some decisions to make, but neither you, nor my father, can pressure me one way, or the other. So, keep your threats to yourself. Mutter them under your breath if you have to, but they'll play no part in my decision."

Jameson hissed through his teeth and left. I stood alone in the alley. I hoped I'd made the right move. Jameson was a dangerous man, at best, and lethal, at worst.

I rode home and spent a restless night in bed. Soon, I'd have to decide what to do. Like Hamlet, I couldn't stay in the middle too long, or my silence would be the same as condoning their treacherous acts.

As I dressed in the morning, I heard a number of horses ride into the yard. A moment later, my father summoned. I checked my clothes, and thrust the Colt into my waistband.

"Come down here, son. You'll like the surprise I have for you this morning."

I went with him to the door. There were several of father's men standing about another man. As we approached, the others stood aside to reveal their captive. I felt as if I'd been slapped across the face. There, not more than a few yards from me, and looking as if he'd been rolled down a mountain, was the doctor from Monroe.

"Let this man go," I demanded, pushing some of the armed men back away from him. "He tended my wounds."

My father watched me with narrowed eyes. He was disappointed and suspicious of my nature. I suppose he wanted me to hate the man. I suppose he'd have been happier if I'd killed him.

"Get away from the wretch," he demanded.

I gave him a look of abhorrence. "The man's a doctor, for heaven's sake."

My father rolled his eyes. "Stand back," he insisted, waving his hand as if to push me aside.

I glared at him. I stared into his small, corrupt, greedy eyes and again saw the evil Tom spoke of. He had the look of a man who did as he pleased, above the law and, ironically, believed that he was doing what was right, that it was properly done. He was a man without guilt, without thought beyond his own desires, for if he desired it, it must be proper.

I'd hoped, perhaps foolishly, that his conscience wouldn't permit an abundance of injustice. I could see, then, that my hopes were for naught. My father had no conscience left.

Old Ezra came up and handed my father a lash.

"Thank you, Ezra," he said, then spoke loud enough for all to hear. "This man has publicly abused my son, and myself and I'll not have it."

The doctor fell on his knees, begging, pleading for mercy. When my father hit him, it struck his face and toppled the man over. I averted my eyes in shame and horror. I heard the lash again and again. With each stroke, I jumped and felt a knife-like pain go right through my innards. I winced and rubbed my forehead.

Tom alluded to the very thing. If I could stand by and watch my father perform such deeds, I was rotten. I shared his guilt and his shame if I could allow it to go on. He was right, I deserved to die if I couldn't stop such selfish evil.

The lashes continued as I thought. The doctor lay on the ground, with his fingers dug into the dust, crawling away and weeping in distress. I felt my chest heave and my breathing come short. Still, the lashes came. Then, the man collapsed in a pile and no longer struggled, or plead. He gave one last breath and remained still. I closed my eyes to it and could hear the slapping of the lash.

"Stop it!" I screamed. "Stop it!" I rushed to my father and pulled the lash from his hand. I threw it to the dust and pushed him in the chest. He barely moved. "Stop it."

"You were right, Jameson," he said, and looked down at me with a pompous sneer. "He hasn't the strength to run this organization. He's weak and incapable. It's his mother's blood in him, I imagine."

I jerked my gun and leveled it at his chest. His sneer didn't waver. Behind me I heard the cocking of several weapons.

I heard Jameson say: "we'll cut you to pieces, Jeff."

"I'm stopping it," I said to my father.

"You've already stopped it," he said. "It was just a test to see if you had what it took. You don't."

"No, I mean I'm stopping all of it, right here and now."

"All of what?"

"All of the murder, the filthy deeds that've taken place while I've been gone. It ends here."

My father snorted and slowly, deliberately blinked his eyes.

"Put your guns away, boys. He won't shoot me. He doesn't have the strength."

Then, he spoke to me in a condescending, infuriating tone. "It takes more than blood to run this organization. It takes a will to do things like this. How do you think I got all of the comforts you enjoy? Do you imagine that it fell into my hands? I had to fight and scratch to put things right. Murder? Yes, I've murdered. A man has to be able to murder to get what he wants. A man has to protect his good name and punish those who abuse it. Even if that abuse takes place as distant as Monroe. I brought this man here to show others that no distance is too great to avenge evil rumors."

"That's not strength," I said. "To do this sort of thing is simply brutal and ugly. It shows a shallowness of thought and ability. It's weakness that causes a man to do such a thing. Do you think you're unique for this? I've seen children with arrows sticking from their bodies and men shot over card games. Those are not the acts of strength, they're the acts of fear and weakness."

"But, you couldn't have done it. It's beyond you to know what a man must do, because you're a child. I hoped the Frontier would toughen you and make you a man. You came back to me as a man, wearing a man's clothes, but you're a child and the sight of you sickens me."

"I learned plenty in the Frontier."

"Like what? Slobbering sentimentality?"

"I learned thirst and hunger and death. I learned murder. But, there's a time for it, a time when there's nothing else to do, but to murder, cold and clear and simple. But, this is the fit of weak old man, who's afraid to hear of his treachery, who's afraid of his own shadow and of looking into the mirror. He's afraid he'll see his own evil reflection, that he might have to face the truth of who he's become.

"I know you, father. I know who you were, once. I remember the way your name inspired respect, not fear. You've confused the two in that twisted mind rotting in your skull. You've spent all the honor you once commanded and you've disgraced not only yourself, but me in the process."

I expected him to walk away and, indeed, he turned at that very moment. I had to bring him back, the moment couldn't pass that easily.

"Do you recall the Bible?"

"Of course," he said, turning back to me, puffing up as if to frighten me.

"Ezekiel 33:13. Do you remember what it says?"

"Refresh my memory of it," he replied, ready for a matching of wits.

"It says: 'When I shall say to the righteous, that he shall surely live; if he trust to his own righteousness, and commit iniquity, all his righteousnesses shall not be remembered; but for his iniquity that he hath committed, he shall die for it'", I said, firing three shots into his chest before I was shot down from behind. I fell flat on my face, unwilling, or unable to break the fall. I smelled the dust and saw darkness sliding over my eyes. I felt death near and was not afraid.

I heard Jameson yelling at one of the men, but it was none of my concern. I lay on the ground, continuing to recite that which followed the passage, because within the rest of it, I found my path back to righteousness.

I kept waiting to lose consciousness, but I didn't. I lay and felt my back grow wet and sticky from blood. I thought I could even feel each spurt of blood issue from the wound.

Some men grabbed my body and lifted my arms and legs. It seemed distant and I heard reassuring voices surrounding me and the pounding of hooves as they went away from the house.

I dwelt on the words of the Bible as if I could enter them, like entering heaven. I concentrated on the passages that followed the one I recited for my dead father. I knew by instinct that he was dead. My shots were accurate and damaging.

There was a calmness. The hurried and excited voices died down to concerned whispers.

"Can you hear me?" Jameson asked.

"Yes," I whispered.

"Good, lie there now and be still."

I felt tired and wanted to go to sleep. Even if it meant death, I wanted to sleep. I'd avenged the souls that cried out for justice and I would meet death on even terms.

I recovered from my slight wound, but my shoulder and a rib were broken. No vital organs were affected by the piece of lead speeding through my flesh. I was fortunate, the doctor said, more than a month ago.

It seemed to me then, that God wasn't interested in my soul. There'd been so many times in the past few months that he could've taken it. Always, he punished me with pain and worry, but left my soul alone. Perhaps, God expected me to pay for the deeds of my father, I thought. There was plenty to do, if I wanted to set things right. Some things could never be atoned for.

I stood at the door, thinking about such things and watching Old Ezra hitching up the buggy. I held a cigar and a glass of whiskey in my right hand. My left was bound up and my body was wrapped to help the rib heal. The Colt was tucked into my waistband.

Jameson came out of the stables and walked up to the porch. He was quite angry.

"Are ye goin' to leave anything?"

"I'll leave enough," I said, staring at him. He'd never liked the idea of using the better part of my father's ill-gotten gains to repay the people that'd been hurt. He thought it'd be sufficient to place an ad in the paper saying how sorry I was for my father's actions.

"You're spittin' on all the work I done to build it up."

"The work you done, should be spit on, Jameson."

"Be that as it may, it was honest work ordered by your father."

"Then, it wasn't honest."

"It was still work, though," he said, spitting a stream of tobacco.

There was a long moment of silence between us. We stared at each other for a bit, then we looked away.

"We have the bank, the store and a piece of the riverboat trade. That'll build the cash reserves."

"But, you got rid of the railroad shares. Those'll grow it better."

"Enough," I said to end the argument.

Jameson kicked the dust at his feet. He was angry, but he didn't have anything to be angry about. In the absence of my father, we'd become partners. It was a better deal than he would have otherwise gotten, which is why I think he didn't have me killed that day. The price of his partnership kept me out of jail for the killing. The local constable looked at us with a knowing grin, but accepted our explanations at what had taken place.

From then on, we were unwilling and hostile partners, but partners all the same. I kept control of the partnership, because I feared he might revert to the old ways of business.

The sun started to set, bringing a brilliance to the scene that was captivating. I saw Jameson wander off toward his buggy.

"Hey," I called, and he turned around, standing between the buggy and the house. He squinted against the last remnants of the sun. I looked down at my fine, new pair of boots.

"I'm thinking of taking some of the capital and going back to Texas. I'm leaving you in charge here. I think there's some money to be made in the cattle business."

"Well," he said, smiling. "I think you're right."

"Don't take it into your head to start doing business like before."

"Aw, Jeff, you know durn well I was just obeyin' orders."

I nodded, but I wasn't reassured. Jameson finally found something he was better at than war: secret war. It was his nature to pursue a violent solution to his problems.

"I'm warning you, Jameson. If I have to come back and take care of things, I will."

He nodded and turned back toward his buggy. I watched him climb in and crack the whip. The white horses leapt to a run and he rushed toward the sunset.

I stood there on the porch, sipped the whiskey and wondered what old Charlie Goodnight was doing about then. I imagined a large herd of cattle drifting lazily into the desert, a cloud of dust hanging behind. I saw the cowboys whooping and waving their ropes to keep the cattle together.

Lord, if I didn't long to be with them.

F&S Press

...would like to thank you for purchasing this book. In conjunction with our company, T.L. Davis would like to offer his thanks by requesting that you fill out the form below, so he might inform you when he will be making a personal appearance in your area.
It is just this sort of policy that makes F&S Press and its authors different from every other publisher in the business.

Look for the next book in the J.D. Wilkes trilogy...

Home To Texas.

Name_____

Address_____

City_____State_____Zip_____

By mailing in this form, you are eligible for a 20% discount for all F&S Press titles, if ordered directly from the publisher. If you choose, you will be informed when a new title is published.

____Yes, tell me about new titles!   ____No, not at this time.